EAT YOU UP

A SHIFTER'S CLAIM NOVEL

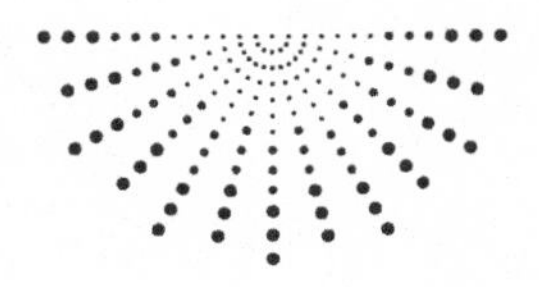

LUCY LEROUX

DISCLAIMER

TITLES BY LUCY LEROUX

Making Her His, A Singular Obsession, Book One
Available Now
Confiscating Charlie, A Free Singular Obsession Novelette
Available Now
Calen's Captive, A Singular Obsession, Book Two
Available Now
Take Me, A Singular Obsession Prequel Novella
Available Now
Stolen Angel, A Singular Obsession, Book Three
Available Now
The Roman's Woman, A Singular Obsession, Book Four
Available Now
Save Me, A Singular Obsession Novella, Book 4.5
Available Now
Trick's Trap, A Singular Obsession, Book Five
Available Now
Peyton's Price, A Singular Obsession, Book Six
Available Now

***

The Hex, A Free Spellbound Regency Short
Available Now
Cursed, A Spellbound Regency Novel
Available Now
Black Widow, A Spellbound Regency Novel, Book Two
Available Now
Haunted, A Spellbound Regency Novel, Book Three
Coming Soon

***

Writing As L.B. Gilbert
Discordia, A Free Elementals Prequel Short,
Available Now
Fire: The Elementals Book One
Available Now
Air: The Elementals Book Two
Available Now
Water: The Elementals Book Three
Available Now
Earth: The Elementals Book Four
Coming Soon

Kin Selection, Shifter's Claim, Book One
Available now
Eat You Up, A Shifter's Claim, Book Two
Available now

CHAPTER ONE

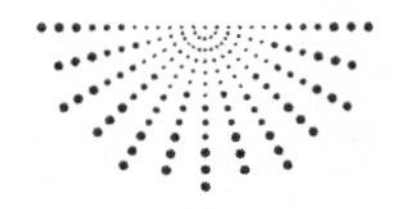

The stewardess leaned over Dmitri, exposing the maximum amount of cleavage as she served him an ice-cold vodka.

"We are so sorry we didn't have any more first-class seats available, Mr. Ivanov. They oversold the flight. Hopefully, though, the seat next to you will stay empty so you can stretch out a little."

The woman's baby blues lingered on his broad shoulders and muscled arms as if she wanted to lick them.

Shifting in the too-small seat in the economy section, he nodded politely. The woman was blatantly broadcasting her interest, but he couldn't summon the will to bed another human woman right now, no matter how silicone enhanced her curves were.

Once upon a time, he would have taken the unspoken offer. As a werewolf, he was used to taking what was offered. And being as he was well-groomed, over six foot, and built like a brick shit-house, he was offered quite a bit. But fucking yet another stewardess in one of those tiny cramped stalls had zero appeal, even if it had been months since he'd gotten laid.

Was it him or were human woman getting boring?

Dmitri dismissed the still-hovering woman, waving away her offer of a second drink and everything else that came with it. He lifted his phone, checking the notes Cassandra, his booker, had sent him on the upcoming Boston job. It was a simple in and out, but he was hoping for a little twist, something to pique his interest. Cass knew that, but after what happened on the last job, she was throwing him a softball, one with a large paycheck.

If it happens again, I'm going to have to talk to her about it. It wasn't as if Dmitri needed the money. His years of high-risk work had come with substantial rewards. Now he only worked to break up the monotony of his too-comfortable lifestyle.

A fresh challenge. That was what he was missing. To a *were* of his age and experience, novelty of any kind was harder and harder to come by. He sighed, wondering what he would find to entertain himself after this job wrapped up.

The scent of a woman—*the* woman—hit him like a freight train. Dmitri tensed, his muscles locking as his heart raced in reaction.

Mate, his wolf growled from inside his mind.

His head told him it was a lie. True mates didn't exist. It was only a human woman, one who possessed an outrageously appealing scent. He'd met a few whose natural perfume attracted his interest before even seeing them. The first had been a grandmother in her sixties, an effective and very quick death blow to his stirring libido. A short but intense affair had followed after meeting the second woman, a young bike courier. But that lady's scent had been nowhere near this...potent.

He took a deep breath to calm down, but immediately regretted it. *Shit.* This couldn't be happening—not when he was about to be trapped for a six-hour flight.

It wasn't the stewardess, of course. Nor was it anyone crammed into the seats behind him in the bowels of economy class. This intoxicating perfume was new. It belonged to someone who'd just stepped on the plane—at the last minute, no less.

His acute hearing heard the airplane door latch as the scent grew stronger. Dmitri gripped the armrests, his fingers digging into the metal frame to keep himself in place. It was necessary. In order to keep from jumping up and tearing the plane apart to find her, he had to exercise complete control.

She came through the door with the stewardess, who threw him an apologetic grimace behind the newcomer's back as she gestured to the empty seat next to him.

At first, all he saw was red wool. The siren was wrapped in a scarf big enough to be a blanket. Then she unwound it, taking off her coat as well as she lowered into the seat next to him.

Her slow-motion descent was like something out of a movie. The woman possessed a mass of dark shiny curls that smelled faintly of almond and vanilla. She was also a trifle more lush than average. Succulent curves were encased in denim and cashmere wool, protection against the blustery San Francisco weather. Perfect *creme-au-lait* skin peeked out from over the edge of a boatneck sweater. The neckline exposed down to the edge of her shoulders...the area a *Were* would place his bite.

Her brief smile and nod damn near stopped his heart. *Hell.* She was perfect.

Dmitri released a shaky breath as she settled in. Their two seats were separated by the aisle from the others in this row, just after the bulkhead. It was the only coach seat capable of accommodating his height. It made for a cozy space, a bubble that would hurtle through the air at six hundred miles an hour. Nevertheless, it wasn't private enough for him to get away with pinning his seatmate to the bulkhead and fucking her brains out.

The woman sat blissfully unaware of his intentions. After buckling in, she sat drumming her fingers on her thigh as the plane taxied and took off. Once they were in the air and reached altitude, the *fasten seat belt* sign dinged off. Once it did, she took out her phone and checked emails for a few minutes until her eyes grew heavy and she dropped off to sleep.

He glanced down, watching the small rise and fall of her chest. Fuck, another bad idea. He was full of those.

Dmitri had stared down the barrel of a gun more times than he could count without breaking a sweat. He'd even been on the wrong end of a grenade launcher once. His mercenary stint had been filled with pulse-pounding danger, but he'd been notoriously cool under fire. Enough to earn the 'Ice Man' moniker from his associates.

If they could see me now... A solitary woman had just done more to undermine his equanimity than a warlord's horde. Sweat was literally beading on his upper lip.

He was also hard as a rock. Dmitri focused on his breathing, trying to stay calm as his neighbor shifted, sending a waft of light honey musk over him. A few minutes later, he nearly bit through his tongue when her head landed on his shoulder.

Dmitri side-eyed the girl sleeping half on his chest as if she were radioactive. She might as well have been. There was no way he was going to make it through this damn flight without doing something unspeakable.

Nina Briggs raised her head slowly. Her week-long conference, along with the sleepless nights that accompanied it, had taken their toll.

Her head was resting on her neighbor's shoulder. Dear Lord, was she drooling on a stranger?

This isn't completely your fault. The massive man spilled over the narrow seat. He wasn't overweight, but he was built a magnitude bigger than average. Perhaps two. Blushing, she leaned away.

He was awake, staring straight ahead at the tiny screen fixed to the bulkhead just in front of them, but it wasn't on. The plane was dark, the lights dimmed so passengers could sleep.

"I'm sorry," she whispered.

He was silent a beat too long. "It's fine," he growled.

The rude man didn't even glance her way as he said it. That was all right with her. Chatting up the passenger next to her wasn't on her to-do list, even if this one happened to be an attractive man with more muscles than seemed humanly possible.

She stifled a desire to check him out again. *You have enough problems.*

Nina touched the bare space on her ring finger with her thumb. It had taken a while to get used to wearing the engagement ring, especially one with a stone that large. Removing it regularly to perform surgery had ensured she never got too comfortable with it, but now, six months later, *not* wearing it was just as odd.

I wonder if Matt gave it to Kate? She wouldn't put it past her ex to recycle an engagement ring, especially since his flamboyant choice cost more than the average car. Plus, she knew Kate had coveted it. That much had been obvious when Nina had shown it to her, the way newly engaged women were supposed to.

What was it they said about pride? *It cometh before a fall.*

She snorted and pulled out her computer, intending to make a few notes about the conference. As the keynote speaker for the cardiothoracic panel, she'd been too busy to do it before. Everyone had wanted to talk about the Brigg's technique, a new surgical method she'd developed, the one that almost guaranteed her the prestigious Downey Fellowship.

Conversation with her peers stimulated a few interesting questions, things she wanted to make note of before she forgot them. She had to do it now because the minute she went back to the hospital, she'd be sucked up in work at the breakneck pace required of a surgeon.

If only work was the only thing waiting for her in Boston...

A wave of pain rose unbidden. Closing her eyes, she counted to ten and focused on what she wanted to jot down until it went away. Nina excelled at compartmentalization. It was part of her professional toolkit, as necessary as her scalpel or stethoscope.

She worked for a few minutes more until the beverage service started. The stewardess took her order by rote.

"Here you go," she said, extending the cup of black coffee without looking at her. The woman's attention was fixed on the man next to Nina. The stewardess was so engrossed that she let go of the tiny Styrofoam cup before Nina had a grip on it.

The coffee spilled all over her tray, running off the sides to puddle in her lap.

Swearing, Nina tried to mop up the mess with a tiny paper towel. Fortunately, the hot liquid lost some of its heat as it ran across the plastic folding tray.

"Oh, dear. I'm so sorry!" She had the stewardess' attention now. The woman fished out a towel, helping Nina clean up. When the worst of it was taken care of, she tucked the tray back in and blotted her jeans.

She glanced at the man next to her. He hadn't moved at all during the incident. He just sat there, holding something to his mouth and nose. Nina raised an eyebrow as the man cleared his throat, extending the item with a little *here-you-go* nod. It was a handkerchief.

"No, but thank you." Standing, she headed to the bathroom to clean up.

Despite her catnap on her neighbor, she was still exhausted. Her dark skin appeared grey under the harsh fluorescent lighting.

It's official. Her outsides now matched her insides. Hanging her head, she let the tidal wave of feeling she'd been holding at bay flood back. A few tears squeezed past her tightly closed lids. Ruthlessly, she scrubbed them away and took a deep breath.

I just need to get through this week. Less than that. Matt's wedding would be over and done in five short days. Once it was, she'd pick up the pieces of her shattered ego and go back to work. In the operating room, she was in total control. That would have to be enough.

Of course, according to her friends and mother, her job was part of the problem. Some doctors, even those who claimed to be madly in love, couldn't take the competition.

And on top of everything else, she was going to have to go through this entire flight with a wet lap.

When she was done feeling sorry for herself, she wandered back to her seat. Her odd neighbor didn't spare her a glance. He did, however, slam the handkerchief back up to his face before turning away.

Frowning, Nina sat, giving her underarms a surreptitious sniff.

All right, so perhaps she was asking a bit too much from her deodorant. She'd been forced to run the last hundred yards to make her flight, but she didn't smell *that* bad.

What a butthead. I *hope I did drool on him.* It would serve him right. Indignant, she returned to her notes, doing her best to ignore the man. That was easier said than done, however.

Despite having one, she didn't need an advanced medical degree to notice the stranger was tense. A quick glance at his face showed he was flushed and damp. The muscles in his forearm were rock hard, the veins popping out in stark definition.

That last was common enough among bodybuilders. Though this guy's musculature was on par with that, she didn't get that vibe from him.

No, this guy was reading as a terrorist.

CHAPTER TWO

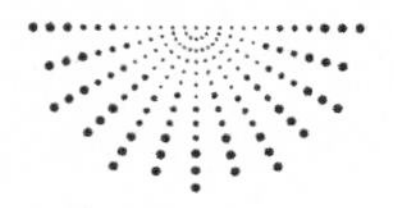

Fear gave Nina's heart a good squeeze. The man's demeanor, the way he watched her from the corner of his eye before furtively darting his attention away, was all very suspicious.

Turning slightly, Nina pretended to work on her computer. Was she overreacting? Some people didn't like to fly. Even men built like oversized Greek Gods could have a phobia. Besides, with the political climate being what it was, security had been pretty tight. What were the chances this man had been able to smuggle a weapon on board?

Pretty damn good if the news was to be believed. Whenever they did tests, a scary number of weapons and contraband always managed to get through security.

She peeked at her neighbor one more time, just in time to catch him doing the same to her. They looked away at the same moment, but she was able to catch the distinctive flutter of a rapid pulse beating in his neck.

Her stomach churned. Nina had seen enough *'see something, say something'* advertisements to know she was supposed to get up and make a report to the aircrew, but this guy was so damn *big*. He had at least sixty pounds of muscle on the biggest member of the crew. The size of his hands alone….

Unbidden, an image of those massive hands wrapping around her neck flashed through her mind. She imagined them squeezing the life out of her. Despite her own generous build, it wouldn't be hard for someone of his obvious strength.

Don't panic, she ordered herself as the airplane dipped suddenly. Nina tensed, and then tried to relax. This was normal.

Unfortunately, it was just the start. The plane hit a large pocket of turbulence. The cabin shook so hard the meal trays rattled.

It was as if the plane had decided to read and reflect her state of mind.

Across from her, the man gripped his armrests as the plane rocked and shuddered. His fingers were white against the metal and plastic frame.

There you go. The giant *was* afraid to fly. Her imagination had simply run away from her. Nina released a pent-up breath. A few minutes later, the shaking subsided. She transferred her attention to her computer again, deciding her notes could wait. Instead, she settled in to watch a bloody action movie she'd rented weeks ago but hadn't gotten around to watching.

Her relief was short-lived. The turbulence had returned worse than before, enough for the *seat belt* sign to turn back on. A few minutes later, the pilot got on the PA system. She instructed the flight crew to take their seats.

"We've hit some bad weather, folks," she announced in a voice far too chipper for Nina's nerves. "For your safety, please remain in your seats. We're going to see if we can get some altitude to pull us above this storm. In the meantime, put your seats back in the upright position and stow your tray tables away."

Outside, the dark grey clouds lit up as lightning streaked so close by she had to shut her eyes. She sucked in a breath. Had it hit the plane?

Nina was still staring out the window when a sudden jolt propelled her forward. Though loose, her seat belt kept her in place, but she did shift enough for the tray to dig into her stomach. Faster than she could blink, a pair of massive hands held her shoulders back before a second jolt could slam her forward again.

"Here, let me." Her neighbor closed her computer, handed it to her, then put the tray away before she had a chance to react.

He didn't sound at all anxious now, despite the brutal buffeting the plane was getting.

"Thank you," she gasped as the plane suddenly dipped, taking her heart with it. She slipped the computer into its sleeve, holding on to the seat in front of her as she stowed it in the vintage leather messenger bag at her feet.

"Are you all right?" her neighbor asked.

The man's deep voice rivaled the thunder outside. For the first time, she noticed he had a pretty thick accent—something Slavic or Russian. And he still hadn't let go.

"I'm fine," she assured him, blushing and nudging his arm off. That small contact was the most action she'd gotten for the better part of a year.

Embarrassed for her previous suspicions, she racked her brain for small talk. Maybe she could help distract him from his phobia… although oddly enough, he seemed calmer the worse the turbulence got.

All around them, the plane continued to rattle and shake.

Whenever the plane dipped more than a few inches, people would gasp. An experienced flier, Nina was certain they would pull out of it soon enough, but it went on and on.

"Hello again, folks. This is your pilot speaking. We've diagnosed a minor problem with our system. It's preventing us from climbing to a higher altitude. For everyone's safety, I'm afraid we're going to have to make an unscheduled landing. The plane will be examined by a technician to diagnose the issue. We've been given a priority slot at Wyoming's Rock Spring airport. It's about half an hour away."

The passengers groaned in unison.

"Damn it," Nina swore. This was the last thing she needed.

"It gets worse."

Nina started, realizing her neighbor was talking to her. "What? Why?"

He pointed out the window. The sky was filled with dark clouds. She leaned forward, but there was no break in the mass, no hint of blue sky.

"This isn't just a storm. It's a blizzard."

Dmitri kept a close watch on his mate's expression as the plane made its bumpy approach to the Rock Springs airport. She looked as concerned as the next person, but he didn't pick up the stink of fear from her that he caught from the other passengers.

A little corner of his heart lit up with pride. His woman had nerves of steel.

Her name was Nina. He'd rifled through her bag when she'd been in the bathroom, so he knew her name and address now. If he somehow lost her, he would be able to find her again.

Dmitri had also peeked at her computer, finding a PowerPoint for a recent medical conference. She'd been the keynote speaker. The woman was a rock star.

He wasn't going to deny who and what she was to him. Her scent was unmistakable. In the few short hours he'd been sitting next to her, that damn perfume had been working its way into his system, imprinting itself on his brain. It had been all he could do not to grab her and claim her then and there.

However, the minute their flight had begun to have trouble, he'd made a complete turnaround. If they had a problem, his lust would have to wait. He had to be ready to protect his mate however he could.

Dmitri didn't fool himself into thinking he was indestructible, but *Weres* were stronger and faster than humans. Their muscle density and heavier bone structure afforded them a good deal of protection during accidents. He'd do what he could to shield her in case of a crash landing.

A few minutes later, they began their rough descent. Dmitri could feel the plane slowing in preparation, but the view out the window was unchanged. The clouds were a thick ominous blanket. He could barely make out the vessel's wings. Snowflakes pelted the small oval window, streaking across the surface.

The severity of the storm was difficult to judge from this altitude, but he'd been through some bad ones in his native country Russia. Though severe, this one didn't appear as bad as some of those. However, if they managed to land without incident, would they be able to take off again?

It was doubtful. They had to be close to the ground now, but the tail end of the plane was swinging like a pendulum. The oscillation wasn't too wide, but it signaled the pilot was having a rough time keeping the plane on a straight course.

He reached for his mate's hand, but she had them gripped tightly in her lap. Chagrined, he pretended to reach for his phone, but then decided it was a good idea. He'd never heard of Rock Springs airport. If this flight was grounded, along with the rest of the airport, then there wouldn't be enough rental cars to go around. In any case, Dmitri preferred to travel in style whenever possible.

He fired off a quick text to Cass, instructing her to buy him a four-wheel drive from the nearest dealership, something that could withstand a Russian winter.

I'll pay a premium to have it delivered to me at the airport within the hour, he texted.

If you land at all, Cass replied.

Dmitri snorted. He knew he wasn't Cass's only client, but his booker's income would take a big hit if he was taken out of play prematurely. He was crafting an equally sarcastic reply when the pilot came over the speaker.

"We've begun our descent, but visibility is poor. Normally, we'd circle a while longer to see if things improved. But given the nature of the problem with our electronics, we've decided to land. Emergency crews will be waiting for us, strictly as a precaution. Nevertheless, I'd advise that everyone take the brace position—heads down."

Nina's indrawn breath was sharp in his ear. He ignored the other murmurs and gasps as the plane began to touch down. A quick glance confirmed they were landing in white-out conditions. He couldn't even see the ground.

"Brace for impact!" The pilot's shout was met with muffled screams from the rest of the passengers.

Nina's lips were pressed shut. The second the plane touched land, it slid haphazardly on the slippery snow-covered runway. Inside, the passengers were jerked violently back and forth. He threw himself across his mate's seat, leaning over to cover her upper body as best he could. His hold kept her safely down, but the tail of the plane fish-tailed, putting them in a dramatic spin.

The squeal of the brakes and continued screams filled his ears. He was still protecting Nina's back, but missed the briefcase flying up from behind them. It struck the back of her head.

Dmitri swore, backhanding the case to the ground as they finally came to a jerking stop.

"Nina, look at me." He cupped the sides of her face, checking her pupils for signs of a concussion.

She murmured something, but her protests were weak, her eyes dazed. Dmitri felt the rising bump on the back of her head, removing his fingers to check for blood. Fortunately, there was none.

The wail of the sirens was muffled by the wind, but Dmitri caught a glimpse of flashing lights from the window.

"I'm fine. Let go." Nina weakly pushed him away. Her big brown eyes blinked at him, but they weren't as focused anymore.

"Not a chance." He hopped up as the passengers began to rise, unbuckling her and lifting her in his arms. Dmitri shifted her, so he was holding her with one arm. He used the other to throw her wool peacoat over her upper body.

He didn't let go until he had to—into the waiting arms of the paramedics.

CHAPTER THREE

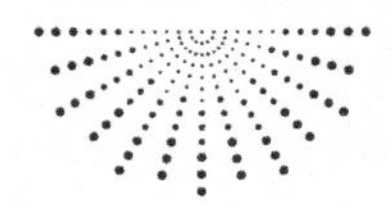

The ice pack wasn't doing anything for the throbbing pain in the back of her skull.

She was inside the airport, being checked over by a paramedic. As far as she could tell, hers was one of the worst injuries. All things considered, the bump wasn't bad. There was also a minor cut at her hairline she didn't remember getting, but it didn't require stitches.

No, it could have been a lot worse. Her seatmate, the man she'd suspected—albeit briefly—of being a terrorist, had thrown himself over her, doing his best to shield her with his body as the plane made its terrifying emergency landing. However, he hadn't been able to protect her from a falling suitcase. Other passengers had bruises, one a likely sprain. Thankfully, no one had been killed.

"You'll have to watch out for signs of a concussion, but I guess I don't need to go over those with you, Dr. Briggs."

She nodded. "I'm fine. You're sure everyone else is all right?"

"Yes, Doctor." The male paramedic smiled winningly. "Except for being stuck here in the middle of a snowstorm that is."

Nina glanced out a window. "It doesn't look that bad now." The sky was almost clear, at least compared to the blinding wall of white they'd been forced to land in.

The man cocked his head to the side as he put away his otoscope. "This is the eye. It's all over the news. What do they call a winter hurricane?"

Her heart dropped in her chest. "A bomb cyclone."

There had been one in Boston earlier this year. She'd spent most of it stuck at the hospital. There had been fewer gunshot patients due to a precipitous drop in crime, but an uptick in traffic accidents. The city had been a mess for days.

How bad could a storm get out here in the Midwest? Didn't she read somewhere that it could get a lot worse without the moderating effects of the ocean?

The EMT was downright chipper. But they were safe and dry for the moment, and he appeared quite young. It was likely one of the most exciting things that had ever happened to him.

"Some people have been talking about getting out before the next part hits, but unless you get lucky, I think you're going to be stuck here, at least for a couple of days. They canceled tomorrow's flights, and it's not looking any better for the day after. So...maybe if it's not too bad out later tonight, you'd like to get dinner? My place is near the Holiday Inn. That's the nearest hotel to this airport."

Nina blinked a few times. It had been a while since she'd been hit on so blatantly. "Err...I'm afraid I'm going to be one of the people trying to make a break for it before the rest of the storm hits. I have to get back to Boston. I have an event there in a few days that I can't miss."

The EMT looked disappointed, but he took her rejection with good grace. "Oh, I'm not sure you should get up, let alone drive. You're sporting a nasty bump. Not to mention the big guy who brought you inside was insistent you wait for him right here. He told you not to move an inch. Don't you remember?"

She didn't. Her head had been muddled for a few minutes there. "He said that, did he?" Her voice was wry.

Mr. Muscles may have carried her out of the plane like a hero, but it might have been a tactic to get out of the plane first. That way he could run and snag a rental car before anyone else. He was probably miles away from the airport by now.

Taking a deep breath, Nina stood. “I better get to the car rental desks. If what you said is right, I don’t have much time.”

The paramedic grimaced. “If you insist on leaving AMA, you better hurry. This isn’t a big airport. There may not be many cars left at this point.”

She hadn’t considered that. “Thanks.”

Grabbing her bag, she hurried to the car rental desks as fast as her throbbing head would allow. Unfortunately, the paramedic was correct. The first agency had a ‘Closed’ sign on their counter. When she finally reached the front of the queue at the second desk, there were no vehicles left.

“Is there any chance you’ll get more vehicles? Maybe tomorrow morning?” she asked hopefully.

The woman behind the counter shook her head. “It’s not likely, ma’am. I’d suggest you get a hotel room before they all book up. If you’d like, I can call the Holiday Inn for you.”

So even the hotel rooms are in danger of running out? Defeated, Nina put her head on the counter. “My mother will never forgive me if I miss my sister’s wedding.”

The woman tsked sympathetically. “I can put you on the waitlist, honey, but honestly your best shot is to run out to the parking garage. Some of the people before you made plans to carpool. Maybe some of them are headed in your direction.”

She was right. It was her only chance. “Thanks, I’ll do that.”

They may have been in the eye of the storm, but that didn’t mean the weather outside was calm. As soon as she stepped outdoors, the howling wind ripped the hat from her head. She had to run to catch it, but it was too wet from the snow to put back on, so she shoved it in the side pocket of her purse.

The garage was just across the road from the terminal entrance. She hurried across, eager to get to the partial protection of the covered building. The car rental spaces were conveniently marked by the company’s logo, but the small cluster of carpoolers she found was headed in the wrong direction. Their car was also full.

"The other rental agency keeps its vehicles across the lot," a man volunteered, pointing. "You should try there."

Nina thanked him and hurried off in the direction he indicated, wondering why she was killing herself to be at what promised to be the most excruciating experience of her life.

The universe is trying to spare me. It had to be why it was throwing up a huge roadblock to returning to Boston. Did she really have to keep trying so hard to get back?

Hiding here in a Wyoming blizzard was so tempting, but she knew nothing short of losing a limb would excuse her in the eyes of her mother and sister.

If you miss it, you'll never hear the end of it... She'd never be able to look any of her relatives in the eye.

They're going to pity you anyway. In fact, they already did. Hastily wiping a tear away, she quickened her step.

"Hey!"

Nina turned, a thrill of fear coursing through her as she caught sight of a massive figure charging her way.

His back was against what little light illuminated the garage. She couldn't see his face, but he was moving too fast, and he was coming for her.

Pivoting on her heel, Nina started to run, but she didn't get far. Big hands spun her around at the edge of the parking garage. A brief impression of dark eyes and cut cheekbones was all she could make out before she was engulfed in a pair of rock-hard arms.

"What—"

Her question was drowned out by a blistering kiss.

Nina's knees buckled as her insides melted. Red swamped out her vision as her whole body responded to the devastating embrace. The pain in her head receded and her breasts swelled, her nipples pressing against the man's chest as she grew wet.

She didn't mean to collapse in the man's arms. It just happened. If he hadn't been holding her, she would have fallen to the ground.

The keen edge of her arousal was new and unfamiliar. Nothing in her experience prepared her for it. Nina was completely blindsided.

The man finally broke the kiss. "I told you not to move."

Huh? "You're the man from the plane."

She recognized her seatmate now. There was enough light at the edge of the parking garage to make out his full lips and sculpted cheekbones. His light brown hair glowed with gold at the edges. Up close, she could tell that his eyes were not blue, but a verdant green.

This near she could also see there was no tell-tale ring around his iris. He wasn't wearing contacts. How was it possible that such a color existed in nature?

"Your eyes are like emeralds," she blurted, then winced. She hadn't meant to say that out loud.

He smiled. It warmed his chiseled and forbidding features, a heat that turned her insides to gooey caramel. "I see you feel better now," he said.

He wasn't sweating anymore, nor did he appear ill. "Are *you* feeling all right? For a minute, I thought you were going to break the armrest up there."

A corner of his lip turned up. "I apologize for making you uncomfortable on the plane. It's better out here in the open air."

"Everyone could use more oxygen," she pronounced stupidly, belatedly realizing she was still in the man's arms.

What was she doing? *Get it together, woman. Haven't you ever heard of stranger danger?*

She pushed away. "Sorry, but you were acting weird."

"I know." He cocked his head, a hapless, disarming gesture. "Again, you have my apologies. But it's better out here where I can stand upwind. You are less...potent."

"Excuse me?" Nina scowled. "You weren't freaking out about flying? All that teeth-grinding, sweaty mugging was about my *smell*?"

Incensed, she moved farther away, but her back hit the side of the wall. The man had her practically pinned against a car.

The expression on the stranger's face was relaxed and a little amused. A bit of his hair fell forward as he leaned closer, his eyes darkening as he stared down—way down. He towered over her.

Warnings from the little piece of her brain still functioning buzzed in her ear like mosquitoes, but it was too difficult to focus on them as his lush lips parted again.

"Allow me to introduce myself," he said with a little old-world bow. "My name is Dmitri Ivanov, and I am your mate."

Nina's head drew back, bumping the car in the exact same spot the suitcase had struck her. "Excuse me, but you're my *what*?"

Dmitri wanted to laugh, but he was too concerned when Nina reached up, touching the back of her head. When she closed her eyes in pain, he put his arms around her, wrapping her close to protect her from the wind until she relaxed, quickly recovering from the minor tap against the frame.

Dmitri cupped her cheek with his palm. He was having a tough time keeping himself in check. True, he'd never laid eyes on her until just a few hours ago, but keeping his hands off her would have been too much to ask. Especially with the way her body was responding to him.

Despite her injury, the signs of her attraction were too blatant to be mistaken. Her pupils were dilated. He could feel her body heating in reaction to his pheromones. Under her shirt, her nipples were hard and round. He couldn't wait to bite them. This close, the unmistakable scent of her arousal wrapped around him like a vice whether he was downwind or not.

"I'm so glad we're finally alone." His voice was guttural and pitched low. Heat pumped off him as Dmitri bent his head to take her lips again.

His mate let out a tiny cry as he took her mouth. His body covered hers, gently pressing her against the side of the car while cradling her head protectively to prevent further injury.

His tongue pressed against the seam of her lips, demanding to be let in. She hesitated for a moment, but her willpower was no match against an alpha's mating call.

He raised his head long enough to check the expression on her face. Nina's eyes were unfocused, thoroughly muddled. He kissed her again, moving to cup her ass.

Her arms crept up his chest until her palms clasped behind his neck. Elated, Dmitri scooped her up, slipping in between her open legs. Nina tasted like honey and walnuts. Dmitri had never realized how delicious that combination could be. The glutton in him spurred him to drink deeper. He ground against her, pulling her legs around his waist while cursing the barrier of their clothes.

Unable to resist, he moved down, deftly undoing the zipper on her pants. Dmitri snaked his way inside, his fingers stroking over her cotton panties, tracing the seam of her wet slit. Her heat almost burned him, despite the barrier of the thin cotton.

For a second, he was tempted to break into the car behind them. He wanted nothing more than to take her then and there, but a freezing cold parking lot was not the place to claim his mate. Growling in frustration, Dmitri broke the kiss, panting as he fought to catch his breath.

The confusion in Nina's expression cleared with the frigid breeze. It snaked through the lot between the cars, finding tiny openings in his clothing and presumably Nina's. The cold didn't bother him, but his mate was human. Their bodies were too frail for weather like this.

Luckily for him, his mate had a body built for something else. He cupped the lush swell of her derriere, relishing the exaggerated curves. Her ass was almost as good as her full firm breasts.

Dmitri considered himself a connoisseur of women. Nina was a rare jewel. Sexy, beautiful, and if the hospital I.D. was to be believed, an accomplished physician.

She was also bright enough to distrust their connection. Nina pushed hard at his chest. He didn't budge, grinning at her until the light in her eyes changed. But when she began to look scared, he slowly put her down, an unfamiliar sensation of guilt filling his chest.

CHAPTER FOUR

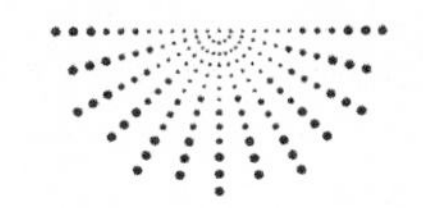

Nina struggled against the man's hold. He let go of her of his own accord, and she breathed a sigh of relief. There was no way she would have been able to break away on her own.

She sidled sideways, moving until she was no longer pinned against the car. Hurriedly, she zipped up her pants.

"I don't know who you are or what the hell you think you're doing, but I have to go. I need to find the other rental cars." Her voice was nowhere near as steady as she'd hoped.

How could she have let a stranger touch her that way? What was wrong with him? Crap, what was wrong with *her*?

A corner of the man's mouth pulled down. "I told you—my name is Dmitri, and I am your mate."

Warning lights flashed in her mind. There was that word again. *He is crazy.*

She backed away. "If you don't get the hell away from me, I'm going to call the police."

Dmitri didn't blink. "I don't think they're going to be able to get here anytime soon. This is a small town. I'm betting whatever emergency services they have are tied up with weather-related business."

Nina continued to retreat, her heart thumping as he followed, almost as if he were tracking her. Each step back she took was mirrored by one of his. "Then I'll go back inside and find security."

"I would never harm you. I only want to get you out of this storm," he said, his tone flawless in its sincerity.

Okay, so he's a committed crazy person. She held up a warning finger. "Why the hell would I believe anything you say?"

Dmitri laughed. The husky sound hit her ears and ran down her spine, making her shiver. It wasn't fear, so she automatically distrusted the feeling. Shoving it away, she spun on her heel, heading back to the main building.

"I can get you to Boston."

Nina turned around. "What?"

Dmitri waved around them. "There isn't a soul in sight. Those few motorists foolish enough to brave this weather have already left. The break in the storm is rapidly closing. I don't think you're going to find much in the way of help inside. The airport is in the process of shutting down."

He pointed to a near-empty patch of asphalt just left of the main building. "While we were…getting to know each other, the staff was leaving the building. Cars from the employee parking lot were departing from over there. Even the ambulances are leaving. There they are making the turn at the end of the road."

Double crap. He was right. While he'd distracted her, there had been a mass exodus. Whoever was left in the airport was going to be stuck there for the night.

She dropped her arms, letting her purse fall to the floor. "Damn it, I need to get to Boston."

"I doubt you'd be able to get a taxi from here at this point. Any driver with two brain cells to rub together is staying home today."

That was probably true, but she still wasn't going anywhere with him. She'd break into one of these cars before taking him up on his offer. Nina didn't think she could trust him. And she definitely couldn't trust herself around him.

Dmitri indicated a boxy SUV in the distance. "I took the precaution of ordering a car while we were still in the air. Given the fact you're trying to get to Boston despite a low-grade concussion, I have to assume your business there is important. You can go back inside and try your luck with the skeleton crew in there, or I can drive you."

Nina clenched her teeth, thinking it over. Something told her he was right. If she wanted to get home, he was her only option.

"I can give you my gun if it makes you feel more comfortable."

Her mouth dropped open. Dmitri held up a hand. "Before you freak out, it goes with this."

He reached into this pocket, fished out a black leather wallet, and flipped it open, displaying a shiny gold badge.

"You're an air marshal!" *Unbelievable.* "I thought you were a terrorist!"

This time, he did laugh aloud. He knelt, opened the rolling suitcase she hadn't noticed at his side, and pulled out a small lockbox. Rising, he gave it to her.

She took it automatically, testing the weight of it. "*Unreal.* Did you seriously just give me your gun?"

Dmitri crossed his arms. "If that's what it takes to get you to trust me, yes."

She flicked her gaze over him, skepticism only getting stronger. "Like you couldn't wrestle this away if you wanted to."

Dmitri put his hands in his pockets. "I'm not going to do that."

A frigid gust of wind hit them, but he didn't react. It was as if it didn't affect him. She was not so lucky. Her teeth began to chatter.

"Tell you what," he said, pulling out his phone. He tapped the screen, typing briskly before handing it to her. "Why don't you follow these instructions to change the combination on the lock? It's easy if you know the current code, which is zero-four-eight-one."

She wrinkled her nose. "What I should do is look up your credentials."

Dmitri lifted a shoulder. "I'm afraid a list of air marshals isn't something you can find on Google. A little matter of national security."

He raised a key fob in the direction of the SUV. The distinctive beep and click of a car unlocking carried over to them. Dmitri pressed another button, and the engine started.

"It doesn't need to warm up, but that will start the heater." He began to walk toward the car.

He moved quickly. Before she knew it, he'd climbed into the SUV. It pulled alongside her a moment later. The vehicle was a hunter green Range Rover, and it appeared to be brand new. Dmitri reached across the passenger seat, throwing the door open.

A waft of welcome heat hit her in the face.

Biting her lip, Nina turned back to the airport building. Through the glass, she could see some of her fellow passengers. One, a woman, was settling on a bench, presumably for the night.

She turned back to the open door. The vehicle was high enough that she didn't need to bend over to speak to the driver.

"All right. I'm coming. But if you touch me, I'm shooting you with your own gun."

Dmitri didn't answer. Instead, he hit a button, the rear door lifting automatically. She circled the car, put her suitcase in the back, and closed the hatch. Taking a deep breath, she composed herself before straightening her shoulders and making her way to the passenger side. Nina climbed into the seat, setting her purse at her feet. She also kept the gun case, clutching it tightly in her lap. Tension stretched over her, keeping her muscles tense. She stared straight ahead, wondering what she had gotten herself into.

CHAPTER FIVE

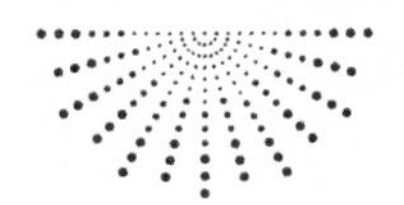

Americans were too trusting. All he had to do was flash a badge at them, and they instinctively believed it was real.

Well, his was technically real. He'd paid a premium for it, and the profile and identity that was crafted specifically for it. Dmitri only used his air marshal cover on certain jobs, quick ones that required the insurance a firearm provided. If his task was a little more involved, he had Cass ship special equipment and arms directly to the site. They would be waiting for him at his hotel or safe house along with his standard pack of provisions.

The latter procedure was neat and clean, but also restricting. In his experience, a client always overestimated the time needed to pull a job. Dmitri liked being able to pop in and out without having to haul a suitcase full of gear around. It was why he only traveled with one change of clothes and, if necessary, the gun. If he needed anything else, he bought it and added it to his client's bill.

He peeked at his mate out of the corner of his eye as he pulled onto the highway. God, she smelled amazing.

Nina was gripping his gun case, holding it between her and the door. It was cute that she thought her actions would keep it from him if he'd been determined to get it, which he wasn't. If holding the gun was what it took to make her feel safe with him, then it would do…for now.

She kept peeking at him from under those dark lashes. They'd been on the road for almost half an hour before he sensed she was finally relaxing.

"So, what do you do?" he asked, a grin playing on his lips. He knew the answer, but was curious about the details.

"I cut people open for a living," she said in a warning tone.

He laughed. "And where do you do this? A hospital or a funeral home?"

"Boston Memorial."

"And do you do this cutting on the living or the dead? Or does Boston Memorial not have a pathology department?"

She huffed. "The living. I'm a surgeon. Cardiothoracic."

Dmitri let out a low whistle. A doctor was one thing, but he'd been expecting something a little more girly like a pediatrician. Well, mucking about with hearts was kind of romantic, he supposed.

"And how long have you been an air marshal?" she asked.

"Oh, a while," he said, keeping his eyes on the road. There was a flare of heat and tangy musk from the passenger seat. His answer frustrated her.

"And it pays well, does it? Or did you win the lottery?" she asked skeptically. "You bought this car just now, didn't you? It still has the temporary plates with dealership name on them."

"I ordered it from the plane. It was obvious the rental agency was going to be wiped out by the time we landed."

"And your profession pays well enough to be able to buy a car just like that?" She snapped her fingers, not even trying to hide her suspicion.

It was a fair question. Government agents didn't make much. He wasn't wearing one of his ten thousand-dollar suits, and he'd been seated in coach next to her. She was smart to be skeptical.

"It does when you moonlight. I combine my pitiful salary with a few side contracts," he replied. "The job I've been hired to do in Boston would pay for ten of these." *And then some.*

He didn't have to glance over to know her expression was dubious. Everything she was feeling was right there in her scent. There was no uncertainty or confusion. She was coming across so clearly. Dmitri had never been so tuned into someone. It was like reading a book that he wanted to eat. He grinned.

"What's so funny?" she asked.

"That you don't believe me, but it's fine. Eventually, you're going to know everything there is about me."

Fear crept into the air. He turned to her. "What's wrong?"

Her dark eyes flashed. "I don't like it when you say stuff like that. A—it's presumptuous. B—it's super creepy."

Okay, no destined mates talk. He was going to have to win her the old-fashioned pre-*Twilight* era way.

He flashed his most disarming smile. "It's a long drive to Boston. I hope you're not going to keep mum the whole time."

Her mouth twisted. "No, I won't be 'keeping mum'. I thought you were Russian? That's your accent, right?"

"I am," he confirmed. "But I've spent a lot of time in the UK, and have lived all over."

"Really?" There was something in her tone that most people wouldn't have noticed.

"Have you ever lived abroad?"

"No. I was offered a fellowship last year to do a specialty rotation in London, but I turned it down."

"Why?"

She turned away, fixing her gaze out the window. "Family reasons."

Hmm. "So, what's happening in Boston that can't wait?"

For a minute, he thought she wasn't going to answer. "A wedding."

His heart reached down to squeeze his balls. "Not yours, I hope?"

"*No*."

Patience was not his strong suit, but Dmitri had done more than one interrogation. Recalcitrant subjects tended to speak when you let the silence stretch.

"It's my sister's wedding."

Ah. Family was apparently very important to Nina. That might complicate things, but it could be worse. As a lone wolf, he had no pack obligations. His only issue was having to share her with her own people. Her profession would necessitate special consideration as well. Big-time surgeons required large hospitals and he liked living near forests, places he could let his wolf run without too much fear of discovery.

You're getting ahead of yourself.

"Are you a bridesmaid or maid of honor?"

"No."

Interesting.

"I take it you and your sister don't get along?"

She turned to him before settling back in her seat. "We used to. When we were small."

"What happened?" he asked.

"We grew up."

Dmitri knew there was more to it than that. Nina didn't sound happy for her sister. A difficult history could explain some resentment, but he didn't peg her as the petty type.

"How does your mother feel about you not being a bridesmaid?"

Nina shrugged.

This was getting nowhere. He fished his flask out of his inside coat pocket, then offered it to her.

"In case you're still feeling cold."

She uncapped the flash and sniffed, her nose wrinkling adorably. "How did you get this on the plane?"

"They don't frisk air marshals. It's thirty-year-old scotch, by the way. Not vodka."

Nina handed it back. "I don't really drink."

"You can't possibly be on call," he teased.

Her sudden shudder caught him off guard. Concerned, he was about to pull over to the side of the road when she snatched the flask back. Viciously, she unscrewed the cap, then took a big swig.

When she finally spoke, her voice was flat, devoid of all emotion. "My mother *is* angry at me for not being a bridesmaid. So is my sister. They say it's necessary, to save face. But I said no."

"Why would you need to save face?"

"Because up until six months ago, the man my sister is marrying was my fiancé."

Nina didn't know what possessed her to confide in Dmitri. She didn't talk about Matthew and Kate to anyone, not even her friends.

Although you don't have many of those. Most of her social circle had been friends from medical school or work, back when she and Matt had been a couple. When they broke up, most of them had sided with her in public, but in practice they belonged to him. He was the gregarious one people gravitated toward. Always a bit shy, she let him do the work of making friends.

Despite what had happened, she could only count on Jodi and Jesse as her friends now. The rest of their social circle just pitied her. Seeing her at work made them uncomfortable, especially when Matt invited most of them to his wedding to her sister.

Imagine if they knew he was using their reception hall. Matt had put them on the list for the exclusive venue almost two years ago. Losing the hefty deposit they paid would have been too much of a waste.

Her parents were deeply troubled by the rift between her and Kate, but Nina wasn't surprised when they accepted their youngest daughter's surprise engagement. Kate didn't even have to go into one of her trademark histrionic fits. Just the threat of one was enough to make them cave these days. Her sister had exhausted them into submission long ago.

"You're better off."

Blinking, she turned to Dmitri in surprise. She'd forgotten he was there.

"I know." And she did, really. But that didn't stop her from feeling as if someone had dug her heart out with a spoon.

"I guess the wedding's going to be kind of rough."

"You have no idea." Attending her ex-fiancé's wedding to her sister at Nina's dream venue, surrounded by all the friends and family who'd been waiting years for *her* wedding…

She couldn't think of a worse nightmare.

"Are you sure you want to go?" Dmitri asked. He gestured to the open road. "I can take you anywhere you want."

"Don't tempt me." She laughed before taking a deep breath. "I can handle it. It's fine."

He snorted. "Yeah, and Russians don't like Vodka. Let me guess… this sister of yours has a long history of stealing your boyfriends."

"No, actually. This is an upgrade for her. Before, she used to just take my toys, then my clothes, and eventually my car—until she crashed it a week later. Our dad bought her a sports coup after that."

"So, she's a spoiled brat."

Nina was regretting starting this conversation. "It's complicated."

Accepting that with a nod, he lapsed into silence. When his phone began to ring, he lifted it and accepted the call.

"Cass? What's up?"

A voice launched into conversation over the line. It sounded like a woman.

"Well, he's going to have to wait. I don't control the weather."

Nina turned away, trying not to listen, but it was impossible to avoid eavesdropping.

Dmitri sighed. "Ugh, well too bad. Turn down the bonus. I can't make it out any sooner. If the weather report I read on the plane is still holding, then there aren't going to be any flights in between here and there."

The voice said something else. "The client can bitch and moan all he wants, it's not going to change." Another pause. "Then he can hire someone else."

This time, the voice got loud. Dmitri huffed. "Relax. He's been shopping this job around for months and he's not had any takers. He's not going to hire someone else in the next three days. It took him long enough to find me."

He clicked off, then turned his attention to the in-dash GPS. "Can you check the weather report for me? The direct route was clear the last time I checked, but that may have changed. Cass confirmed the detail about the flights. All planes are grounded in Wyoming and neighboring states. The storm is worse now than when we were forced to land."

She did as he asked. Her stomach knotted as she perused the weather app, and then raised her head to glance out the window. The sky was too dark for midafternoon. "I think we have a problem. The storm is in front of us now. And behind us. It's kind of everywhere."

Nina bit her lip, noting the rapid rate snow was falling now—or rather, was sweeping sideways. The wind had picked up while she'd been wallowing in self-pity.

"How bad is it?"

She scanned the report again. "Bad."

Dmitri drummed his fingers on the steering wheel. "I thought we had a shot at outrunning the blizzard, but I guess I was wrong. We're going to have to stop and take shelter somewhere soon, probably for the night."

The words were appropriate. Even the delivery—it had just the right degree of concern and regret. But Nina had a sneaking suspicion Dmitri was pleased with the turn of events.

CHAPTER SIX

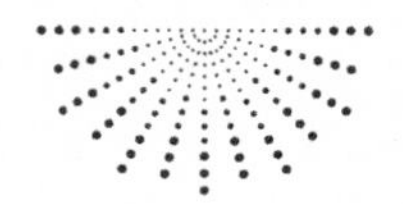

The crease between his mate's brows deepened when he took the next turn. She cast a nervous glance at the sky before squinting at the road ahead. Visibility was fucked. Even with his superior visual acuity, he could only see a few feet in front of them.

Dmitri kept driving as fast as he dared, but he'd been forced to reduce speed due to the conditions. He couldn't afford to stop, though. The temperature in the car was going to drop like a stone once he turned the engine off, and he'd have to soon if he wanted to make it to the next gas station when the weather improved.

"Don't worry. The cabin Cass lined up for us is only a few more clicks away according to this," he said, tapping the display.

He didn't take his eyes off the road, but the sound of Nina gulping was like a little knife to his soul. "It's going to be fine."

"Who are you trying to convince?" Nina sounded calm, but her elevated heartbeat and the spike of adrenaline in her blood was messing with his equilibrium.

Come on, where the fuck is this place?

A few miles passed in tense silence. "Maybe this Cass lied and there is no cabin."

"Of course there's a cabin. Why would you say that?"

Nina gave him an *are-you-kidding-me* look. "She could be pissed you're spending the night with another woman."

"Cass isn't my girlfriend. She works for me."

"Really?" Disbelief pulled her full lips into a frown.

"Why the skepticism?"

"Because she sounded really annoyed with you. I don't like my boss all the time either, but I know well enough to bite my tongue when he's pissed me off."

Nina didn't strike him as someone who held back much in life, but she *was* going to her ex-fiancé's wedding to her sister...

"Hmm, that sounds nice. Unfortunately, I've known Cass for years and years, so she has no qualms in sharing her opinion. Quite loudly, too. And since she gets paid on commission, she has a vested interest in getting me to Boston ASAP."

"Ah."

Wondering if Cass was his girlfriend had to be a good sign, he decided. At least it distracted her from their predicament.

That last was getting worse. He was driving at a crawl now. His superior vision was useless in the wall of white that was the road.

"How much longer?"

He checked the GPS. "Two clicks," he said, breathing a sigh of relief.

She didn't share his feelings. "In this weather, that's like a hundred," she muttered, drawing in a short breath. "The car may not make it much farther."

"Don't worry. We can walk to make it the rest of the way. I have an excellent sense of direction."

Nina's snort was the only answer.

"Never underestimate a Russian in winter."

"I think you're confused. It's *Russian winters* you have to watch out for." She cast another anxiety-ridden glance out the window. "Just ask Napoleon and Hitler."

"Relax. I've tangled with General Winter before." As long as the GPS was accurate, he'd be good crossing ten miles with her on his back, but there was no point in telling her that. The skeptical scientist in her wouldn't believe it until she saw it.

The distance to their destination grew smaller and smaller. However, the snowbanks only grew. They were piled high from storms earlier in the week.

When it reached the approximate height of Nina's waist, he began to search for a place to park. He couldn't tell if he was still on the road but leaving it where they were might be a bad idea, particularly if they were going to depend on a snowplow to get them out.

A sudden warning jostle shook the Rover. "I think we ran over a rock. I'm taking that as a sign we are no longer on the highway proper. But if this is correct, the house is only a couple of hundred yards away."

"Okay." Nina's gaze drifted down to the gun case, her fingers tightening. "I'm keeping this."

He was going to have enough to carry with their bags. "Suit yourself but use the strap. You're going to need your hands free."

Dmitri climbed out of the car. His dense body sank up to his thighs in the deep snow. He was around the car and opening the back to reach for their bags before Nina got her door open. Shouldering both bags, he hustled to the passenger side.

Nina was out, struggling in the deep snow.

"Are you sure you don't want to wait in the car? I can come back for you," he said, raising his voice as the wind shrieked. Sharp flakes pelted their faces like tiny knives.

"No. Let's do this!" Nina yelled as she waded, half pushing, half-crawling.

Heaven save me from stubborn mates. Rolling his eyes, he fished out his goggles from his bag—his only concession to the storm.

Widening his stride, he overtook her in a blink. He grabbed her wrist, urging her to hold the back of his coat. "Don't let go. I'm going to make a path. You follow," he ordered, turning his head so she could see him.

Squinting against the wind and snow, Nina nodded. The small pull of her holding him was all the incentive he needed. With a suitcase in each hand, he began plowing through the snow in the direction of the house.

It better be there, he thought, consulting the map in his head, overlaying that on the uninformative terrain in front of him. He counted paces in his head impatiently, aware their progress was too slow. Nina was going to be an icicle by the time he got her indoors.

Determination propelled his feet, picturing them indoors drinking hot Russian tea. Visualization had always helped with difficult tasks. For fun, he threw in a few images of a naked Nina, which had the added benefit of sending flashes of heat through him.

It didn't last. He was feeling General Winter's bite. Nina stumbled behind him. Dmitri whipped around, tossing the suitcases aside.

Despite making a path, it was too difficult for her to go on. "Hold on," he shouted. The wind had picked up. When he scooped her up, she let out a little shriek, but she didn't protest. He hefted her higher, tossing her over his shoulder in a fireman's hold. The gun case banged him in the hip.

Free to move now, Dmitri redoubled his efforts. "We're almost there."

He wasn't sure if she heard him. The wind carried his words away.

The cabin should be steps away. He could feel Nina's heart pounding. Her anxiety was infectious, but he'd never been one to succumb to fear. Dmitri's reaction was to get angry.

He almost ran headfirst into the cabin. Relieved, he laughed aloud and knocked on the wall. "We're here."

Dmitri maintained contact with the wood as he rounded the corner to find a door underneath a roofed porch. According to the specs Cass sent, this was the back door that faced a lake, now wholly obscured by the storm.

A smack on his lower back reminded him to put Nina down.

Her mouth was slack. "*Damn.* How strong are you?" She waved in the direction they had come. "That should have been impossible."

Dmitri grinned. "Not impossible. C'mon, we have to find the key box. It should be under the porch on the right."

She put her hand on his arm. "What about the bags? If you don't get them now, they could get buried. We might never find them. I can search for the key box on my own."

He cast an assessing glance at the sky. The snow was still coming down fast and hard. "All right, but when you find it, open it and get inside. It's got a combination lock."

He rattled off the code before jumping off the porch to backtrack for the suitcases. "I'll be right back."

The suitcases were easy to find. The storm hadn't been able to cover his wide track yet, despite its best effort. He returned to the cabin a few minutes later to find Nina lying on the snow next to the porch.

His heart dropped to his gut before he noticed she was still moving. *Stop overreacting.* Nina was on her stomach because she'd had to dig to get to the box. She was struggling, reaching for something he couldn't see.

The wooden porch creaked under his weight, Her eyes met his.

"I accidentally pushed it farther away," she shouted, fighting to be heard over the wind.

"Here, let me." He helped her up, noting her wet gloves. The thin fashionable leather wasn't meant for digging in the snow. His long arms fished out the box in no time. Nina was jumping up and down to keep warm as he opened it.

After he unlocked it, he hustled Nina inside, snatching their bags and closing the door against the fierce wind.

Their shelter was a single large room. Two padded wooden chairs faced a fireplace stocked with wood. On the left, there was a tiny kitchenette. A single bed was against the far wall.

Dmitri pulled Nina to him, then methodically began to pull off her clothes.

CHAPTER SEVEN

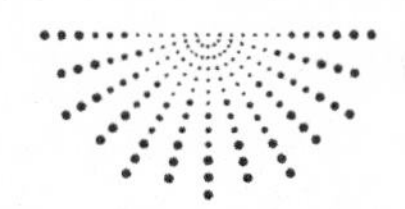

Nina froze as Dmitri began to run his hands all over her. She found her tongue as he began to strip her.

"What are you doing?"

"You're wet," he said, removing her coat. He started to pull at her gloves. "You need to get out of these clothes. Check and see if there are blankets and sheets in that chest." He indicated the one at the foot of the bed.

"I can undress myself," she protested, trying to back away to safety.

Dmitri succeeded in tugging the glove off, engulfing her fingers with his giant paw. Heat burned through her near-frozen digits, and she gasped aloud.

"Are you sure about that?" Dmitri's voice was smug. He took her other hand, rubbing it until the blood slowly began to course through them again.

"You need to take better care of these. Aren't you a surgeon? You can't afford to get frostbite."

He held her until the pins and needles stopped. Blushing, Nina peeked at him from under her lashes. "I can't believe how warm you are." He hadn't been wearing gloves, and he was still hot to the touch.

He did all the work getting us here. His blood was pumping fast from all the exercise. That explained it. She hadn't quite convinced herself, but he was right. She needed to get out of her wet clothes.

This was no time for modesty, but she was still embarrassed. "Can you turn around?"

Dmitri nodded politely. "I'll start a fire."

He went to kneel by the fireplace. Nina hurried to her suitcase, pulling out a change of clothes before tugging off her pants. Her shoes and socks were soaked through. Down to her bra and panties, she practically sprinted to the linen chest, pulling out a thin blanket. Once she wrapped it around herself, she made her way to the wooden chair, then huddled there as the burly Russian got the fire going.

His body blocked her view, but the distinctive snap and crackle of flames buoyed her spirits. "That is officially the best sound in the world," she muttered, drawing the blanket closer to hide her body when he stood and turned around. "Is there electricity? Maybe a generator or—"

Nina lost her train of thought when Dmitri unfastened his pants. He toed off his boots and tugged the black jeans down, revealing a skin-tight pair of red boxer briefs and thick muscular thighs.

Heat flooded her cheeks. Her neck hurt as she nearly gave herself whiplash by jerking her head back up. Dmitri was big in every way. *Every way.*

He turned to hang the pants on the set of fireplace pokers next to him. His shirt followed soon after.

The man's chest was a literal work of art. His back could have been carved from marble, but when he turned around, she had to bite her lip. Either he was a mutant or he spent all his time in the gym. Nina blinked owlishly at his chest, telling herself she was wrong. Humans couldn't have a ten pack, could they?

Dressed only in his boxer briefs, Dmitri sat in the chair next to her with a casualness she envied.

Why on God's green earth would he be embarrassed or shy? If she had a body like that, she'd be an exhibitionist, too.

"Feeling better yet?"

"Um, yeah," she said, shaking her head to stop the replay of anatomical charts running in her mind. Nina raised her toes, trying to get them closer to the fire.

"Here, let me." Dmitri slipped off the chair, kneeling in front of her. She didn't have time to protest before he grabbed her feet, using his massive hands to warm them up.

Nina was mortified. "You don't have to do that," she said, trying unsuccessfully to pull away.

"It's no problem." His dark slumberous gaze sent adrenaline coursing through her. Little hard bits of her soul started to soften and melt.

Nina abruptly pulled her feet away. "I'm fine now. I better see if I have cell reception here. I need to call home."

Dmitri nodded, staying put as she went off in search of her phone. He stretched out in front of the fire languorously, like a cat basking in the sun.

She had to tear her eyes away. There was a single bar on her phone, but she gave up trying to call after a few failed attempts. It wouldn't connect. She didn't know if it was the storm or a reception dead zone. Dmitri had mentioned this was a summer vacation spot. If there weren't people here year-round, there might not be many cell towers.

Sighing, Nina decided her feet were dry enough. She pulled on socks and pants under the blanket, doing her best to ignore the near-naked man lying in front of the fire like a living bear rug. She made sure Dmitri wasn't peeking before pulling on a clean sweater. Then she investigated the cabinets.

Uh-oh.

"Dmitri, there's no food."

Well, of course there *wasn't.* People rented these out during the summertime. They would bring their provisions with them.

When she turned around, Dmitri was pulling on his pants. He reached for his T-shirt. "I was warned about this. Cass said there's a general store on site. It'll be locked for the season, but it should have canned and dry goods. It's only a half-click away."

"*No*. Don't even think about going back out." She tried to tug the shirt away, but it was like playing tug-of-war with a giant.

"I'll be fine." He pulled the shirt back on, winking at her as he tucked it into his waistband.

"I'm not that hungry," she insisted. "In fact, I could stand to lose a few pounds."

"Don't you dare. You're perfect." Dmitri's growl was roughly amused. He put on the ski goggles before donning a scarf and hat. "I'll be back in twenty minutes. Stay by the fire."

He was gone before she could reply.

For the next twenty minutes, Nina paced back and forth, going to the window periodically to check for Dmitri's large form, but the visibility was only marginally better than when they arrived.

He's going to be fine. For Pete's sake, the massive Russian had carried her here. His physicality was superior to the professional athletes she'd seen come through the hospital. He was unreal, more akin to an artist's rendering of what men should look like.

Stop it. The last thing she needed was an infatuation for a man she wasn't going to see again in a few days.

Keep the fire going. He was going to need to warm up fast when he returned. Nina tossed another log on the flames before returning to her vigil at the window. How much time had passed?

She checked her phone. It was over twenty minutes now, closer to half an hour.

There might be a lot of reasons for the delay. Dmitri might have gotten distracted picking stuff out at the store. She always lost track of time shopping. Of course, technically he was stealing, but if he didn't leave cash for their supplies, she'd mail them a check as soon as she arrived home.

With each minute that ticked by, she grew increasingly nervous. A quarter of an hour later, she was convinced something terrible had happened. Nina squinted out the window for signs of movement, mentally willing Dmitri to appear, but from this vantage point, she could only see a very narrow slice of the terrain.

Pulling on her shoes and coat, she went to the door. She made sure it didn't lock behind her before stepping outside.

Nina spotted him immediately. He was too far to make out clearly in this haze, but she could see his black leather-clad arm waving at her.

He wasn't getting any closer. His substantial form seemed frozen in place. Had he gotten stuck somehow? *Crap.*

"I'll be right there!" Nina ran inside, throwing on her scarf and gloves again. They may have still been wet, but it was better than nothing in the driving snow.

Her feet sank into the fresh powder off the porch. Instantly, she was freezing again, but she couldn't afford to stop. What if Dmitri had stepped on a bear trap under the snow? He could be bleeding out, just a few dozen feet away from the cabin door.

By the time she was halfway, her thighs were burning. Only a few more feet, she promised herself. "Are you hurt?" she yelled, wondering why Dmitri hadn't stopped waving.

She reached out, only to touch slick plastic. What the hell? Up close, the form stopped appearing human. She pulled the plastic away, revealing a mound of bricks.

Swearing aloud, Nina turned back to the cabin, eager to get inside before Dmitri returned and caught her being so stupid.

The thick snow was even harder to get through on the way back.

I thought I was in better shape than this.

As a surgeon, she spent a lot of time on her feet. A reasonable degree of physical fitness was required. She'd even started working out with a trainer to build endurance.

If Brad could see her now, he'd want to expand her workouts. *I may just let him,* she thought, struggling the last few feet before the porch.

Was it her imagination or was the snow finally slowing down? It appeared so. At least it was no longer coming at her sideways, but falling delicately the way it should when viewed through the comfort of a window. Preferably when wrapped in a blanket drinking cocoa.

The wind was also starting to die down. That was why she heard Dmitri yelling at her.

She spun toward the sound, ready to explain what an idiot she'd been, when she heard a whooshing sound. She glanced up just in time to see a wall of white come crashing down on top of her.

Pulse racing, Dmitri dug frantically through the pile of snow underneath the porch overhang. What the hell had Nina been thinking coming outside?

His shopping trip had taken a bit longer than he'd expected. The map of the campground area wasn't to scale, and the general store was farther than estimated. Once there, he'd picked the lock and helped himself to whatever looked good, leaving a wad of bills to cover the lot before closing up and hurrying back. He'd been just in time to see a thick layer of snow slide off the slanted porch right onto his mate's head.

I should have come back faster. If he had, maybe Nina wouldn't be buried.

"Nina! Are you okay?"

There was no answer. *Shit.*

Another fistful of snow revealed a bit of black hair. Roaring, he redoubled his efforts, digging her out with care. His nostrils flared, smelling for blood. There was only a trace, thank the Mother. He checked her head and spine for injuries before scooping her up—leaving her useless little hat behind in the snow.

Dmitri carried his unconscious mate inside. She'd already hit her head once today. What were the fucking chances of being hit again?

Thankfully, the only bump he found was the same one as before. Her pupils appeared normal, and she was breathing evenly.

"When you wake up, I'm going to spank you so hard."

The arresting mental image made him stiffen. *Don't even think about it.* He should go back outside and dive in a snowbank, but he had to take care of Nina—starting with stripping her wet clothes. Otherwise, she might get hypothermia.

He laid her on the bed, his eyes running over her still form. Even in a coat, he could make out her bountiful curves. *Damn it.* This was a test of nobility he did not need.

Dmitri dug out an extra sheet and threw it over Nina, undressing her through it by feel. When the sheet accidentally slipped, he tugged it back in place in a herculean effort of will.

Off went her coat and blouse. Working rapidly, he tugged off her pants, shoes, and socks. He left the bra and panties on, yanked back the covers, and slid her beneath them.

Fucking hell, her skin was cold to the touch. Grunting, he stripped down and slipped into the bed with her. He knew from experience that the best way to warm her up was to use his own body. Despite being out in the snow for far longer than she, he was radiating heat, thanks to the workout his hormones were getting.

He settled Nina against him, enjoying the silky feel of her skin too much to feel guilty about it. His only real problem, aside from the raging hard-on, was keeping his hands to himself.

CHAPTER EIGHT

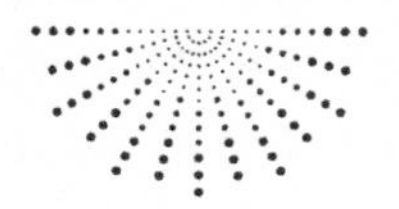

The warmth was downright luxurious. Stretching languorously, Nina reveled in the heat. After being cold for so long, it felt almost sinful. And the room's smell was amazing. It made her want to breathe in deeper. She burrowed under the blanket. She almost never slept without a nightgown, but it felt good. She liked the way her skin tingled against the pillow as she rubbed against it.

The pillow groaned.

Nina's eyes flew open. The realization that all but her underclothes were gone and she was in bed with Dmitri slowly trickled into her confused mind. He was shirtless, his incredibly sculpted chest just inches away.

Dmitri rolled, lying on top of her. Blinking fast, she finally focused on his scowling face.

"Why the hell would you go outside?" he asked.

"Um..." For the life of her, she couldn't remember. All she could think about was the way his thickly muscled arms were like a cage, trapping her against the mattress.

A rush of liquid warmth between her legs surprised her. She was having a hard time catching her breath.

"I'm waiting for an answer, Nina."

Dmitri's hot breath fanned across her cheek. His accent had grown thicker, making his W's sound like V's.

She squirmed underneath him, hyperaware that the tips of her breasts were pressed against his chest. "I...uh... *oh God.*"

Her insides were turning to molten lava, but he wanted an answer... What was it?

"The bricks!" she squeaked. "I saw the tarp flapping, and thought it was you waving."

The crease in his forehead deepened. "I've been told I'm built like a brick shit-house before, but you literally confused me for a pile of *bricks?*"

Her heart was thrumming now, but she wasn't afraid. If anything, his deepening aggression was making her hotter.

"I couldn't see that well." Her voice was a thready whisper. "It was snowing too hard."

"You scared the crap out of me," he said, his accent thick enough to cut with a knife. "You realize I have to punish you, right?"

Dmitri's head lowered until his lips were grazing her cheek. Tingles of electricity sparked where he touched her skin.

"I..." Words formed in her head, but they stubbornly refused to make sentences. The nonsense gibberish kept flowing, but all that came out were squeaky whimpers and increasingly rapid panting.

An inhumanly hot man was lying on top of her. Something like this had never happened.

What do I do?

You have sex. Lots and lots of it... She was supposed to attend her ex's wedding to her sister in a few days. If anyone was entitled to a rebound fling, it was her.

Dmitri's mouth came down on hers. It was just like the parking lot. All resistance was blown to smithereens in an instant.

His tongue parted her lips, tasting in teasing sips before he pulled his head back. A deep rumble came from his throat.

"Delicious," he growled.

The second kiss burned through her. Her body arched involuntarily. Dmitri undulated over her, slipping between her parted legs like a contortionist.

The thin material of his boxer briefs was little barrier at all. His hot, hard length pressed against her soaked panties. Heartbeat skyrocketing, she rubbed against him mindlessly.

It was as if someone had taken control of her body. All thought, all reason, was gone. Her tongue frantically pushed against his, tangling and twisting. He was delicious, too, an instant addiction.

Cool air hit her as Dmitri moved down her body, stripping her bra off. His fingers dipped into the waistband of her panties, tugging them to her ankles before sliding them free. His head bent, tongue taking a hard lick at her parted lips.

Writhing, Nina grabbed his hair reflexively, tugging on it. *"Please, please…"* She had to make him stop before she exploded. Suddenly, that was terrifying.

Dmitri moved back up, nudging her legs wider with his knee. He settled between her thighs, his underwear lost somewhere along the way. His bare cock grazed her wetness, sliding over her lips, sending jolts of pleasure straight to her brain.

She couldn't stand it. Sex should not be this intense—and he wasn't even inside her yet. At this rate, it was going to kill her, but she didn't care anymore. She sucked on the skin of his neck, still wanting more

"I can't," she gasped, finding enough breath to push the two words out.

"You can, love." Dmitri's eyes were hot. "But you need to calm down. Slow your breathing or you might hyperventilate."

He waited for a beat while she fought to obey. She took one deep breath, and then another, clawing at his back to have something to hold onto. The racing of her heart slowed a fraction and she let go, sinking into the mattress.

Dmitri took hold of his cock, adjusting her slightly before resting the head of it against her clit. Her eyes began to drift closed in anticipation, but she caught Dmitri shaking his head. "I want you to watch me take you."

Holy hell. Despite an aversion to being told what to do, her eyes flew down, unable to resist.

He was huge. Not monstrous, thank God, but bigger than anything she'd ever seen in real life—not even at the hospital. Granted, she didn't operate on prostates, but over the course of her career, she'd seen enough to know this man was blessed.

He began to move, his shaft sliding over her clit. Her body responded instantly, growing soft in anticipation. Nina opened her legs a fraction wider to reveal her pink inner lips.

His smile was smug, but it dropped away quickly. His focus was on her pussy, which was laid out like a feast before him. He pumped his dick, turning the head a deep rose color. The satin tip parted her folds, running up and down until she squirmed beneath him.

Dmitri bent to press a kiss to her forehead before leaning even closer. He fit himself to her entrance, pressing against her. "I was going to put my mouth on you first, to make it easier to take me. But this can't wait anymore. I have to be inside you."

Nina held her breath as he flexed his hips, pressing his cock against her entrance. He felt larger than he looked. Her mouth gaped. "*Oh, God.*"

The cry was involuntary, ripped from her when his cock breached her, the bulbous head popping past the ring of muscles constricting her entrance. It was more intense than anything she'd ever experienced. She felt like a virgin being opened for the first time.

Dmitri flexed his hips, driving inside with a loud growl. He swallowed her gasp with his lips, withdrawing and thrusting in again, deeper. A third stroke and his entire length was inside, flush to his balls.

Overwhelmed, she flinched. Her instinct was to push him away. He was too large for her, but her body wouldn't let him go. Instead, she tightened on him, trying to hold him inside her.

It was like grabbing at Quicksilver. He slid in and out easily now. She was wet and warm around him, meeting his thrusts—as much as he would allow. She only had a little room. His hips fixed her to the mattress as his tempo increased.

Refusing to be passive, she clawed at his back, using her sheath to caress and stroke him back, thrust for thrust.

"You're driving me crazy," he whispered. At least, that was what she thought he said. His accent was so thick now she could hardly understand him.

No, she was the crazy one. She'd lost her mind. Nina had never had a one-night stand in her life—had never even considered one. Now she was in bed with a near stranger, a perfect human specimen with a cock from the gods.

Her head hit the headboard and Dmitri swore, pulling her down the mattress. Concerned, he touched her head, but she hadn't even felt it.

"*No*." She wiggled, trying to push at his arms and hips. "Don't stop. Don't ever stop."

This time, the jackass laughed. "Don't stop what?"

His cock was thick inside her, but he wasn't moving and none of her efforts budged him.

Dmitri bent his head, pulling out far enough so his lips could reach her breast. He lathed her nipple, licking and sucking into his mouth.

"What do you need, baby?"

A tiny part of her brain was screaming something about willpower, but she ignored it. Any self-respect she might have had long since crumpled to dust.

"I need you to fuck me," she panted, whimpering as he thrust once very slowly.

He was still amused. "If you want, I can go down on you instead. Should I fuck you with my tongue?"

"No!"

Nina was near her breaking point. She could feel the orgasm just beyond her grasp, an explosion. A few more strokes of his cock, plundering deep, was all she needed. She'd do it herself, rubbing and twisting against him, but he was too strong. She was pinned to the mattress.

"*Please*," she cried, clutching at him.

"Say it."

"Say what?"

"Say that you're *mine*."

"Huh?" The rusty gears in her mind turned slowly until she understood. Dmitri was holding her orgasm hostage until she told him *what?*

A single stroke teased her. "I said tell me you're mine. Now. Forever. Your mind, body, heart. I want it all."

She stared at him. He was serious. She wanted to tell him he was crazy, but that wasn't what came out.

"Why?"

"Because I already know you belong to me. But you need to know it, too."

Nina gaped, her heart picking up speed.

"Now, Nina." The veins in his neck were corded as if he was under great strain. Good. He should be hurting, too. But this kind of pain was pleasure's twin, and she could end it by saying two words.

Dmitri was too impatient to stay still. He began to thrust, slowly this time… She sighed in relief, wrapping her arms around him, but he wasn't ending their little standoff. His pace stayed in the same maddeningly even tempo, just enough friction to keep her hungry.

Shit. Little warning shocks of electricity ran through her body, but the build was too slow. She tried to stay strong, but Dmitri was too smart for that. He knew what he was doing. Nina was on the brink, her body poised for flight, but until he let her, it wasn't going to happen.

Just say it. Hell, she felt like his already. What difference did it make?

Her lips firmed mulishly.

His eyes hot, Dmitri pushed all the way in, grinding right against her G-spot, breaking down her resolve the best way he knew how. Red swamped her vision, and she pulsed around him. Moaning aloud, she writhed, trying to force him to speed up, but he held her down, not letting her break.

The tension built, and she sobbed aloud.

"*Nina...*" Her name was hissed as both prayer and warning.

Fuck. She couldn't stand it anymore. "*I'm yours,*" she gasped.

His breath expelled in a shaky rush, and he closed his eyes, murmuring something in unintelligible Russian.

She didn't understand what he'd said, but her heart skipped a beat. Dmitri pressed her into the bed and began to stroke in earnest, harder and faster. Her whole body rocked, the metal frame of the bed grinding and squeaking as if it were going to break.

Nina accepted each thrust greedily, wiggling and twisting to rock in counterpoint until he swore, and she felt the head of his shaft pulsing. Hot jets of seed filled her, coating her sheath as she splintered, shattering and falling to the ground like a shower of sparks.

Dmitri fucked her through their orgasms, wringing every ounce of pleasure from her body until she was lying prone on the bed, emptied and broken like the fiery wreckage of an exploded star. He landed on top of her with a shudder, his open mouth at the base of her neck. For a long moment, his teeth grazed her, but after a minute he let go, falling to her side with his arms wrapped around her.

Her last thought before passing out was absurd, the product of the fevered mind of a woman who'd just had her brains fucked out.

He was going to bite me.

CHAPTER NINE

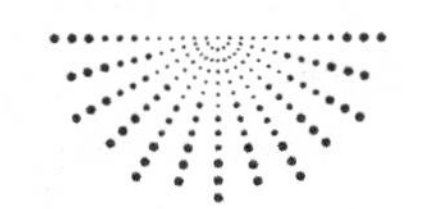

His mate had the most beautiful skin. Dmitri had been studying her face for nearly an hour, ever since he woke up.

He couldn't believe he'd slept at all. He wasn't the kind to drop off after a bout of sex. Usually after he rocked some female's world, *she* would fall asleep, exhausted from trying to satisfy a *Were* in his prime. Once the woman was in dreamland, no doubt reliving their encounter, he would find his clothes and make a quiet exit.

The first time with his mate and he was out like a light.

I needed the rest. Nina had sapped his strength in a single round. Her curvy and fragile human body was so small he could carry her in the crook of his arm, but she may as well have been a damn wrecking ball.

At least he didn't have too much on his plate at the moment. His meeting Nina on a plane had been less than ideal, given his inevitable reaction to her, but the timing couldn't be faulted. Except for the Boston job, his schedule was wide open. Of course, Cass wouldn't agree, but she was a bit of a pessimist, especially if the job had a six-figure payday attached like this one.

This weather delay had Cass's panties in a twist, but he'd never failed to deliver on a job, so she could simmer down while he handled the work at his own pace. Once he wrapped up the job—few days max —he'd be able to focus entirely on his mate. Maybe he'd take her home to seal the deal in the traditional manner of the men in his family.

His mother would have been pleased with Nina. She was special. Calling her a firecracker would be an insult. No, she was TNT wrapped in C-4. Which was why he needed to secure her as soon as possible...

Dmitri had known her for less than a day, but he was already willing to bend his world around her.

There were two types of male *weres*. Those who sought out the mate bond and those who ran from it. He'd done neither. Since he was technically rogue, he was used to passing through other packs, coming and going as he pleased.

He'd seen a fair number of shifter couples come together. Some welcomed the all-encompassing bond. They saw it as an end to loneliness, and a chance for a truly intimate connection. It made them complete. Others, often men like him, went down hard, fighting it every inch of the way.

Dmitri learned a lot from observation. He hadn't been in a hurry to find his true mate, but he'd always known that when he did, he'd take what life offered. It was his way. *Laissez-faire* didn't work for economies, but it did for the way he lived.

If life was giving him Nina, he was smart enough to take her, now and forever. She was more than a gift...she was a promise. Of what, he only had part of the answer. Time would give him the rest. He was looking forward to it.

Unable to help himself, Dmitri caressed the creamy skin on Nina's hip. He knew he should let her sleep, but her siren's call lured him in even in repose.

Hunger roared, and his touch grew aggressive. She had slept long enough.

Nina's nose wrinkled. She sighed, eyes fluttering open. Dmitri watched her face as she woke. He knew the exact moment she hit full consciousness. In his arms, her entire body tensed when she realized where she was.

She peeked down, then snatched up the blanket to cover her bare breasts. Her bashfulness was adorable.

"I'm naked," she whispered in a hoarse voice, sounding as if she couldn't believe it.

"Making love is easier that way. Don't get me wrong—even if you were dressed, I could work around whatever you were wearing. I've been known to get creative when presented with obstacles..."

She clutched the blanket closer, flushing a delicate rose, but her body quickened and heated deliciously. The predator in him licked its chops.

He bent to take her lips, but she put a hand on his chest. "We shouldn't."

Dmitri shifted, enjoying the way her silky skin felt against his much rougher body. "Why not?"

She wanted him—that much was clear in her scent. It wrapped around him, teasing his senses and making him hard.

He turned on his back, taking her with him. She landed on top, breasts pressed to his chest.

"B-because we can't." Her eyes were clouded with confusion and lust, but she didn't try to move.

Dmitri stroked her hair. "Tell you what. You can take me this time. I'm nothing if not fair."

He shifted, bringing his cock to rest against the silky skin of her inner thigh. She gasped, her eyes widening as he rolled his hips, rubbing a little so she could feel the breadth and width of his long length.

A little sound escaped her, something between a squeak and a huff of disbelief. Her fingers splayed on his pecs, and she started to stroke down his abs as if counting the ridges. Hungry now, Dmitri focused on her lips, so rosy and swollen from his earlier kisses.

"You're miles away from home, Nina," he murmured. "Think about what you want for a change. I bet you don't get a chance to do that too often."

It was a bit of swing, but he saw her eyes flare with heat and need. The tip of her tongue flicked to lick her upper lip. Confident he had her now, Dmitri pressed on her back, guiding her forward for a kiss.

She met him with a whimper, a tiny tremor running through her as he took advantage of her parted lips to slip inside. He stroked her tongue with his, teasing until she was kissing him back. Gripping her hips, he adjusted her until her wet heat was sliding over his shaft without actual penetration.

He pressed his head into the pillow, exulting in the feel of her—the way her weight felt on his lap and the delicious friction of her pussy on his cock.

Dmitri wasn't the kind to enjoy the anticipation of sex. He liked fucking too much to waste time on foreplay. His past partners hadn't been the sort who minded. But a mate was different. She had to be savored. He could honestly do this all day.

Nina, however, had overcome her reticence. Tiny teeth biting into her lip in concentration, she reached for him, rising enough to fit the head of his shaft at her entrance.

"*Oh, oh, oh.*" Nina panted, her breasts heaving as she settled onto him, swallowing him inch by inch into her tight little channel.

It was better than Nirvana. The high of every drug he'd ever taken paled in comparison.

"That's it, baby. Ride me." His growl was unintelligible even to him, but she understood. Tentatively, she began to move.

There was such a disparity in their sizes that she needed help at first. He leaned against the pillow, letting her crouch over him at an angle so she could back onto his cock with ease. But they weren't mates for nothing. Soon enough, she adjusted, catching and setting a rhythm that stole his breath.

"*Hell.*" Dmitri's jaw clenched, his eyes nearly rolling back in his head as the vise of her muscles tightened on the downstroke.

Not one to be outdone, he bent his head, urging her close enough to take her breasts in his mouth. He lathed the bud, grazing it with his teeth, then sucking until she cried out and fell against him.

Dmitri pushed her up, turning his attention to the other breast. As he rolled her nipple between his teeth, he reached between them, pressing on her clit with the pad of his thumb until she was gyrating on his lap. Her moans were like music to his ears.

"Louder, baby. I want you to be louder," he urged, pausing to bite the delicate lobe of her ear before taking control of her hips. He grabbed them, pushing and pulling until she was riding him hard, driving up and down on his lap.

A few moments later, Nina screamed, her eyes closing as her pussy spasmed around him, going soft and silky with her climax. Her orgasm started to tip him over the edge, but he moved, pulling out and turning her over until she was on her hands and knees beneath him.

Palming one of her breasts, he thrust into her from behind, barely missing a beat. He fucked her fast and hard, slamming into the creamy skin of her backside with audible slaps. Electricity shot through the base of his skull. He had to bite his tongue to keep from howling aloud as he came, pulsing and shooting his seed into her, driving it deep into her waiting womb.

He collapsed, breathing fast, before rolling to his side, his arms thrown around her to pin her against him. Pulling her in tight, he refused to leave her body until she made him.

That didn't happen for some time, but she eventually pulled away, turning to face him.

She was so easy to read. Her face gave away everything she was thinking.

Never let her play poker against Cass.

"I have no idea what I'm doing," she whispered.

"I beg to differ. I think you do everything *very* well."

She tsked and smacked his arm, regretting it instantly. "Damn it," she said, shaking out her smarting hand. "What the hell are you made out of?"

"Sugar and spice and everything nice."

Nina smirked. "That's girls. Boys are made of snips and snails and puppy dog tails."

Dmitri scowled. "Is that how that saying goes? I object. And what the hell is a snip?"

Shrugging, she giggled. "I think they mean like a leftover bit of something."

He hmphed and pulled her closer, stroking her hip despite strong hunger pangs. It wasn't until her stomach growled that he reluctantly rose.

The bag of supplies he'd borrowed from the general store had been forgotten on the table.

"I'm afraid there's not much of a selection for our meal. Nothing fresh. They only had canned stuff in stock, but there are peaches and chili." He paused, inspecting the due dates on the label. Only a month or two past. They would do.

When Nina didn't answer, he turned back to see her sitting up, huddled under the blanket. "Please tell me you aren't a vegetarian."

"No. I'm just feeling a little…weird."

Concerned, he put the can down. "Is it your head?"

"No, I mean…um…" She gestured to him. "I don't do this sort of thing a lot. I'm not into casual sex."

"Nina, it's time to face the facts… There is nothing casual about this."

Dmitri took the cans to the kitchenette stove, turning to hide the fact he could open them without using a can opener. He threw her a smile over his shoulder. "As a matter of fact, I think I should be your plus one to this wedding."

"That's sweet of you to offer, but you can't come." Her tone held a note of wistful finality.

"C'mon, love. You shouldn't have to face the firing squad alone. Take me along. Introduce me to the family. Make your sister eat her heart out."

Nina laughed. "Someone has a healthy opinion of themselves."

His back still to her, he flexed his gluts, making them dance for her. "Is your ex a big guy? Handsome and built? Rich?"

Even if he was, he wouldn't compare to Dmitri—not the way he planned on treating her. A mate was a wolf's greatest treasure. He was going to make sure she knew it.

"No, of course not! I mean, he's average. Not like you."

Facing her, he tried not to smirk as she stumbled over her words. "I mean, he's attractive. And he has family money, but that doesn't matter. I can't take you. I don't have a plus one to the reception."

"Your sister stole your fiancé *and* she is denying you a plus one to their wedding?" Damn, that was cold. He shuddered. "Makes me glad I'm an only child."

Nina fidgeted. "It's not like that. I didn't ask for a plus one. I also didn't exactly get a formal invitation—just my mother ordering me to be there. I'm not exactly on speaking terms with my sister. Besides, no one would believe I met someone so soon anyway. Matt and I were together for years. Since med school. My relatives would take one look at you and think I hired an actor...or a hooker."

Dmitri stirred the chili, deciding it was hot enough before digging around for bowls. "They won't think that. Trust me."

Even if they did, Dmitri wouldn't let them think it for long. Anybody making snide comments about his mate would have to answer to him. As for the rest of the lot, he was going to be a permanent fixture in Nina's life. Her relations might not buy their relationship right away, but it wouldn't take them long to see he wasn't going anywhere.

He held out a bowl of steaming chili to his mate. "Don't worry about anything now. It's going to be a little while before the roads are clear enough for us to get out. Until then, eat, rest, and recharge."

Her stomach growled, and she took the bowl without complaint. He watched with satisfaction as she began to eat.

This was only one of the ways he was going to take care of her. She'd soon learn the others once they left this cabin. Until then, they were stuck here, and he was going to make the most of every minute.

CHAPTER TEN

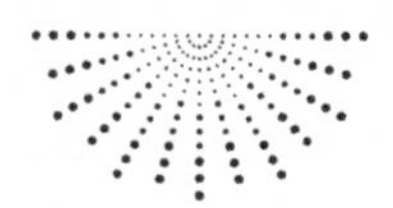

Nina shifted in the seat trying to relieve her discomfort. Only a few hours of driving and she was already stiff and aching. Or maybe that was all the sex? She squirmed again, parts of herself she was usually unaware of throbbing. And it was definitely not from the long car ride.

Over the past two days, she'd had more sex than the entire rest of her life combined. She'd lost count of the times she and Dmitri had come together, or the exact number of orgasms she'd had. Of course, now she was hurting in unfamiliar places.

No one should be able to go on and on like that, she thought, peeking at Dmitri from the corner of her eye.

Her gaze flashed to the steering wheel…those big hands holding the black leather-bound circle brought a flood of memories back—fingers on her breasts, on her ass, in her body. Blushing furiously, she turned away.

I must be insane. A few days ago, this man had been a complete stranger.

But now he'd touched or sucked every inch of her body. He'd fucked her in all the positions she'd heard of and a few she hadn't. He probably knew her body better than she did. She'd certainly never gotten herself off as fast or as hard as he had. And he was several orders of magnitude better in bed than her ex.

The man may be a professional escort. How else did he know how to do all that? He'd played her body like a fiddle. If he did charge money, women would throw their last dollar at him. And he'd deserve it.

He's an air marshal, not a hooker, she reminded herself. The man's protective instincts were real. She'd seen them multiple times, first on the plane during the emergency landing, then at the cabin with the way he fed and cared for her. Selfish people wouldn't have gone out of their way to ensure her safety and comfort like that. Even in bed, he'd been generous, always seeing to her pleasure before his. She wasn't used to that.

Matt hadn't been selfish, or at least she hadn't thought so at the time. But he'd been her first. Nina was only now starting to realize there was so much more to sex and intimacy than she'd believed.

Stop right there. Despite what Dmitri said, he was nothing more than a fling. She'd just been dumped by her fiancé for her sister. She was rebounding hard. Thinking he was serious about all this 'you are mine' crap was dangerous. Once they were back in Boston, the countdown to the end would start.

Maybe he would call her...and maybe he wouldn't. But whatever interest he had in her would fade soon enough after he went back to his own life. It was a fact. Men got bored and left when something better came along. This time, she was going to be ready. For as long as Dmitri stuck around, be it days or weeks or a few months—she'd shield her heart.

What's left of it...

"Don't even think about it."

Startled, Nina turned to watch Dmitri smirking knowingly. What the hell was he? The world's best lover *and* a mind reader to boot?

"What?" she asked.

"I can see the wheels turning. You're plotting something," he said. "If that something is how to ditch me so you can go to the wedding alone, forget about it. I texted Cass about proper attire. My best suit should be ready and waiting at my hotel when we arrive."

A sneaky little part of her was happy to hear he still wanted to go, but she knew it would cause more problems than it solved. Plus. from his assistant's frequent calls, it seemed more likely Dmitri would need to go back to work the minute they got back.

Her lips parted as another thought occurred to her. "Why does an air marshal need an assistant?"

"Hmm?" Dmitri's eyes were back on the road.

"You said Cass worked on commission. She sets everything up for you. She got you this car, and now a suit. But aren't air marshals part of a government agency? If Cass worked for them, she wouldn't be paid on commission. What am I missing?"

Not to mention the price of this vehicle on such short notice. It had to be astronomical.

Dmitri pursed his lips and leaned back. "I told you I only do the marshals part-time. Cass helps me facilitate those private jobs I mentioned."

Nina wrinkled her nose. "Are government agencies that strapped for cash? Because I wasn't aware that was a job you could do part-time."

His shoulder lifted. "You know how it is. The national debt is out of control. Staff gets furloughed. We find outside work."

"Oh." That sounded reasonable…sort of. Except for the fact airport security was through the roof these days. Shouldn't there be more work for air marshals, not less?

"What do you do on those private jobs?"

He drummed his fingers on the steering wheel. "A little of this, a little of that."

Nina's mouth turned down, but Dmitri just smiled. "We should be past the borders of the storm by now. It's almost dinnertime, and there's got to be a decent diner or two up the road. Want to eat?"

As if on cue, her stomach growled, so she didn't argue when he found a place to eat. Aware the wedding was in less than twenty-four hours, she tried to rush him through the meal, but Dmitri seemed determined to get her life story. By the time her meal was over, he'd managed to work all the details of her childhood out of her, right up to high school. She expected his interest to wane once they were back on the road, but he kept asking questions, making her repeat things as if he were trying to commit them to memory.

Eventually, she passed out in the passenger seat, somewhere around the time they hit the Pennsylvania border after he'd managed to wheedle out the Cliff Notes version of her relationship with Matt. When she woke, she was sitting in the car alone in front of her apartment building.

What the hell? Why hadn't Dmitri woken her when he hit Boston? And how did he even know where she lived?

Nina started to get out of the car when Dmitri walked out of the building's front doors, his arms loaded. He waved the bags at her when he saw she was awake.

"I think I got everything," he said, dropping his load in the backseat. Nina twisted her neck to watch.

"Is that my bridesmaid dress?" she asked aghast as he threw a garment bag on top of her suitcase. "How did you even get inside my apartment?"

Dmitri climbed into the driver's seat. He held up her keys. "Is that what's in there? I thought you weren't going to be a bridesmaid."

Nina snatched them back. "I'm not, but try telling that to my sister and mother. Did you take my keys out of my purse? And how did you even know where I lived? Never mind, stupid question," she added in a mutter. "If you went through my purse, you got the address from my driver's license."

He shrugged, turning on the ignition. "You were sleeping. I thought I would check things out—make sure the coast was clear before carrying you upstairs. But when I saw your place, I changed my mind. I decided we should stay at my hotel suite."

Was he joking?

"This is my *home*. This is where you leave me. If you want to see me after this, we can go to dinner if you're still in town."

Shaking his head, he started the car. "I think you should stay with me. At least for now."

Nina covered her face. "We have been driving forever. I just want to go upstairs to my apartment and take a bath."

"But it's not your apartment."

"*What*? You know it is." She waved to the backseat. "Or did you find my clothes somewhere else?"

"That apartment isn't yours. It's the one you shared with your ex."

Nina whipped her head around. How did he know that? Matt had taken his clothes and personal items. He'd left their joint purchases behind, saying he didn't want any of them.

"It's my place now. He moved out over six months ago."

"And yet, he's still all over the place. I can smell him on everything. It's faded, true, but the taint is there."

Okay, he was definitely insane. Nina opened her mouth to tell him so, but Dmitri forestalled her.

"You deserve a fresh start, a five-star hotel, and a bed with cotton sheets too high a thread number to count. I'm staying at a suite in the Caislean. Come with me, stay as long as I do. You can take a bath there. According to the website, it has a jacuzzi tub. All the suites have them. The hotel also has a full spa. We can have a masseuse waiting for you. Just say the word."

She started to shake her head when he offered his hand, palm up. "Think about this—none of your relatives will know where to find you."

Damn, he was good.

"How many of them flew in for the wedding again?" he asked innocently.

She huffed. "Fine," she said, reaching out to shake firmly before letting go. "Drive. But don't expect polite conversation until after I get in a tub."

He pulled away from the curb. "One bubble bath coming right up."

"It better be a freaking huge one."

Dmitri smirked. "You already know it is."

She smacked his shoulder. "You know I meant the tub. And *ow*."

Chuckling, he snatched her smarting hand. He raised her fingers to his lips, then kissed them. "The tub is big enough to swim in. As for that other thing, well, let's just say it's a good thing the tub fits two."

Nina flushed. "I'll need to get ready at my place tomorrow. All my things are there."

"I brought everything you might need."

"Well, not my black dress, I bet, which is what I'm wearing. Not that yellow monstrosity." She gestured at the garment bag in the backseat.

"Yellow would be amazing on your skin tone."

"Not in that shade," she muttered.

"I'm guessing your sister is a bit of a bridezilla. She can't let anyone outshine her, huh?"

"No comment." Outshining Kate had never been the problem. *I wanted her to shine. We all did.*

"Doesn't matter." Dmitri shrugged. "I think we can do better than a little black dress. I know the hotel has some choice couture shops."

"I'm not buying a new dress for this."

"How about a whole new wardrobe? Just say the word and it's yours."

The car pulled up to the Caislean hotel, a luxurious high-rise just outside the financial district.

He was being either very sweet or very annoying. Nina hadn't decided yet. "I don't want a new wardrobe. Really, I don't need anything."

"You may not *need* it, but let me ask you this... What do you *deserve*?"

CHAPTER ELEVEN

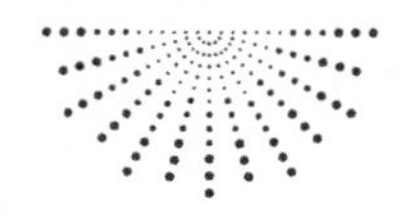

Are sex comas a thing?

Nina rolled over in the king-Sized bed, every muscle in her body pleasantly fatigued. She knew coming to Dmitri's hotel suite meant they would have more sex, but she hadn't realized he'd want to go all night. Somewhere before dawn, and her fifth orgasm, she'd had to tell him to stop. She needed sleep.

He'd wrapped his arms around her and dropped off immediately, snuffling lightly in his sleep. Exhausted, she'd done the same.

What time is it?

Crap! Nina had forgotten to set an alarm. Panicked, she sat up in bed. It was empty save for her. There was a note propped up next to the lamp.

Hello love,

I had to go out for a few hours for the job that brought me to town. I can't make the church service, but I'll meet you at the hotel to take to you the reception. Wait for me.

Yours,

Dmitri

"Shit!" The church service! What time was it? Nina jumped out of bed, searching for her cell phone. The clock confirmed her worst fears. The wedding started in twenty minutes.

Ignoring the many texts and voice mail alerts collected on her screen, Nina ran, dashing to the restroom for a quick rinse in the shower. On the way, she knocked over a rectangle-shaped box at the foot of the bed. A pile of dark red silk spilled out. Nina snatched it up before it could fall to the floor.

It was a dress, a deeply sexy one. And it was in her size. The damn thing had even been altered at the bust to give her a little more room where she needed it.

There was nothing overt or improper about it. The dress was tastefully cut, but the material was so fine it would mold to her body like a second skin.

She couldn't wear this...could she?

Well, it was this or the bridesmaid's dress and she would be damned before she wore that. Hurriedly, Nina showered, dressed, and gathered her hair into a clip, hiding the glory of the dress under a black wool coat. The doorman waved down a taxi for her. She left for the service just as it was scheduled to begin.

"St. Paul's church off Harvard Square, please."

Nina checked her phone's clock a million times as the cab crawled across town.

Their progress was slow enough she could safely jump out without hurting herself. The temptation to do just that was overwhelming.

Stop that. Just go and get it over with. It would be better in the long run.

The cab hit a pothole, jarring her hard enough to whip her head forward. *Ow.* Nina collapsed in the seat, letting her head fall back to stare at the roof of the cab.

"Why the hell am I doing this to myself?" she muttered. The universe did not answer.

After what felt like an eternity, she arrived. She threw money at the cabbie, then hurried up the church steps before the vehicle had come to a complete stop.

Her intention to slip in unnoticed was foiled by the loud noise her heels made on the stone floors. The church was strangely silent. Ahead of her, Matt and Kate were standing in front of the priest, their hands joined, but when she walked in, they turned to the door.

Her eyes met her sister's and she nodded once, hastening to sit in the last pew in the church, aware every eye was on her. She didn't look at Matt, staring straight ahead to the first pew where she guessed her parents were sitting.

In front, the priest coughed and continued the ceremony. Numb and still catching her breath from the morning's mad dash, she focused on breathing…just in case her body rebelled and decided to stop.

The minute the priest pronounced the couple man and wife, Nina slid to the end of the pew away from the aisle. She didn't want to be right next to it when her ex and her sister walked past with the rest of the bridal party, an assortment of her cousins and Matt's friends from high school.

It didn't help. Even with the distance between them, her sister stared daggers at her. Matt was worse. His expression of gracious pity made her blood boil.

"I thought you were going to stop the ceremony!"

Blinking, Nina turned to find her teenage cousin Carina kneeling at her side. "What? Why would I do that?"

"You ran in just when the priest asked if anyone objected."

Nina stifled a groan. *Perfect*. Could this get any worse?

"That was an accident. I arrived as soon as I could. I'm lucky to have made it at all after my flight was diverted to Wyoming."

Carina waved for her to move over, squeezing in the pew beside her. "I heard that from your mom, but I should warn you a lot of the relatives think she's making it up because you weren't coming. And then you run in just then—"

"*No*. It was just bad timing. I really did drive all night to make it back."

Almost. She would have been on time if she'd stayed at her place.

Of course, if she had, she would have been wallowing the entire night instead of enjoying multiple orgasms.

"I know you can take whatever her highness and that scumbag dish out," Carina assured her in a hiss. She craned her neck to check behind her. "People are giving you the eye as they leave. And your mom is going to give herself whiplash, gesturing that way with her head. I think she wants you to come out and take pictures with everyone."

Bile rose up in Nina's throat. Swallowing hard, she plastered a smile on her face. "In a minute, after the crush passes. I need to check in with the hospital. I was supposed to be back at work yesterday."

"I'll try to run interference with your mom." Carina leaned over, hugging her fiercely before slipping away. Nina stood, scanning for a side exit. When she didn't find one, she texted the charge nurse at the hospital from the pew before taking a deep breath and heading outside.

She posed for one photo, staying on the other side of her parents, as far away from the happy couple as possible. But she didn't need her mother's pinch to remind her to smile. As soon as it was over, she stepped away, discreetly evading the crowd to stand off to the side with Carina and a few of her younger cousins.

"What happened to you?" one of them asked, pointing at her head. Nina reached up to the bruise where the suitcase had broken the skin. There was a tiny steri-strip bandage at her hairline, one she hadn't applied herself.

Dmitri. He must have put it there in her sleep.

"It was quite an adventure getting here." She regaled them with details of her trip and the scary emergency landing, adding that she and her friend Dmitri ended up driving back together.

She fingered her phone as the crowd thinned, debating getting an Uber back to the Caislean hotel. The ceremony had been bad enough, but the reception promised to be ten times worse. *Dmitri did offer to go with you...*

Well, it was more like an order. She could go back to the hotel to wait for him.

No. Nina didn't need a shield. Besides, who knew how long Dmitri's business was going to take. She was better off doing this alone.

Nina was under enormous strain. Dmitri could see it in the line of her shoulders and the tight smile she wore as she spoke to a man and woman at the edge of the empty dance floor.

The reception was in a small and tastefully appointed dance hall a few miles from the church. He should have been annoyed Nina ignored his request to meet at the hotel, but he knew what it must have cost her to come on her own. It was written all over her face.

Damn his new client. The man had insisted on getting an update on the job first thing that morning. Since he didn't have any news, Dmitri had felt obliged to get things in motion.

It had taken longer than he'd intended, but he still would have been on time to meet Nina at the hotel had she chosen to wait for him. But his stubborn little mate was a glutton for punishment. She would be the type to insist on doing everything on her own.

Not anymore, Dmitri thought as he crossed the room to meet her.

The bride was working the crowd with a man in a black tuxedo, the groom presumably.

Vindication flooded him. Nina had unquestionably traded up.

The ex was average in every way. His height, hair, face, even his middling brown hair. *She won't miss him.* He would see to that.

Dmitri knew he was cutting a fine figure in his bespoke Hackett suit. It had been tailored to accommodate his wide shoulders and narrow waist. It fit him to a T, and people were noticing. He could feel the bubbles of curious interest following him as he strode across the room, stopping to nod and smile at a familiar-looking couple stationed near the cake—Nina's parent's no doubt. She was the spitting image of her father.

His examination was cut short by a well-manicured hand. "Hey there, handsome," a drunk bridesmaid said, leering up at him.

"Hey there, yourself," he said with a laugh, but he patted her head as he excused himself. He continued, sidestepping a couple standing and talking on the dance floor.

Despite the wisdom of making a good impression, he bypassed the parents, making a beeline for his mate. *And not a moment too soon.*

The happy couple was closing in on Nina's position, no doubt ready to make a spectacle of greeting her. He could see the bright false cheer all over the bride's face. Underneath, she was spitting nails. The man was harder to read, but he was going through the motions as well, greeting people with the joviality everyone expected from a groom. His facade only cracked when he glanced in Nina's direction, his eyes sweeping over her from head to toe.

The little prick. Nina's dress was for *him*.

He saw the moment Nina realized they were coming. Her speech slowed and she tensed, the move so slight he doubted anyone noticed. Without appearing to hurry, he rushed over, sliding in next to her and interrupting her conversation with a man and woman her age. He bent to kiss her cheek, wrapping his arm around her possessively.

"I see I got here just in time," he murmured.

"*Dmitri.*" Nina swayed a little, leaning into his embrace. Her eyes clouded over as she gazed up at him. Her relief was palpable.

The sounds of the crowd faded. Dmitri forgot their audience as he realized how much he'd missed her.

"I thought you were going to wait for me," he said in a low voice.

Nina's mouth quirked. "I never agreed to that."

The timbre of her voice changed as she relaxed in his hold. She might not have wanted him to come, but she was happy to see him. More than happy. The spike of pheromones in the air said as much. It kindled an answering response in his blood.

He sighed, pulling her in close. Just being in her presence was enough to make him hard…

Dmitri was debating finding a convenient closet somewhere for a more meaningful reunion when someone loudly cleared their throat.

Blinking, he laughed at the young couple watching them with avid interest.

Nina was blushing. “Oh, I’m so sorry. Dmitri, these are some old friends from med school. This is Jane and her husband Dale. We were all in the same year together.”

Dmitri nodded, oozing charm. “Please excuse us. You know how it is when you haven’t seen each other for a few hours,” he said with a nod. He extended his free hand. “I’m Dmitri Ivanov, Nina’s fiancé.”

CHAPTER TWELVE

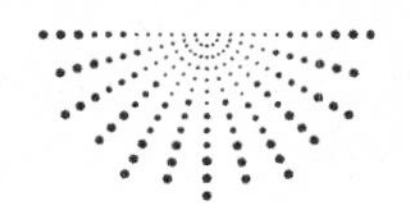

Jane's eyes, always a little protruding due to a minor thyroid issue, almost bugged out of her head.

"He's your *what*?" she gasped.

Nina nudged the impossible Russian hard with her hip. *"Dmitri,"* she hissed in a warning tone.

He pulled her in closer, the smug expression on his face almost enough to make her scream. "I know, I know. We're not supposed to say anything for a few more weeks. Sorry, *dusha moya*. It slipped out."

He turned to her—make that Matt's—best friends, and leaned in conspiratorially. "You'll keep that to yourselves, I hope."

Nina watched, wide-eyed, as Jane and Dale took it all in. And this pair of vipers would have been the biggest skeptics. Despite her claim they were old friends, these two had been staunchly on Matt's side since the breakup. They'd come up to her, with condescending grace, to wish her the best and to see how she was 'holding up'.

She knew these two well. What they really wanted was to pick at her pain like parasites. But now they were derailed.

"How long have you been engaged?" Dale asked, measuring Dmitri's biceps with his eyes as if he couldn't help himself. Though he was above-average height himself, it must have seemed like the Russian towered over him.

It wasn't just Dmitri's size or his broad chest. The man was an overwhelming presence—an alpha personality who made betas like Dale want to follow. The latter was drinking him in like a puppy.

With that little prompting, Dmitri launched into a romantic story of meeting in the park near her apartment months ago. He was so smooth, his lie flawlessly delivered. Nina held on to his arm, stunned as he weaved a simple and yet touching tale, springing in little facts about her life to give the whole thing an air of veracity.

The details caught her off guard until she remembered his relentless questioning over the past few days. Had he been preparing this story the whole time? It was too well-crafted to be off the cuff.

What had she gotten herself into? Nina's stomach tightened, her grip on Dmitri's arm loosening. Sensing her withdrawal, he turned and covered her hand with his, a gentle touch that soothed and comforted.

Unbelievably, the vipers were buying the whole thing, hook, line, and sinker. The Russian was a damn snake charmer.

Woman, get ahold of yourself. Being an amazing liar was a *bad* thing.

"Does Matt know?" Jane asked bluntly, snapping Nina out of her reverie.

Dmitri shrugged as if this was of no importance. "My only concern is when we tell her parents."

He laughed and held a finger up to his lips, making a shushing sound. "It won't be long now. Spring weddings on my family estate are a long tradition, so we're putting the notice in the papers in a few weeks—after the sister's honeymoon, of course. We wouldn't want to upstage the happy couple."

He gestured meaningfully at the not-too-distant bride and groom.

Nina glanced up long enough to see Kate watching them with pinched lips. She avoided Matt's gaze, preferring to face his friends instead.

"Speaking of your parents, darling, I think it's time you introduced me." He waved casually, leaving the pair and heading in the direction of her parents, bypassing the bride and groom with a cordial nod.

The pair ignored them. Kate turned her back, making a show of greeting a third cousin with too much enthusiasm.

Nina gritted her teeth, keeping her attention fixed on the Russian charging across the room. "Oh, no you don't," she whispered, trying to pull him to the doors.

He wouldn't budge. "You're going to want to introduce me to your parents now."

"And why is that?" She stopped short in the middle of the dance floor.

"Because the second I get you alone, I'm finding a private place so I can fuck you till you scream," he said, just loud enough for her to hear. "That can be before I meet your parents or after...your choice."

Holy hell. Nina flushed. "We are not doing that here," she insisted, but her voice was as weak as her knees.

Before she could think straight, Dmitri had dragged her to her parents.

"Zandra, Ricardo," he said, greeting them by name with his hand outstretched.

"Er, hello," her mother said, exchanging a sideways glance with her father as they shook hello.

He greeted her father in turn, launching into a steady stream of small talk and compliments on the loveliness of the wedding.

She didn't know who was more surprised, her father or her mother, but he broke down their surprise and skepticism the same way he'd done with Jane and Dale.

Within minutes he had them eating out of the palm of his hand.

It was so skillfully done Nina was convinced he *was* an actor. She was tempted to ask who had hired him, but her priority was getting him away from her family.

"Excuse me, Mom. Dad. I forgot the gift in the car," she lied when her father invited him to go fishing on his boat. She tugged at the big Russian's sleeve. "Will you help me?"

He came, but not until after he'd shook her father's hand again and kissed her mother on both cheeks, Gallic style. After that, he followed willingly, allowing her to pull him out the doors without a struggle.

"I hadn't realized you'd driven here," he said when they were alone. "Where is this gift?"

"I didn't buy them anything." Her focus had been getting through the event. Buying a gift hadn't crossed her mind.

"Well, in that case, it's a good thing I had the Caislean concierge send something—a nice little porcelain set. It's a traditional Russian wedding gift."

She stared. "*Why?*"

His eyes were soft on her face. "It's expected. Not that I think they'll last given the way your ex was eye-balling you. I give it a year at most."

What? "Whether they make it is no longer my concern. You're the only problem I have at the moment."

"Me?" he said with an injured air of innocence.

"Yes, you," she said from behind gritted teeth. "The only reason I'm not kicking your ass is because you didn't tell my parents we are engaged, too."

"That can be easily remedied, you know," he said, grinning back at her as he led her down the hallway. "I believe I'd like to see you try. I'll even bend over for you if you like, but I can't promise you won't forget what you were trying to do. My ass has been known to distract members of both sexes."

Nina stopped, closing her eyes to pray for patience. *The worst part —it's probably true.*

"Where are we?' she asked, opening her eyes. She'd been on autopilot, letting him pull her along with no heed to their surroundings.

They were in a nondescript hallway. The music from the main hall was distant.

Dmitri rapped his knuckles on a door marked *supply closet.*

"I scoped this place out earlier," he said, leaning in to put his mouth next to her ear. "This room is empty..."

"Absolutely not."

Nina's fingers dug into the wall behind her. "This is crazy. Why can't I say no to you?" She moaned as Dmitri pressed her against the closet wall, his mouth fluttering up and down her neck. Her legs were wrapped around his waist, her panties soaked and shoved to the side to make room for his fingers while he supported her with his other hand. Her heat was almost enough to scorch his skin.

"Because you don't want to," he murmured, turning his attention to her lips.

Her lower lip was an unholy temptation, but fortunately for him, there was no need to abstain. He bent his head, nipping it.

"Hey, no biting," Nina said, pinching him in retaliation.

"Sorry." He licked her lip, soothing it before sucking it gently.

One taste wasn't enough. Dmitri deepened the kiss, wanting more, while his fingers worked their magic, teasing and opening her for his possession.

"We have to stop. I can't do this here." The words were weak, broken by another moan as she writhed in his grasp.

"Are you sure?" His tongue snaked out, licking the soft spot near her ear. "Think about what memories you want to make tonight. This could be the day your ex-fiancé married your sister…or this could be the night your new fiancé fucked you senseless in a closet."

She hesitated, then threw her arms around his neck. He kissed her again, but not to silence her objections. Those were over. "Tell me you want me," he whispered, sucking an earlobe.

Nina strained against him, fingers digging into his back as he pressed a digit past the tight constriction of her entrance.

"*Oh, God,*" she gasped.

"Good enough."

Dmitri removed his hand from her tight pussy to open his pants. Pushing down his boxer briefs, he pumped his cock, touching it to her heated softness before pinning her to the wall and stroking in deep.

The ride was hot, fast, and furious, but he was motivated. Dmitri wanted to mark her, to brand her permanently.

Seeing his mate's ex in the flesh was enough to stoke his competitive streak. But he was serious about making this night about them.

She'd been hiding it well, but he knew Nina was hurting. He'd seen the way she'd averted her eyes, refusing to make eye contact with the groom. Dmitri didn't need to look into her eyes to see her pain. It was there in the set of her shoulders, and the tightness around her mouth.

He didn't like it.

It's okay. He was fixing it. By the time he was done with her tonight, she wouldn't remember the bastard's name.

"Dmitri," she gasped as he pumped into her hard.

That was a hell of a good start.

He thrust a little slower, easing out of her with deliberation. He wanted her to feel him—the thickness of his length, every ridge and vein.

Damn. He'd never been this hard or hot for anyone else before.

Her musk was intoxicating. Dmitri was almost drunk on it. He was pretty sure she was in a similar state. That was why he was here with her now—why she hadn't pushed him away. She couldn't. The burgeoning mate bond wouldn't let her.

Under normal circumstances, a woman watching her ex marry someone else would be a wreck. Most would be holed up somewhere licking their wounds, or at least drinking themselves into oblivion. Nina was too strong for that. Her family had demanded she be here, so she came and somehow managed to hold her head high.

By rights, she deserved to do this on her own. She was more than capable, but Dmitri wasn't about to let her flay herself alive, not when he could ease her.

And easing her he was...

Nina clamped down on him, going all silky soft around his cock as her orgasm blew through her. Her fingers trembled on his shoulders, her head fell back, and her body pulsed, milking his shaft for all he was worth.

Dmitri saw red, the highly focused storm of his orgasm rushing over him. His heart pounded, and he was an inch away from biting her and making their bond permanent.

Not yet. Not tonight. Tomorrow, Dmitri promised himself. *And not a moment later.*

His neck corded, trying to hold off his climax, but it was impossible. He let go with a hiss, pumping his seed in hard spurts as he clamped his jaw shut to keep quiet. If he hadn't, his roar would have been heard all the way down to the dance hall.

He slid down the wall with her in his arms, cradling her in his lap until she regained her senses.

When she did, she groaned. "I did not just have sex at my sister's wedding."

"*We* had sex," he said, the back of his neck prickling in disquiet. "Actually, we made love."

She pushed away, tears shining in her eyes.

"Nina, don't get upset." He stroked her back, then frowned as she scrambled to her feet.

"This is not me. I don't care what today is. I don't have sex to get back at anyone."

Dmitri hurried to stand, closing his fly in the process. "That's not what we were doing. This wasn't revenge sex." At least, he hoped not. "You're with me because you're mine now. It doesn't matter that you were his before. That's over. *I* am your future."

Nina stared up at his face. He knew she couldn't see his features clearly in the dark, but he could see her with crystal clarity. "You know you sound crazy right?"

He laughed. "I am crazy…about you. I love you."

She froze for a beat, staring in the general direction of his eyes.

Something in the air shifted, and her lips parted. "*Shit.* You're serious, aren't you?"

CHAPTER THIRTEEN

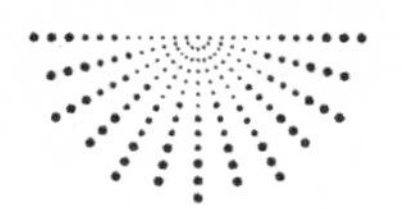

Nina stumbled to the bathroom in a daze. A bizarre cocktail of shame and hope was fizzing in her brain like champagne.

Don't forget, you hate champagne.

She needed to clean up before anyone saw her. Her inner thighs were wet with Dmitri's seed, face flushed and sweaty.

She almost tripped opening the door to the restroom. Breathing too fast, she stared at herself in the mirror before turning on the sink to splash water on her heated cheeks.

What the hell had she been thinking? She hadn't even asked him to wear a condom. Not just now and not at the cabin.

I was right. I have lost my mind. Not once in all this time had she even entertained the idea of consequences. *What kind of a doctor am I?*

She could well be pregnant now or worse. Dmitri appeared healthy but considering how fast he'd jumped into bed with her, he had to be a prolific lover. He could be teeming with STDs under the surface.

"Shit, shit, shit." She had to talk to him. Better yet, she needed him to give her a blood sample. *STAT.*

Grabbing some paper towels, she proceeded to wash up, her

cheeks flaming. Cleaning up after a clandestine sexual encounter was a new one.

You need to get ahold of yourself. Of all the problems in her life, this one shouldn't even rank. As long as none of her relatives saw her stumbling from the closet *en dishabille*, it wouldn't even be a blip.

And surprisingly enough, the fact she was at her sister and ex's wedding wasn't the biggest issue. What felt like a much greater one was the look in Dmitri's eyes when she left the closet without saying 'I love you' back.

He wasn't lying. There was no way for her to be certain of that, yet she knew it was the truth.

Nina should be screaming, running like hell in the other direction. But even as she thought it, she knew the only direction she was going to be running toward was the one he was in.

Crap.

How the hell had this happened? Nina was damaged goods, but she should have enough sense not to let another man near her right now.

But Dmitri was here tonight. He'd literally crashed into her life. After what he'd just said, it was getting clearer he meant to stay. That was why he'd insisted on coming to the wedding. It had been a calculated move to let everyone know.

This is too fast. Nina had to get her bearings, or everything was going to spin out of control.

After a few minutes, she had herself in hand. She repaired her coiffure as best she could, grateful she wasn't in the wedding party. The bridesmaids had elaborate hairdos she wouldn't have been able to replicate even with a hot iron and hundreds of YouTube tutorials.

Back when this was supposed to be her wedding, Kate was going to be maid of honor. Nina had asked her at her mother's insistence, but with poor grace. In the back of her mind, she'd expected her younger sister to find a way to make Nina's big day all about her. Nina snorted. Was this irony? She was a gifted doctor, but wasn't great with idioms, metaphors, and the like. Her English teacher would be disappointed at how often she had to Google definitions for those. One thing she did know...this should hurt more. She'd been one of the walking wounded for the better part of the year. But now she was either numb or too spent to think straight. *I guess I can thank Dmitri for that.* Nina took a last look in the mirror. She was presentable. Well, presentable-ish. But if her memory of past weddings was right, the hall lights would be dimmed now that the dancing had started. Her state might go unnoticed if she made her goodbyes quick.

Hesitating at the door, she reconsidered, but no…she had put this off long enough. She was going to speak to Kate—to publicly congratulate her baby sister on her wedding day.

When she pushed the swinging door open, it hit Matt on the shoulder.

"*Nina.*" Reaching for her, he took hold of her upper arms, pulling her to him.

Nina swiveled her neck right and left to make sure they were alone before pushing him away. "Don't you dare touch me," she hissed.

His eyes softened, meeting hers with a beseeching plea. "Nina, I made a mistake," he whispered, glancing over her shoulder at the main hall doors.

Aghast, she drew back. "You better be joking asshole."

"I'm not! I'm so sorry about the mess I made, but this was a huge mistake. Can we go somewhere and talk, please?"

"*Hell, no.*" Nina couldn't believe it. "You just married my baby sister."

"She's not who I thought she was. But I don't need to tell you that. She's a spoil—"

Despite what Kate had done, her protective instincts rose just as hot and as fierce as they had during their childhood. She held up a finger, wagging it in his face. "You finish that sentence and you lose a testicle."

She was the only one who got to criticize her sister, period.

"Nina, she seduced me. I'm sorry I let her, but *she* started it. How can you defend her? And who the hell is that guy you are with? I know he's not really your fiancé like everyone is saying. Did…did you hire him, so you wouldn't have to come here alone? Because if you did, I totally understand."

Wow. "You are unbelievable. Fucking unbelievable."

Matt was half a foot taller than her, and outweighed her by at least forty pounds, but she was seconds from wringing his bloody neck.

"Nina-bear, don't swear," he chided, still casting furtive glances over her shoulder.

Someone was there, but a quick glance confirmed it wasn't Kate or her parents. It was Edward, Matt's father. He scowled at her as if she'd ambushed his son. "What's all this?" he asked.

Nina ignored him, turning back to Matt and leaning in. "You have made your bed," she hissed. "If you don't lie in it and make my baby sister the happiest woman in the world, I will *end* you."

She pivoted on her heel, storming past a glowering Edward to find her sister.

When she did, she found Kate with Dmitri, the two standing in the corner away from the dancing crowd. His gaze was focused in her direction, but his face was hard, almost angry.

She paused in her tracks, but realized his attention wasn't on her. His gaze was trained just over her head. Puzzled, Nina checked behind her, but the only person there was Edward. His second wife, Constance, floated to his side and Nina turned away.

Kate watched her approach, her lower lip tightening petulantly. But her sister didn't turn her back this time.

She joined them with a nod, ducking under the arm Dmitri held out for her.

"There you are, love," he said brightly, but bent to whisper in her ear. "Any longer and I was going to start hunting you down."

Suddenly, his expression darkened. He took a deep sniff before his face cleared and he grinned. "I was just wishing your sister a traditional Russian blessing for a happy and fruitful marriage."

"That's nice," she said, watching her sister with a tight expression.

Every eye on the room was on them, but Nina didn't care. She also wasn't mad anymore. Just tired.

Kate was beautiful, as always. Her fine features were made up perfectly and her gorgeous hair was loose, showing off its curl and shine.

"You look lovely," Nina said. "I'm sorry I was late to the service."

"I understand. Your new boyfriend explained. I hope your head feels better. Thanks for driving so far to make it," Kate said softly, eyeing the big man suspiciously, but she reached for Nina's hands, gripping them tightly.

It was the first time they'd spoken since the big blow up all those months ago.

"I wouldn't have missed your wedding," Nina said, blinking a little too fast. Impulsively, she hugged her sister.

"Did you take your pill this morning?" she asked in a low voice as Kate returned her hug.

"Of course." Kate sighed, a tinge of exasperation in her tone. One minute and they were back to their normal roles. "And my regular appointment with Dr. Gandhi is the day after we get back from the honeymoon."

"Good." Nina leaned back, placing a hand on Kate's cheek. "Don't forget to take a vial of spare meds in your carry-on just in case your checked luggage gets lost or delayed."

"Yes, Mom." The tone was classic Kate, annoying baby sister. "Are we okay?" she added in a whisper.

"We're fine. I love you," Nina said, surprised to find she meant it.

"Darling, we should go," Dmitri interrupted gently, nudging her with his arm. "You have a very early day tomorrow."

Kate blinked, as if she had forgotten the massive man standing next to them.

"You're going to have to tell me how you two met later," she said, giving Dmitri an incredulous once over. "Mom and Dad are having a cow over him, discreetly of course..."

Grinning, Dmitri took Nina's arm.

"It's a long story," she said weakly as Dmitri leaned over. He gave Kate a big kiss on the cheek.

"Until next time, little sister."

They were in the Range Rover before Nina started breathing again. Dmitri was watching her closely.

"What?" she asked.

"I expected more fireworks."

She leaned back, stretching her shoulders. "I think everyone was. However, I love disappointing people." Unexpectedly tears stung at her eyes, but it wasn't the same as before.

"I'm never disappointed in you," Dmitri murmured after a moment of silence.

She sighed. "You just met me. Give me time."

He didn't appear to know how to answer that, so he focused on driving.

"I want to spend the night at my place."

"That's not a problem."

"Alone."

"Problem," he growled.

"Dmitri, I'm very tired. I need a little space."

"You can have space tomorrow. Tonight, you need me."

"I—"

He turned the steering wheel, pulling over to the curb before twisting to face her. "She's sick, isn't she? Your sister?"

Nina took a deep breath. "She has a congenital heart condition. One that is inoperable—at least for the moment. It has to be monitored closely."

"*Ah*... So the lifelong patient ended up a spoiled brat, one who only now realizes she went too far by stealing your milksop ex-fiancé. And you're a—"

Nina held up her hand. "And I'm a doctor who went into cardiac medicine to find a cure for her condition. Congratulations, you figured me out," she snapped. "It's hardly a complicated story. Please take me home now. And I'd like my things returned from the hotel in the morning. I do have to go to the hospital early, but you can leave my things with the doorman."

He was quiet. "The Caislean staff can have your things sent to you within the hour. And I can sleep over there if you want, but I would like to see you tomorrow. What time are you done at the hospital?"

"I have no idea," she said, letting her head loll to the side.

"*Nina*."

Drained, she could barely turn her head. "Hmm?"

"Let me take care of you tonight. We can just sleep. I know how tired you are."

At this point, she might not make it to the elevator of her building without help. "Fine. But in the morning, we are going to have a long talk."

Dmitri didn't even flinch. "I look forward to it."

His mate was dead to the world less than two minutes after he got her into her apartment. Nina had been so tired she'd passively let him strip her red dress off and put her to bed without a word.

He didn't think that kind of submissiveness was going to be all that common for them, but it was just as well that she was asleep. He needed to think. Dmitri had a very big problem.

What the hell had his client been doing at the wedding tonight?

He had recognized Edward Lawrence instantly. The prominent Boston businessman had hired him through a dark web backchannel. The man had insisted on remaining anonymous, setting up his down payment through a proxy to protect his identity. Despite those precautions, Cass had uncovered his real identity in less than five minutes.

Wait a minute. Wasn't Lawrence the last name of the groom? Dmitri swore under his breath. Upon reflection, the resemblance between the two men was clear.

His client was the father of Nina's ex.

CHAPTER FOURTEEN

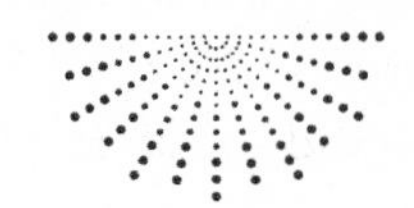

Nina woke to the smell of waffles. Bleary-eyed, she sat up, struggling to focus on her surroundings. She was home, not the Caislean hotel. The bright sunlight reflected off the honey pinewood floors beyond the forest green coverlet on her bed. Her overstocked bookshelves lined the walls on three sides of the room.

Her phone was on the bedside table, plugged into its charger. *Dmitri, of course*. She could hear him moving in the kitchen. Bowls and dishes clattered as he made breakfast.

Nina collapsed back on the bed, unsurprised to find herself naked except for her panties under the sheet. She pulled her phone off the base to check the time. Nine AM. She had slept eleven hours. That had to be a record. She hadn't gotten more than six or seven in a single stretch since med school. Thankfully, she didn't need to be at the hospital until after lunch.

They probably weren't expecting her in at all. The entire staff was aware of the wedding. Some had even been guests, although she hadn't spoken to many of them.

Nina had been quiet since her break-up with Matt. It had been too difficult to act normal, so she hadn't even tried. Not that it would have made a difference. Most of their coworkers had expressed sympathy with her, but only on the surface. In practice, they were team Matt.

Maybe her withdrawal was a good thing. Shutting down and not sharing at work might mean she could get away with everyone believing Dmitri *was* her boyfriend. Only her good friends Jodi and Jesse knew she had rarely left her apartment since the breakup. And they had graciously lied to everyone at work on her behalf, making up stories about rebound hookups that hadn't happened.

Nina made a mental note to take her friends to coffee to tell them the whole story. *Damn.* How did she start explaining Dmitri?

So much for this being a much-needed rebound fling… Well, when had she done relationships right anyway?

That included the one with Kate. When her baby sister had been diagnosed with her condition, Nina's caregiver switches had been flipped. They were still on full throttle all these years later. The Matt fiasco hadn't changed that.

She was still hurt, but losing him wouldn't end her relationship with her only sibling. True, it would never be the same, but the sting was less intense, and she had Dmitri to thank for that.

As for Matt himself, she would get through seeing him at family events, provided he overcame whatever misgivings he was having now. *He better…or else.*

"Hungry?" Dmitri was in the doorway of her bedroom, holding a loaded tray. His hair was damp, and he was wearing loose cotton pants.

His chest was bare. Her mouth watered, and not for the waffles he'd made for her.

"How did you do this?" she asked, pulling the sheet up to her neck as he set the tray down over her legs with a flourish. These thick golden treats hadn't come from the freezer.

"I don't have a waffle iron. And where the hell did you find fresh berries because I know it's not from my fridge?"

"I made a grocery run this morning," he said, picking a strawberry off her plate and popping it into his mouth. "Your fridge was empty."

"It usually is," she said, her voice just a notch above sandpaper. She cleared her throat. "My job doesn't leave me a lot of time to cook."

"Not a problem. As you know, I'm a good improviser." Dmitri waggled his eyebrows, making her smile despite her determination to stay in a bad mood. "Eat, *dusha moya.* You need your strength."

She was starting to recognize that expression in his eyes. "Don't even think about it. I am all sexed out."

"No one is ever all sexed-out. At least no one who is sleeping with me. It's like a replenishing well," he said, giving her an exaggerated wink. But he didn't make a move to touch her. Instead, he pushed the tray closer before waving a bottle of maple syrup in her face.

"I can think of several uses for this that is far more interesting than waffles by the way."

Nina suppressed a laugh. He was incorrigible. "I have to go to the hospital at noon, so that's a definite no."

One eyebrow cocked, bemusement crossing his features. "You know I can count the number of times I've heard that on one hand." He smirked. "Well, it's more like three fingers...and one of those turned into a yes the minute the woman's husband was in the bathroom."

Nina sniffed disdainfully. "You hit on a married woman?"

Dmitri shrugged, then stretched out next. Appearing every inch a lazy Roman emperor, he picked another berry off her plate. "I was at loose ends in a bar in Slovakia. The woman was making eyes at me all night. I thought she was alone. Turns out she was just waiting for her man to be out of sight. I took back my offer to rock her world by the way. There are enough single women in the world not to have to mess with the married ones."

He narrowed his eyes. "Except for you. Had you been married to the useless drip I saw yesterday, I would have taken you from him."

"Not touching that one," Nina muttered, focusing on her waffle, wondering how many women there had been. The number had to be astronomical. "Do you have any communicable diseases?"

Dmitri snorted, almost choking on a strawberry. "What...no lead-in?"

"I'm a doctor. What I've been doing with you—having unprotected sex—it's beyond irresponsible. Especially after this rather gross rundown of your past sexual history."

Nina put her fork down. "In fact, I'm starting to get nauseated the more I think about it."

"Baby, you don't have to worry about it. As I told you earlier, I'm clean. I've been out of commission in the boudoir department for a while. My last security detail went south, and I spent the last few months recovering. This is my first job since—" He broke off. "I actually landed in a huma—London hospital in the beginning before transferring to a specialist in Colorado. Between those two places, I got poked and prodded just about everywhere. Do you want me to make a call to get the results to whatever bloodwork I got done?"

Was he serious? "Uh... You know I'm a doctor, right?"

"Of course." He smirked, continuing to nibble off her plate.

She smacked his arm when he reached for the last strawberry, popping it into her mouth before he could snag it. "Giving me your medical records is not like handing them to anyone else. I'll be able to understand them. I might end up knowing more about you than you do."

He shrugged, a corner of his mouth pulling up. "I'm not scared."

Nina took another big bite, shaking her head at him. *He offered, and it's the quickest way to get those burning questions answered.*

"Fine, then. Make the call. But don't say I didn't warn you."

Dmitri got up, leaving the room and coming back with his cell phone. "It's too early for Colorado. Kiera won't be at the clinic yet, but London should be no problem."

"I'm going to take your word for it." In her experience, a patient requesting his own medical records was not a high priority for any medical facility unless the case was critical. She had enough time to shower and get ready for the hospital before he was done.

He left the room to make his request. She could hear the deep rumble of his voice, but no words. It was oddly comforting.

Nina started to polish off the last bit of her breakfast. Before she could finish, Dmitri was wagging his phone in her face.

"What's this?"

"My medical records."

"*What?*"

"Haven't you ever seen a PDF before?"

She snatched the phone from him. "Of course I have. But there was no way you got them that fast."

He shrugged. "I paid my bill in full. Cash. They were more than happy to help."

"Huh." Nina blinked, turning her attention to the screen. She scrolled down. They *had* done a cursory STD check—just the basics, but there were no red flags.

The tension in her shoulders eased...at least until she read farther down.

"What the hell!"

Dmitri started toying with her hair. "Hmm?" he murmured.

She pointed at the screen. "You were *poisoned*?"

He leaned back on the bed, putting his arms behind his head. "I told you the job went bad."

"*Dmitri.* A dose of strychnine this large should have been fatal, even to someone your size. How the hell did this happen? And how did you survive?"

The man yawned. "It was unavoidable. When I interrupted an attempt on my client's life, I breathed in the toxin. I lived. So did the client by the way."

"That's unbelievable." She turned back to the screen, rechecking the numbers. It was a miracle he survived.

"Wait, what is this?" Nina kept going, speed-reading the remaining lab results. All his other levels were way outside the standard range. The testosterone reading alone was cause for concern, and what the hell was going on with those protein levels?

Her lips parted, and she stared at him wide-eyed, her heart in her throat. "Dmitri, I think you're ill. These test results are not normal."

He shrugged. "I had just been poisoned."

"No, some of these readings would have been unaffected by the poison." She reached out, touching his arm. "Sweetie, I think you need to come to the hospital with me. You need a full workup."

She could tell he was trying not to smile. "Do you call all your patients sweetie?"

Nina sniffed. "Sometimes. Just the children and some of the women."

He scoffed. "Then definitely don't call me that. I prefer my love or dearest heart."

Her lips firmed. "Seriously?"

"Well, perhaps not. Those sound better in Russian. We'll find something else for you to call me, *dusha moya*."

"Don't try to distract me. You need to see a doctor."

"Oh, I'm seeing a lot of my doctor," he said, practically purring. He reached for the sheet, and tugged it down to reveal the deep V of her cleavage.

Frustrated, she snatched his hand and bit it.

He laughed delightedly. She spat him out, glaring at his smug face. "You're not taking me seriously."

"I'm very serious about you." He traced the top curve of her breast, eating her up with his eyes.

"I assure you I'm fine, love." He took the now-empty plate from in front of her, setting the tray on the bedside table before crawling over her. "If it makes you feel better, I can have the specialist I saw in Colorado give you a call. She can tell you all those other tests are normal for someone like me."

Someone like him? "I'll believe that when I hear it from her."

Despite the bulk of Dmitri's body, she was able to wiggle her hands free to change apps on his phone.

There were one or two pictures of her asleep in the cabin, but nothing else. Not even a selfie.

"No other pictures?" She'd expected to find hordes of women, his many past bed partners in living color.

He took the phone back with an *I'm-not-stupid* expression on his face. "You're not dealing with an amateur."

With that, he tossed the phone aside, drawing back the sheet and replacing it with his own body.

"Until Kiera is able to get in touch, allow me to demonstrate my full recovery. I think you'll find me quite fit..."

CHAPTER FIFTEEN

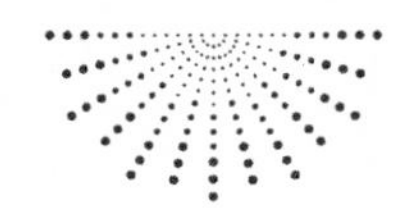

A very relaxed Dmitri dropped a flushed but well-satiated Nina at the rear hospital entrance a few minutes before her shift. He hadn't let her go without a big and deeply possessive kiss first.

The fact they were spotted by several members of the staff was a bonus. Dmitri knew Nina's ex also worked in the hospital. He wanted her coworkers to know she had traded up.

Cass buzzed in on his Bluetooth before he'd cleared the hospital parking lot.

"Are you done playing house yet?" she asked waspishly as he pulled into traffic.

"No. Not by a long shot."

There was a pause. "Are you telling me what I think you're telling me?

He laughed. She knew him so well. "And what might that be?"

Cass snorted. "C'mon. Since when have you spent more than a weekend with a woman? You're on what—day four now? You met your mate, didn't you?"

"It's day five actually. And yes, your guess is correct. The doctor in question, Nina Briggs, is *mine*."

"Whatever. I don't think the client cares that you just met your life partner. He wants the item he paid you six figures to retrieve, and he wants it yesterday."

The tone was harsher than usual, but Dmitri could detect the trace of pain behind them.

"You'll meet someone someday," he said softly. "You just need to have a little faith."

This wasn't jealousy. He and Cass had never been a thing, but ever since her accident, Cass had grown into her natural pessimism. He doubted that she even expected to find a mate.

Sadly, she was likely right. There weren't a lot of wolves out there who'd look twice at a shifter in a wheelchair.

"Oh, shut up," Cass snapped. "I'm beyond stupid things like that. A mate is just a fuck buddy you can't get rid of later when you want to be alone. And I prefer flying solo."

Dmitri sighed. His scheduler and friend had been a hermit too long, ever since she'd self-ostracized herself from her pack after the accident. He knew what would make her a little happier—the second half of her finder's fee.

"I just called to tell you I'm going to acquire the item for our client now. This job will be wrapped up in a couple of hours, tops."

"Good. This jerk has been up my ass for days now."

"I thought you enjoyed that sort of thing," he said, clicking off before she could think of a comeback.

Minutes later, he reached his destination, a choice Back Bay mansion on a wide tree-lined street. The house was protected by a state-of-the-art security system, but Dmitri always did his homework. He had the route all mapped out.

He spent a few minutes studying it from his car until the pre-determined window of opportunity opened.

Getting in was a little more difficult than he'd anticipated, but nothing Dmitri couldn't handle. Dressed as a well-heeled jogger, he hopped over the five-foot wrought-iron fence in one smooth leap.

At least there were no dogs to deal with this time around. There had been a whole pack of Rottweilers on a case the previous year before the poisoning.

Not that dogs were ever a significant issue. Even the most highly trained guard dog cowed in the presence of an alpha *Were*. Nevertheless, dealing with a bunch of frightened animals could complicate his exit plan, so he was grateful there weren't any around.

Dmitri slipped on his black gloves. The shaded dormer window on the attic level was his chosen point of entry. It was inaccessible from the ground floor, but the branches of a convenient pine tree were just close enough for a short jump.

He timed the thump of his landing in time with the passing of the local garbage truck. As long as someone wasn't in the attic on the other side of the window, the noise of his landing should be adequately masked. Or at least, he hoped that was the case. It was hard to mask all sound—his muscles were too dense. But he'd tried to move more quietly ever since that thing in Toulouse.

Using one hand, he held onto the jutting window frame, fishing out the spell stone from the gear bag strapped to his belt. He set the small flat stone on the sill. If it was wired into the security system, it would flash with an oily iridescence and heat up. Once it cooled, it meant the system was deactivated.

He'd paid a premium for the stone from Salvador, one of the few reliable witches he knew. They were friends of a sort, but Salvador, like him, didn't work for free.

Dmitri tested the heat of the stone with his finger. It was cool to the touch, which meant it was either defective or the window wasn't wired into the security system. He decided to bet on the latter, slipping the stone back into the bag to save it for another job. They were a one-time use charm.

It's now or never. He held his breath as he gripped the bottom of the sill with two fingers, exhaling slowly when no blaring alarm sounded.

Dmitri did another quick recon of the grounds to make sure he was unobserved before sliding his leg over the sill and slipping inside.

The attic was hot, cluttered, and dusty. He picked his way through the mishmash of old furniture and boxes until he was over the trapdoor entrance that led downstairs.

Focusing, he went into stealth mode, ghosting through the second story like a wraith. He was little more than a shadow. There wasn't even a creak of the hardwood floors to give him away.

According to his intel, the safe was in the master suite behind a genuine Renoir. He'd bribed the team that had installed it for the specs before coming to town. *A quick in and out.* That was how he rolled. Now he just had to make sure the house was empty. Genevieve Burgess, an old-money grande damme and retired witch, was away cruising the Caribbean on her private yacht.

He'd reached the hall to the master suite before he sensed something was wrong. His hearing didn't pick up anything. It was silent. No heartbeats, no breathing. But something wasn't right.

Dmitri paused, his acute sense of smell picking up the trace of copper too late. Outside, the distinctive wail of police sirens began to scream up the drive.

He threw open the door to the master suite. One glance was enough to tell him she was dead, bludgeoned by the blood-stained statuette lying next to her prone body. Behind her on the far wall, a priceless Renoir was tossed carelessly to the floor, the hidden safe behind it open and empty.

"Well, fuck me."

T*his is humiliating.*

Panting, Dmitri licked the hand the homicide detective cautiously extended toward him.

"Good boy," the man said, visibly relieved at getting all his fingers back.

It was an escape of last resort—one Dmitri had never had to employ until now. But desperate times called for desperate measures. He was posing...as a pet.

Not many people would believe a massive wolfhound wasn't a threat, but the obscenely wealthy were known to be eccentric in their choice of animal companions. Some kept lions; others kept monkeys. He was betting his life on the old stereotype working.

Unbeknownst to her friends and family, Genevieve Burgess had just acquired a wolf.

But Dmitri had to sell it, which was why he was reduced to playing the playful pup. Though he'd only had a minute to prepare, he carefully set the stage, fishing out a framed photograph of himself in wolf form, a diamond-studded collar, and a slightly used tennis ball.

He'd set the photo on the desk next to the body, picture facing the door so it would be the first thing the cops saw. When they opened the doors, he was sitting on his haunches next to the body and whining, the diamond collar around his neck shining in the bright sunlight. The gear bag was tied just under the collar, almost invisible in the thickness of his fur.

"Whoa, what the hell?" the first officer through the door had sworn, nearly dropping his gun. Dmitri had whined again, wagging his tail.

A female office joined the man. "Holy shit, that's a big one," she'd said.

You have no idea. He'd thrown the pair a lopsided grin.

That worked better than I thought it would.

In minutes, the cops had been checking their pockets for treats. He'd been allowed to nose around the crime scene while they did their assessment. Death by bludgeoning. They were here responding to an anonymous tip—of course.

Eventually, a dog-loving officer took him downstairs for a few surprisingly invigorating games of fetch, until the special detail of animal control arrived.

Dmitri allowed himself to be put in the truck. The minute the dogcatcher walked around to the front seat of his truck, he shifted back to bipedal form. Then he waited until he heard footsteps, timing it to give himself the best chance before rearing back. All out of spells, he punched the lock with his fist, jumping out and darting across the street to slide under the ambulance parked there.

Crawling naked from vehicle to vehicle, Dmitri worked his way down to his SUV down the street.

Pissed off, he yanked a clean shirt and pair of pants from the back of his car. The coroner's vehicle passed him on its way to the mansion as he pulled away. He had Cass on the phone the minute he got clear of the crime scene.

"I thought you vetted these jobs," he snapped after swearing a blue streak in her ear.

"What the fuck are you going on about?" she growled. "I laid everything out for you, a total softball of a job—just what you needed to come back after that mess of a last case."

"Well, your softball was a setup. The old Burgess crone was dead, her safe empty with the cops on the way."

"*What?*" Cass swore—longer and far more colorfully than him. "Wait, that doesn't make sense. That asshole was just on the line calling for an update. Before I could tell him you were on site, he offered a bonus, another ten grand if you could deliver the item tonight. If he was trying to set you up, why would he do that?"

"Most likely because he had no intention of following through," Dmitri said with a sniff, turning the corner sharply. "But it doesn't matter. I'm on my way to see the bastard now. Don't take any more of his calls. Leave this to me."

Cass sighed. "Whatever you do, don't get caught."

"Oh, don't worry. I won't." There was no way that was happening twice in one day.

CHAPTER SIXTEEN

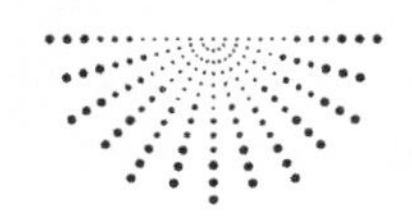

Dmitri stalked his prey at his place of business. He watched Lawrence meet with a client through a telephoto lens, searching for a window of opportunity to confront the man alone.

It wouldn't be difficult. According to the dossier Cass had worked up, Edward Lawrence was a creature of habit. He worked in the financial district, meeting clients for whiskey-laden convos until five sharp, after which his car picked him up to take him home. Then he spent an hour in his office before taking a shower and dressing for dinner at a variety of five-star restaurants or for a formal six-course meal at home.

What a douche.

Dmitri was waiting in Lawrence's home office at quarter past when his client waltzed in, picking his nose.

"Charming," Dmitri observed, making sure his voice carried.

"What the hell is this?" Lawrence stopped short, pulling out his cell phone. "Who let you in here?"

"I'm the thief you hired." Dmitri leaned back in the chair. "Now close the fucking door."

The man's expression shifted. "I thought I was supposed to get my item by special courier?" Lawrence closed the door behind him, his eyes lighting with greed as he came toward him. "Give it here. I want to see it."

Dmitri took a deep sniff, considering the man on the other side of the desk. There was no hint of deception, but all that meant was he hadn't asked the right question yet.

"It wasn't there," he said in a flat tone his friends would have recognized as a warning.

Lawrence sniffed and narrowed his eyes. "I thought you were supposed to be the best. That's what I paid for. How is it that the best can't handle a simple break-in?"

"Oh, I handled it. I also handled it when I found old lady Burgess dead on the floor and her safe busted open," he said, standing and reaching over the desk. He picked up Lawrence by the collar and hauled him bodily over the mahogany surface, letting his feet dangle inches off the floor.

Dmitri put his nose right up into Lawrence's face. "It was a setup. If I find out you had anything to do with it, I'm going to toss you off the nearest high-rise."

Lawrence sputtered, kicking his legs, releasing the acrid scent of fear tinged with trace amounts of urine. "I don't even know your real name. Why would I set you up? I just want the item!"

Dmitri evaluated the claim with a sniff. There was a chance Lawrence was a practiced dissembler. The majority of men in his position were good at lying, but most couldn't do it well enough to fool his nose.

He released him, letting the man fall to the floor. Incensed, Lawrence scrambled to his feet, dusting himself off and rearranging his clothing in a huff. "I had nothing to do with this other theft or the death of Genevieve Burgess, but I wasn't the only one who was unhappy she won the bidding war. Doubtless the others involved have been searching for it."

Dmitri crossed his arms. "So, this item was recently auctioned off and you lost?"

Lawrence nodded. "It's been in a private collection for years, but was sold to the highest bidder after the original owner was killed. And any of the other participants could have found out she had it and sent another thief after it like I did. She didn't cover her tracks all that well —not like I did." He gave Dmitri another sour look. "Well, like I assumed I did. I guess that hacker isn't worth the money I paid."

Dmitri ignored that. "I want to know what the item is." It wasn't part of his modus operandi to demand that kind of information, but most of his jobs didn't involve murder.

Lawrence screwed up his nose. "That wasn't part of the deal."

"Neither was having competition. That's the sort of thing I require my clients to disclose before I accept a job," Dmitri said, jaw tight.

"If you hadn't been late, this wouldn't have happened." Dmitri could see Lawrence working himself up, but he wasn't having it.

"My agent already explained the delay was unavoidable. Of course, if I'd known I wasn't the only person going after the item, I would have made other plans."

And the old woman wouldn't be dead.

Lawrence skirted around him, flopping down in the leather chair behind the desk. "I still want the item. I can pay more. I'll throw in another twenty-five grand if you get it back from whoever took it. But it has to be this week. Tomorrow at the latest."

What was the rush? Dmitri stayed on his feet, towering over Lawrence instead of going around to the other side of the desk to sit in the chair facing him.

"If you expect me to track whatever this item is now, I need to know what the hell *it* is."

His client drummed his fingers on the table before fishing out a set of keys from his briefcase. After he opened the small side drawer in the antique desk, he removed a manila envelope.

Dmitri tore it open. Scowling, he held the picture out. "What the hell is this? A crown?"

Lawrence snatched it back, turning it around. "You're holding it backward. It's a necklace."

Dmitri squinted at the photograph. If that was true, it was the ugliest necklace he'd ever seen—more like a rough collar made of poorly cast metal, bronze judging from the color.

"This is what I've been after?" Not much surprised Dmitri these days, but this wasn't what he'd been expecting from the price tag attached to this job. This so-called necklace looked like a rejected Renaissance costume piece.

"It's a very valuable antique," Lawrence snapped. "Are you going to finish the job or not?"

Dmitri thought about it. As much as he disliked the man, he'd made a commitment. And his curiosity was piqued. He wanted to know what the hell was so special about this crappy collar.

"I will find it." Turning his back, he headed to the door.

"*Wait.*" Scowling, Lawrence got to his feet, running after him. "I recognize you now! You're that male esco—man who came to my son's wedding reception. You were his ex's date."

Dmitri paused at the doorway. "That's right. But I wasn't there on false pretenses. The woman Nina Briggs is mine now. If your son goes anywhere near her or tries to get her back, I'll break him in half."

He left, slamming the door behind him.

CHAPTER SEVENTEEN

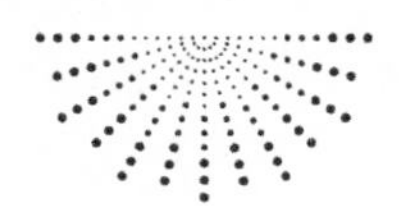

Nina could feel her successful-surgery high rapidly disappearing as Dr. Meredith Carlson picked apart her presentation to the American Cardiology keynote after the fact.

"I'm aware the talk on the Brigg's technique was well-received," she said in her nasal voice at the tail end of the staff meeting, interrupting the otherwise-universal congratulations. "But that doesn't mean it was ready to present on a national stage. I believe it needs further refinement. We have to think of the hospital's reputation."

She always does this. Nina wanted to throw her tablet at the woman's head. The others were on their feet, shuffling to the door. That was typically when Dr. Carlson chose to criticize Nina's work. She always timed it so that everyone heard it on their way out after discussion had been tabled and nobody wanted to keep talking.

Nina opened her mouth to argue, but her mentor forestalled her, coming to her defense.

"I disagree. Ultimately, the decision was mine, not yours," Dr. Phelps said dismissively. "Nina's work and her presentation were excellent, as always. We were doing other hospitals a disservice by not sharing her findings, but I can go over the many requests for her to teach a seminar on the topic at our next meeting."

Dr. Carlson's pinched her lips and nodded shortly, sweeping out of the room, her pristine white lab coat flying out behind her like a cape.

Nina waited for the others to exit before rolling her eyes at her mentor. "Why is it that the biggest chauvinist in this hospital is a woman?"

Carlson was in some ways worse than Doctors Kelso and Ryan, the sexist and mildly racist co-chairs of surgery.

Dr. Phelps clapped her on the back with his big paw. "She's part of that old school, back when there was only room for one female doctor in any given department. Try not to take it personally," he said.

"Sure thing, boss," she muttered. It was an easy thing to say, but he wasn't the one having to constantly put up with that kind of crap.

I really hope winning the Downey shuts that woman up. "Is Dr. Strickland still out of town?" she asked.

Nina had stopped to see the head of the fellowship committee first thing that morning. She'd been hoping to give him a report on the success of her talk before pressing him for a date on the committee's decision.

"I didn't know he was out," Phelps said, checking his phone for the time. "Must have been a last-minute thing. Don't worry. I'll follow up with Kelso on that."

"Thanks," she said, waving half-heartedly as he headed back to his office.

Totally drained, she dragged herself to the nurses' station.

"Carlson being a shit again?" her friend Jesse asked, leaning against the counter.

"Is the sky blue?"

With a grin, he held up a tin of cookies. "My mom made your favorite."

"Ooh." Nina grabbed a macadamia nut and chocolate chip cookie, taking a bite. She moaned almost as loud as she did in bed. Not too long ago, these cookies were the closest she got to sexual fulfillment.

"Want another?"

She laughed, reaching to take another one—she could afford the calories. "Always, but then I have to get back to work. Tell your mother I love her, and she needs to come out with us one of these nights."

He nodded. "Speaking of, Jodi said she'd meet us at Red's a little late. She's dying to interrogate you about the big guy you took to the wedding."

Of course they would have heard about Dmitri. Everyone at the hospital was talking about him.

"Consider me forewarned," she said, saluting before going to do her rounds.

Nina wanted to sink into the booth and drink the entire pitcher of fruity goodness, but she couldn't. After so many days away, she was on call. Restricted to sipping a single glass of Red's special sangria, she sighed, closing her eyes to savor the taste.

A sharp poke to the ribs broke her reverie.

"Don't even think about going comatose," Jodi admonished. "I know it was a long shift, but you gotta spill, girl. Tell us everything about your new man."

Nina blinked, reluctantly lowering her glass. Jodi and Jesse were watching her with wide eyes.

Jesse leaned forward. "Are you sure he's really not an escort? Cause if he is, we won't say a word." He put his hand over his heart. "We swear."

She laughed. "He's not a prostitute."

Jodi leaned over. "Of course he's not." She gave Jesse a sneaky side-eyed glance.

Nina's mouth dropped open. "You don't believe me!"

These were her best friends. They'd proven their loyalty during the post-breakup drama with Matt time and time again, and here they were doubting her word.

"Sweetie, we are here for you. We know how hard it must have been facing that crowd alone, and we don't blame you for paying someone to pretend to be your boyfriend."

"I didn't, and Dmitri is not an escort," she insisted, deciding to laugh instead of cry.

The two shared a pitying glance. Nina shook her head, deciding she could afford a second sangria if she ate something. She took a much bigger sip of her glass, then reached for the pitcher.

Jodi threw an arm over her shoulders and squeezed. "If you want it to be convincing, you need to find a regular-looking guy next time. Don't go for the top-of-the-line body builder."

"Jodi," Jesse admonished, nudging her with his elbow.

"I'm sorry, but someone with those arms and shoulders just isn't believable." Jodi waved dismissively before downing her own glass. "But it doesn't matter. What we need to do now is get our stories straight—your couple backstory and why he isn't around anymore. I vote we say he was called back to Russia because one of his parents died. Did he mention a mother or a father to anyone at the wedding?"

Jess nodded, his mouth full of sangria. He swallowed with a gulp. "Good idea! If he didn't mention either, let's go with mother. That's more touching, and fewer people would question it."

Tears sprang to Nina's eyes. It meant a lot that her friends were willing to go to bat and lie to the rest of their coworkers like this, but it was also unnecessary.

She hugged Jodi impulsively, catching and grabbing Jesse's sleeve to include him in the embrace. "I love you, guys."

Jesse scooted over, making it an effusive group hug. "We love you, too. And we've totally got your back on this."

"I know. But Dmitri is real—well, not all the relationship stuff he was telling people at the wedding. I just met him on the plane. We almost crash landed, I had to hitch a ride with him, and we...."

She trailed off, her face heating.

Jodi froze, but Jesse was almost jumping up and down in his seat. "You slept with *him*!" He whipped out his phone, pointing to a picture of Dmitri in his suit.

Nina snatched it from him. "This is from the wedding. I thought you didn't go!"

Jesse took his phone back, mooning over Dmitri in all his custom-suited glory before handing it to Jodi. "I didn't. At least five different people sent me pics of him that night."

Jodi held her phone up. "I got seven."

"*Oh.*" Nina waved that away, partially refilling her glass. "Well, um, we did get close very fast. My head is still spinning. But he embellished at the wedding too much, telling everyone we're engaged, which is a huge problem. He's in Boston for work, but I don't know what happens after that."

"Oh, Momma. I didn't get one from this angle." Jodi sighed dramatically, almost licking the screen of Jesse's phone. "I can't believe you hit that."

Again and again and again. Nina blushed. "It's crazy. I don't do stuff like this."

"Well, it's about time you did. You needed to show Matt that you're a vibrant beautiful woman who can do way better than him."

Something like a *pfft* escaped her. "Oh, who cares about him?"

"Sweets, he married your sister. You have to care a little...or a lot."

Nina shrugged. "I know this sounds weird, but I'm kind of done with that whole mess. I'll put up with him when I have to, of course, but I have to deal with Dmitri now."

That wasn't how she'd intended to put it, but her relationship with the crazy Russian was too new and overwhelming for her limited communication skills. And she didn't know what to say about it anyway. Other than he was possessive and planning on being a permanent fixture in her life.

Nina gave them a quick rundown of meeting Dmitri, mentioning in abbreviated detail the accident, as well as being forced to hole up in a cabin on their way back to Boston.

After she was done, she straightened in her seat. "I think that's enough about the new man in my life. Let's talk more about that later, once I have an idea of what the hell I'm going to do with him. I want to hear about that tricky bypass you pulled off earlier today, Jodi. The charge nurse said it was awesome work."

Jodi, another surgeon, beamed and launched into the story. Jesse, a surgical nurse, ordered them a big plate of nachos.

Her friend was wrapping up her account when the food arrived. "Even Dr. Strickland complimented me, and you know what a hard-ass he is."

Nina frowned. Dr. Strickland was the former head of the department. He was also leading the committee deciding on the Downey fellowship.

"Wait. I thought Strickland was out. I dropped by his office, and his secretary said he wasn't in."

"That's weird," Jodi said. "I saw him twice today."

Jesse turned away, averting his eyes. Nina leaned over, gesturing with her glass. "I know that look. What do you know?"

He winced. "I think Strickland was avoiding you."

She put down her glass. "What? Why?"

His shoulder's tightened. "Because your talk in San Francisco went well. We've been getting calls about it from the press. A few papers want to schedule an interview with you. And some potential patients want to schedule surgeries."

Nina had expected that, but why in the world would it be a reason for one of her supervisors to avoid her? "Yes, and..."

Jesse winced. "Well, I'm not sure about this, but I suspect Strickland was hoping it would go badly so they'd have an excuse to give Matt the fellowship."

"You're not serious," Jodi scoffed. "Matt's half the doctor Nina is. Less than half. Nina has more talent in her pinky finger for fuck's sake."

That was a bit of an exaggeration. Matt was an adequate doctor, but he'd always come in second to her. *And wouldn't getting the Downey be the perfect way to show me up?*

Jesse picked up his drink, worrying his teeth with the straw. "You're still the front runner, of course, but I heard a rumor Edward Lawrence might be offering to make a big donation to the hospital."

Nina's stomach sank. Was that true? Was Matt's father trying to buy his son *her* job?

CHAPTER EIGHTEEN

Dmitri swept in the bar across from Nina's hospital with a clear conscience. Sure, he'd tracked her phone to find her location, but only because she hadn't mentioned she was meeting friends for drinks after her shift.

He spoke to Cass after dealing with Lawrence. She was researching the auction Lawrence had lost, including its other participants, as well as the background of the ugly collar thing.

It was the best he could do for now. Until he heard from her, he was free to spend what time he had with his mate, who appeared to be commiserating with some friends.

Excellent. Getting to know Nina's friends was almost as important as winning over her parents.

The buxom waitress was happy to show him to Nina's table, but she seemed disappointed when he greeted his mate with a hearty 'my love'.

Nina was mid-sip when she spotted him. She choked a little, coughing and checking her friend's reactions. So did he. He caught admiring glances from the man next to her, but the other female appeared startled.

"Dmitri! What are you doing here?" Nina asked.

He slipped into the booth next to her, wrapping an arm around her to demonstrate to all the men in the room who she belonged to.

"I finished my appointment earlier than expected, so I ran down to the hospital to see if you wanted to join me for dinner. A nurse pointed me in this direction. I wanted to meet your friends," he lied, turning his megawatt grin on the hapless pair staring at them with open mouths.

The man was excited to see him. His eyes were shining, and he might have been blushing. But the woman smelled frightened. Dmitri cocked his head, taking a surreptitious sniff.

Well, I'll be damned. Nina's little female friend was a shifter. Something small—a cat species, maybe a lynx. He focused on her, making his smile wide, showing a lot of teeth.

The woman's eyes flared in terror. She gulped and started to sweat, glancing at the door as if preparing to bolt. Deciding to stop torturing her, Dmitri extended his hand.

"Dmitri Ivanov. I am Nina's mate. Any friend of hers is a friend of mine."

"O-oh," the woman stuttered, understanding straight off. She coughed. "That's uh, wow. Um...wow." Hesitating, she stared at him and then hurriedly shook, dropping his paw as soon as politeness allowed.

Nina nudged him hard in the ribs. "In America, you're called a boyfriend, not a mate. Dmitri, these are my best friends, Jesse and Jodi."

Dmitri smiled, pressing a quick kiss to her hairline. "My mistake, *dusha moya*."

He turned back to the others, greeting them properly, and engaging the young man in conversation while doing his best to put the lynx shifter at ease.

Jodi watched him with wide hazel eyes while Jesse peppered him with question after question. Dmitri answered them all, his arm securely around his mate who, despite her initial reaction, seemed to be enjoying his presence. Nina cuddled against his side unconsciously, instinctively reaching to touch him the same way he did to her.

Despite the lynx's caution, Dmitri instantly warmed to Nina's friends. He ordered a bottle of the bar's finest vodka, which his mate eschewed, but the others enjoyed very much.

The liquid lubrication did wonders for Jodi's mood. Soon, she was delicately shoveling nachos in her mouth and warning him to take care of her friend with the most charming slur.

The vodka also loosened the man's tongue. Jesse was the one who told him about his mate's troubles at work. His ears pricked when Edward Lawrence's name came up.

"Why didn't you tell me you were competing against your ex for this job?" he asked in an aside when Jodi stumbled to the bathroom.

Nina shrugged, but couldn't hide her disappointment. "He was always a contender, but I was under the impression the fellowship was a lock for me. I underestimated the role politics might play." She took a deep breath. "But it's better to know. Now I won't be surprised."

He scowled. If his mate wanted this job and she deserved it, then he would help her secure it.

"I can have a talk with this Dr. Strickland, to level the playing field," he suggested.

"Oh, hell no." Nina was adamant. "The last thing I need is for you to threaten my boss."

He grinned, pleased she was coming to know him so well.

"I'm serious," she said, poking him in the abdomen and then wincing.

"I will earn this job on merit or not at all," she added, sucking on the injured finger.

"But merit might not work," Jesse interrupted with a pout. "I say you let Dmitri 'walk' Strickland to his car one of these nights," he said, adding air quotes.

There was another and more effective option. "I was thinking of offering a competing donation instead. I can offer to match Lawrence Senior's offer." It wasn't as if he didn't have the money.

Nina wagged a finger in his face. "*No*. I'm serious...and you couldn't afford it anyway. Matt's family is old money. The obnoxious snobby kind."

How wrong she was. "Actually, my private commissions pay well. I wouldn't even notice the funds were gone," he assured her.

It was a gross understatement. At this point, he might be able to buy the hospital outright without concerning himself about lining up more jobs.

"Then sure, whatever," Nina said, waving airily.

He brightened. "Really?"

"*No,* not really," she said, smacking him lightly. "Leave it alone, Dmitri. You trying to fix my mess will not only fail, but it will also make me look weak at work."

Jesse was disappointed. "Are you sure? I bet dangling Strickland off the building would change his mind about taking Daddy Warbucks's donation."

His mate mock glared at her friend. "Don't encourage him."

Jesse waved his glass at him. "And you don't listen to her. Be encouraged!"

Dmitri was starting to like Jesse quite a bit.

Jodi returned from the bathroom at that moment. "Yes! Do it. What are we encouraging?"

"Nothing," Nina told her before pointing at Jesse. "And you better stop that."

She waved a hand over Dmitri to encompass his entire body. "This right here is an unknown quantity. Do not egg him on. It's bad enough he told everyone at the wedding we were engaged."

Dmitri grinned, lifting and kissing her palm. As far as she was concerned, he'd do what she asked. Privately, he'd reach out to this Dr. Strickland and take whatever steps he had to nullify Edward Lawrence's interference.

He turned to her friends. "She still thinks I'm joking. But we will marry and soon..."

Nina groaned, letting herself fall forward. Dmitri reached out to check her forehead's progress before it could strike the wood.

The drunk lynx cheered, lifting her glass in a toast. Half the contents spilled over her hand as she shouted loud enough for everyone in the bar to hear.

"To Nina and the wolf-man. May you live happily ever after!"

Nina wanted to be annoyed at Dmitri for crashing her night out with her friends, but the nibbling little kisses up and down her neck on the elevator ride kept her too breathless to scold him.

"Stop," she muttered when the doors opened to reveal the old retired couple from across the hall. Flushing, she pushed away from him, ducking her head in embarrassment.

"Hello, Mr. and Mrs. Isakovic." She almost ran to her door, aware her shirt buttons weren't done all the way.

Nina expected Dmitri to be right behind her, but he had paused in the hallway. She frowned as she realized the couple wasn't talking to each other. They were speaking to Dmitri in their native tongue.

Mrs. Isakovic, a reserved and sour old woman, was openly beaming and feeling Dmitri's arms, chattering.

She turned to Nina. "Finally, a nice boy for you," she said in her thick accent.

Turning as a group, the three of them went to the Isakovic's door.

"I'll be right back. I'm just going to move a couch for them," Dmitri said.

"All right." Bewildered, Nina rubbed her eyes and opened her own door. He was back in a few minutes, holding a plateful of pastries.

She couldn't believe it. "Mrs. Isakovic gave you food?"

"It's *tulumbe*. You'll love it."

Shaking her head, she wondered if there was a person alive who could resist Dmitri's charm. She'd picked up the Isakovic's mail and watered their plants for an entire month last year when they went back to the Old Country to visit family, and she'd received nothing but a tersely written thank-you note.

"Where did you learn to speak Serbian?"

He shrugged, setting the plate down and following her into the bedroom. "It's close to Russian. Now, where were we?"

"Moving a couch for septuagenarians gets you in the mood?"

"Around you, I'm always in the mood. And I think it's sweet to see a couple who has lasted the test of time still happily in love."

Nina cocked her head. "Are you always such a romantic?"

"Only with you. Allow me to demonstrate." Dmitri pushed her back until she landed on the bed.

She was naked in ten seconds flat.

"Did Kiera call you?" he asked, pulling off his shirt.

Nina's brain fizzled as she caught sight of his chiseled pecs and the defined grooves of his ten-pack abdomen. "What?" she asked blankly as he started on the zipper of his pants.

"I asked if Kiera called you. Did she answer all your questions and assure you that I'm healthy?"

Blinking, she raised her head. Thank God he'd reminded her. "Oh, yes, she did. And frankly, I have more questions now because little of what she said made sense."

His brow lowered, confusion evident. "How so?"

Nina focused on his eyes to avoid getting distracted. "She kept saying those test results were normal for someone like you. And that's exactly how she said it—'someone like you'. Which begs the question, are there *more* like you? Because the only way those results make sense is if you're part of a super-soldier program."

He laughed. "Well, I can think of some bits of me that are super-sized," he teased, unzipping slowly.

She giggled, despite the little jump her heart gave as he pulled his jeans down and set a condom on the bed next to her. "Why don't we finish this discussion later?" he suggested, his voice low and full of gravel.

Now she was completely confused. "*Wait*. I thought the whole point of giving me those test results was to have sex without protection?"

"That was before you were ovulating," he said, crawling over her.

"And even though I have every intention of putting my baby in you, I think we should wait. I'm not ready to share you yet."

Holy shit. Everything Dmitri said was unexpected. And the words were so cheesy. Yet after they came out of his mouth, they transformed into something capable of reducing her to a melted pile of goo. She didn't even stop to ask *how* he knew she was ovulating.

Nina stroked his bare chest. He was so warm her palms pricked as if the heat were burning her.

"I don't understand how you do this to me," she whispered.

He pressed his lips to hers in an aggressive kiss. "It's magic," he said.

Nina laughed again, stroking his broad shoulders with hungry hands. Dmitri didn't laugh with her.

"You'll understand soon," he promised. "I want to go for a drive this weekend. I have something to show you."

"What is it?"

"Later. You have to see it to believe it. But once you do, you'll know we're meant to be. *Forever.*"

He stopped talking then, dipping his head to take her mouth more aggressively. Her vision blanked out. All she could do was feel.

His hands roamed over her body, caressing her curves wherever his lips didn't reach. She bucked as he took one nipple in his mouth, then the other, sucking and grazing them with his teeth. Her pulse beat in time with her breath, her heart nearly seizing when he parted her legs, fitting his thick shaft to her entrance.

His possession was a little rough, but she didn't care. Nina wrapped her arms and legs around him, trying to get closer as he ground against her, working her pussy with deep hard strokes. All too soon, she was there, clenching around him with a mindless shout as her orgasm powered through her.

Dmitri flipped her over until she was on all fours, panting. "This time, I want you to scream my name. Louder."

She was happy to oblige.

CHAPTER NINETEEN

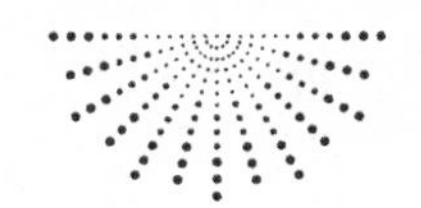

Dmitri couldn't believe it. Cass had come up empty.

He'd been up for hours, ever since Nina had been called into the hospital for an emergency surgery shortly before dawn. He dropped her off himself despite her insistence she could summon a car, then he'd gone back to the Caislean for a few more hours of shut-eye and to wait for Cass's message.

"What do you mean—there was nothing on the collar?" he asked when she finally got in touch.

His assistant's frustrated hiss could have cut glass. "I told you. I found plenty on the auction. I've confirmed Edwards, Genevieve Burgess, and another man named Wilcox participated. I am close to getting the last one. But the collar itself is a no go. Nothing on its provenance or history, not even on the dark websites that have been reliable for this sort of thing in the past."

Well, fuck. "I need to know what that thing is. I can't even tell what the stones in it are from that picture."

They looked like rubies, but could have been garnets. Regardless of their size, they couldn't account for the amount Edward and other auction participants had spent.

Dmitri was racking his brain to explain why everyone was so

crazy to get their hands on the collar when the silence on the other end of the line was interrupted by an impatient grunt. "Earth to Dmitri. You done wool-gathering? Or is your mate there?"

He glanced at his watch. "No, she's probably cutting someone open around now. She got called into the hospital."

Cass whistled, reluctantly impressed. "Are you really going to stay with her?"

He pulled the phone away long enough to scowl at it. "Why the fuck would I leave her? You just said it—she's my mate. Where she goes, I follow."

She clucked her tongue. "Simmer down, doofus. I meant are you going to stay in Boston with her? Think about it. It's a big city. You'd be an urban wolf and frankly, I don't see that. I know you. You need to run. Do it in town and you'd have trigger happy humans taking shots at you all the time. That or they'd be freaking out and calling animal control. Access to the woods is not easy when your mate has to go work in a downtown hospital at all hours."

Trust Cass to find the black cloud on the horizon. "I haven't thought that far ahead. Nina hasn't even seen me shift yet."

"Well, maybe she should. If it doesn't melt her little human brain, then you can bring up what a terrible idea living in Boston is for you."

He grunted, mulling it over. After last night, he knew her job was under threat. What if, instead of taking steps to level the playing field, he did nothing? She'd even asked him not to interfere. He could be selfish and bring up moving if she was passed over for promotion.

Dmitri owned property all over the world. He even had some on the Pacific coast near Portland. The edge of the land wasn't that far from town. Instead of living in the cabin in the middle of the property, he could build a big house at the edge. From there, it would be an easy commute to the city center. There was bound to be a hospital she could work at. In all probability, there would be several that would kill to have a superstar of her caliber.

Don't go there. Nina deserved that prestigious fellowship. She'd worked all her life for it. He couldn't live with himself if he didn't at least make sure no one stole it out from under her.

"How many bidders were there in the auction again?"

"Four. Edwards, the Burgess woman, Wilcox, and another party I haven't identified."

Dmitri started gathering his gear. "Get me Wilcox's address. I'll start there while you track down the final name."

"What about the collar? Any other ideas where I should start?"

He'd have to mark this in his calendar—the day Cass asked for help. It might have been the first time. But in this case, he had a better idea.

"I have another source, one I should contact directly. Alec Broussard."

Cass gagged. "Not the *vampire* Alec Broussard."

Dmitri shrugged, even though she couldn't see him. "He's a friend. And he's an expert in antiquities with a photographic memory. He has access to museum collections around the world. If anyone has heard of this ugly thing, it'll be him."

"Suit yourself. You know…it's a good thing you're not part of a pack. Consorting with bloodsuckers would get your ass kicked out."

"I'm well aware," he drawled. "That's why I prefer being a lone wolf. Text me Wilcox's address. If he has the item, I want to know ASAP."

His phone buzzed moments later. "Done. You won't have to go far."

He found out what she meant when he put the address into Google maps. Hammish Wilcox lived in a penthouse in a building down the block.

Dmitri didn't get a chance to break into Wilcox's place that morning. He was sidetracked by an irate vampire.

He had emailed Alec Broussard before he set out, never expecting the vamp to get in touch less than a minute later.

"Where is it?" Alec asked, almost yelling.

"Hey." Dmitri held the phone away from his ear. "Sensitive hearing here. Can you watch the volume?"

"Sorry. But I need it back. It's extremely dangerous."

Dmitri set down his bag, taking a seat on the bed. "Back? Is it yours? And it's a necklace. How dangerous can it be?"

"It's not a necklace. Well, it's supposed to go around the neck, but that thing is not an adornment. It was stolen a few months ago from the Elemental archive, along with several other items."

"Fuck," Dmitri muttered. As if this couldn't get any worse, here was proof it could.

There were only four Elementals working at any given time—Earth, Air, Fire, and Water. Four were more than enough, though. The bad-ass female warriors kept the supernatural world in order, making sure the populace maintained their Covenant with Mother Nature. The latter was basically the ten commandments for the magically inclined.

Dmitri heard rumors about a dangerous Elemental artifact ending up in a shifter pack earlier in the year. The idea that more than one was out in the world was enough to make him want to update his will.

"So it's a weapon, like that staff that caused so much trouble in the Maitland pack not too long ago? The one that killed one of their enforcers?" Dmitri was a lone wolf, but he was on good terms with the Maitland clan and he'd heard about their dilemma.

"No. It's worse. That collar was confiscated from the Delavordo family."

Double fuck.

Witch lines rose and died out with regularity, just like shifter ones, but seven families had stood the test of time, founding dynasties that survived to this day. The Delavordos were the worst of the lot, yielding some of the most notorious black witches the world had ever seen.

If this collar was theirs, it was evil.

"Can you cut to the chase? What does this thing do? I'm burning daylight here."

If Wilcox was at work, these were precious hours Dmitri could be spending casing his place.

"So, you don't have it yet?" Alec asked.

"Not yet, but I will soon."

"I take it you were hired to find it."

Unlike his mate, Alec knew his true profession. He'd even hired him a few times. "I was. But the first person I was supposed to acquire it from was dead and the item was gone."

"Who was it?"

"Genevieve Burgess."

"Damn it, Dmitri. Why didn't you tell me about this earlier!"

"Hey, I can't run all my jobs past you on the off chance it involves a witch or Elemental business. I certainly didn't expect it on this one. The man who hired me is human."

"Are you sure?"

"Yes," he hissed indignantly. "And how dare you insult my sense of smell."

Alec snorted. "Could he be a practitioner in disguise? Maybe he's masking himself."

"Not a chance. I would be able to smell the magic of the charm. There was nothing like that on him."

"I don't know; there's some crazy masking spells out there these days. Remember Toulouse?"

He did, but Dmitri was sure this was nothing like that. Edwards was human. *Period.*

"He wouldn't have had time to cast a spell or activate a charm," he added. "I caught him off guard."

"All right, I believe you. But that thing can't stay out in the world. If you find it, you have to return it. It can't go to your client."

"Yeah, yeah. I know."

Cass was going to hate missing this commission, but even she would agree it was better not to get on the Elemental's shit list. Any one of them could knock him on his ass with one hand tied behind their backs.

Also, they were the good guys. If they said this thing belonged under lock and key in their care, he wasn't going to argue.

"Damn, I can't believe Genevieve is dead," Alec muttered.

"Did you know her?"

"I met her once a few decades ago. She seemed like a nice woman, for a witch. She liked to collect antique porcelain. And though she was a known practitioner, it was nothing questionable. I wouldn't have pegged her as someone who would buy a Delavordo artifact."

But as a member of the Burgess clan, she would have some idea of what it did and how to use it.

"So, what *is* it?" And why would a human like Edwards want it so badly?

Alec was quiet a beat too long. "I wish I knew the answer to that. Regrettably, the records for the collar are incomplete. Given what happened, they were probably intentionally misplaced or destroyed. It's been hell trying to piece together a complete list of items stolen, let alone what they all do."

"Shit. I had no idea it was so extensive a theft."

Not to mention, a thief of Dmitri's caliber should have heard about a heist of this nature. *The Elementals must be pissed.* When they found the person who stole from them, it was going to be a bloodbath.

"Well, the Elementals and their archivists obviously aren't eager to spread the word," Alec confessed. "I trust you'll keep this under your hat."

Like he had a choice. "Believe me, I value my life too much to do otherwise." And there was Nina to consider.

Fuck. The truth hit him hard. Dmitri had just met his mate. Tangling with black magic artifacts was the last thing he should be doing.

But the case already involved her through her connection to Edwards, albeit peripherally.

Keep it that way. Screw the money from the commission. Keeping Nina safe was his priority.

His phone buzzed. Cass had worked her magic. He had the last name—Carlton Lang, a millionaire banker with a sprawling townhouse on Beacon Hill.

"Alec, I'm going to get back to you. I have a couple of leads I need to follow."

"All right. But be careful. Take every precaution you can when you find the collar. It could be cursed. I wouldn't even touch it."

"Wasn't planning on it," Dmitri muttered before clicking off.

He didn't need the warning. Knowing the necklace came from the Delavordo clan was enough. Whatever the necklace did, it had bad mojo written all over it.

CHAPTER TWENTY

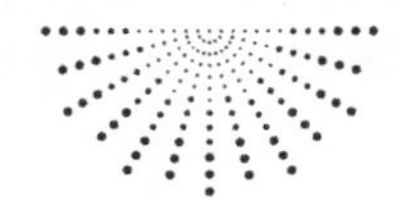

Lang was a dead end. Dmitri had watched his house for more than a day before determining the man wasn't even in the country. After taking the precaution of breaking into his home to plant listening devices and hidden cameras, he refocused his efforts on Wilcox—in between bouts of lovemaking with his mate.

Nina was at the hospital quite a bit. But despite her continued stellar work there, she was on edge. She didn't say so, but he knew the fact they hadn't announced the winner for the fellowship was bothering her.

He didn't like seeing her worry, but the long hours apart gave him plenty of time to find the collar. But getting into Wilcox's place was more of a challenge than he'd anticipated. The old man was retired and an invalid.

Bedridden for the better half of the last decade, the octogenarian was a retired real estate mogul who'd started out as a slum lord. Wilcox built an empire by gentrifying low-income tracts. The fact he'd displaced thousands of people in the process hadn't kept him from gracing dozens of magazine covers in the eighties and nineties.

Karma had caught up with him, however. The rapacious old fart hadn't been able to buy his way out of the slow and painful death sentence.

The mark rarely left his home, a palatial penthouse in a six-story Atlantic Avenue building. Unlike the private homes of the other bidders, this one was protected by armed guards in addition to a state-of-the-art security system, including fingerprint lock access to each individual floor. There were also a superfluous number of closed-circuit cameras. The only time Wilcox left his suite was a regular appointment to see his doctor every week.

Sometimes the simplest solutions were the effective ones.

Determined not to waste a second more than he had to on this case, Dmitri decided to cut to the chase and rent a unit in the building, giving him access to the security office. One quick after-hours visit and he created a few useful blind spots, making covert entry to the penthouse possible. Then he waited for his window of opportunity.

Dmitri began his op the minute he dropped Nina off for her shift at the hospital on Friday. It was the middle of the day, and there was a lot of traffic in and out of Wilcox's building. The wealthy residents were getting ready for a long weekend away.

Dmitri took advantage of the bustle and confusion to slip into the building unnoticed, casually mixing in with the crowd. He went up to his apartment, bypassing the inside to lounge in the sun of his own private balcony. Once there, he poured himself a big shot glass of vodka, then activated a small spell stone and dropped it into the glass.

Obfuscation spells were fairly common in the witching world, but getting a well-crafted one that would successfully mask someone of his size took some effort to craft. They didn't make people invisible precisely, but they strongly discouraged the beholder from noticing them. Unfortunately, his contact Salvador insisted the most effective way for someone his size to deploy the stone was to take it internally.

Swallowing a stone a little larger than a quarter wasn't too terrible when there was a bottle of vodka handy. It had taken an entire bottle the first time, which had made the subsequent job remarkably interesting, to say the least. The real drawback had come later when the stone made its ignoble exit.

Enough. He checked his watch, deciding the stone had enough time to take effect. Dmitri donned his custom-made gloves, an extra-large leather pair with special pads for added grip.

The ledges of the apartment were narrow by human standards, but it was more than adequate for a shifter with an unnatural tolerance of heights to make his way. Finding handholds for paws his size was more of a challenge, but he managed, scaling the building like an oversized Spiderman.

He'd timed it perfectly. The setting sun was low enough to hit the windows of each building almost horizontally. The obfuscation spell was supposed to make a person's eye skip over him, but it never hurt to have a little extra insurance. Anyone focusing in this direction too long risked permanent sun damage to their vision.

The penthouse-level balcony was too far out of reach for a free-hand climb—a security measure no doubt. His problem was easily remedied. Dmitri scaled a few more stories until he reached the roof. From there, he was able to jump down to the Wilcox's balcony, something no human would have been able to do without ropes.

After that, breaking in was child's play. Most people didn't lock their balcony doors.

The rooms beyond could have been located in any of the Back-Bay mansions he'd seen earlier in the case.

Dark hardwood floors shone with a subtle glow. The rooms and walls were sparsely decorated in a minimalistic and hard-edged modern style. He paused in the main salon below a genuine Mondrian—the only color in a sea of chrome and grey.

Dmitri sniffed. No matter how fancy the trappings were, it wasn't worth living monochromatically just to make a statement—*I'm a rich a-hole who can afford to hang an overpriced placemat on my wall.* But then, he had always hated modern art.

I hope Nina appreciates the masters. He made a mental note to introduce her to the Russian artists he loved. She'd know Chagall and Faberge, of course, but probably not Brullov or Shevchenko.

He was cheerfully making plans when multiple male voices drifted out of the bedroom.

Bollocks. Wilcox was supposed to be at his regular doctor's appointment. Biting back a sigh, Dmitri beat a strategic retreat back to the balcony.

What now?

Logic dictated that he walk away, but he hadn't swallowed that damn rock for nothing. He had to take a closer look at what he was dealing with.

Expelling a frustrated breath, Dmitri hopped over the balcony railing, precariously balancing on the thin ledge. It was too small for him, but he managed to hold on with the tips of his fingers.

He poked his head around the corner of the building for an unobstructed view inside Wilcox's bedroom.

There were four men in there. The old man was lying in a wide hospital bed, the head of which had been raised to allow him to sit up. He was talking to two lackeys, security judging by their clothing. Both men were muscular and wearing the mid-range dark suits preferred by bodyguards everywhere. A young African-American man in salmon scrubs was fussing with Wilcox's IV line.

Damn it. There were too many of them. He no longer had a choice but to come back another day.

In truth, it would be a simple matter to take out the guards, but he wasn't about to strong-arm the poor guy forced to wear those scrubs, or the old man himself. Annoyed, Dmitri was about to make his way back to the balcony when a rush of movement inside stopped him.

At Wilcox's nod, the two men in suits turned and grabbed the male nurse, forcing him down on his back at the foot of the bed. One struck him over the head with the butt of his gun, a Colt Defender.

The nurse stopped moving.

His jaw clenched as Wilcox raised a shaky hand. One of the bodyguards moved out of his line of sight, returning with something held in front of him as the second supported the nurse, keeping his upper body stretched across the bed.

Dmitri recognized the collar from the photograph Edward Lawrence had shown him. It was a butt ugly thing—and viciously made. The roughly hewn piece was a dull yellow color with jagged spikes jutting *in*. Anyone wearing it would have the spurs partially embedded in their neck.

The stones laid into the bronze collar were a dark blood red. Their deep fire marked them as real rubies. He could tell as much, even at a distance. But there was something unsettling about them—a hint of menace. It was palpable, even from the other side of the thick glass windows.

Dmitri hated the thing on sight. The whole collar needed to be melted down. *Right*. If it were that easy, the Elemental crew would have done it a long time ago.

"Do it," Wilcox yelled loudly enough to be heard through the thick glass.

The second bodyguard fitted the collar on the still form of the male nurse while the first man continued to hold him down. Dmitri tensed, wanting to leap through the glass to help, but there was no way he'd be able to break it without specialized tools. He winced as the metal spurs of the collar cut the vulnerable skin of poor man's neck.

Wilcox raised a hand. His lips moved, but now his voice was too low for Dmitri to make out.

The unconscious nurse convulsed abruptly, jerking and shaking violently. He would have slid off the bed if he hadn't been pinned down.

The fit ended as abruptly as it started. The young man arced, his body tightening like a bowstring, then he collapsed. The central ruby flashed, glowing in the dying sunlight.

At first, Dmitri assumed the extra shine was a trick of the light, but the sparkle didn't dim when one of the guards lifted it. He removed it from the still nurse, holding it out to Wilcox with a great show of solemnity.

Wilcox's trembling fingers took the bloodied collar. He waved away an offer of help from the guard, fitting it around his neck on his own. Once the points were pressing into his own skin, he let the guard fasten it.

Clasping the collar shut was like wrapping barbed wire around the man's own neck. Dmitri winced as Wilcox squirmed, visibly trying not to breath as the spikes dug into his flesh. Blood mingled with blood as the light in the stone flickered, catching fire. It was glowing brightly, like an ember heated by the wind. And then its radiance began to fade, transferring to Wilcox at the point where the blood of his victim mingled with his own.

The subtle shimmer raced up Wilcox's veins, highlighting them with a muted luminescence. The wave passed down his body, into his frail arms, and up over his head. The blue veins sparkled, blazing red-orange momentarily. Once the light faded, so did the prominence of the veins.

Wilcox's body shed the infirmities of old age in minutes.

The near-translucent quality of the skin on Wilcox's arms and temples shifted, growing more opaque before Dmitri's eyes. As he watched, the tremble in the man's hands ceased and his labored breaths became deeper and easier.

He didn't grow young before Dmitri's eyes. It was subtler than that. Wilcox's sallow skin color deepened, his flesh rippled, filling out and growing almost supple. Strong wiry muscles moved underneath. As he swallowed, Wilcox's lips firmed, and his fingers stopped shaking. The time-ravaged invalid was gone. In his place was a man in peak physical condition for his age.

The stones in the collar were dulled as Wilcox pulled them aside. He set the collar on the bed before starting to rise.

The bodyguards tried to help him, but Wilcox waved them away once again. When one brought a walker, he smirked.

"Stand aside," he ordered in a firm voice.

With borrowed determination, he slid one leg over the side and then the other until he was standing unaided—something Dmitri guessed he hadn't been able to do on his own in years.

The young man was still lying at the foot of the bed. His glassy eyes stared straight at the ceiling. Dmitri studied him for signs of life, but his chest didn't move. He was dead.

"Get my suit." Wilcox waved at the closet.

Then he began to dress as if the body wasn't there. One bodyguard ran to the closet, pulling out a set of formal clothes.

Dmitri understood then. After sucking the life out of an innocent young man, Wilcox was going to celebrate out on the town.

Who could blame him after so many years of being bedridden?

Dmitri's fist curled. He pulled his black balaclava down over his face.

I can.

CHAPTER TWENTY-ONE

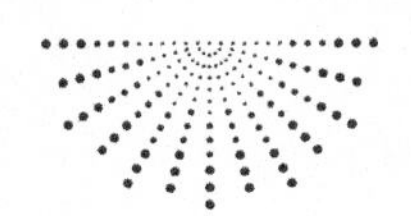

Dmitri punched the back of the bodyguard's neck before the man had a chance to turn around.

The guard had been grabbing a set of keys—no doubt to drive Wilcox to whatever evening entertainment he'd chosen. The man himself was coming out of the bedroom.

"Put that in my safe," Wilcox said, his head turned to the guard remaining in the room.

He turned just in time to meet Dmitri's fist. Bones crunched underneath the heavy weight. He crashed to the floor like an automaton disassembling. His head hit the flagstone floor with a hard, satisfying rap.

The last bodyguard rushed out of the hall holding a steel box. His adversary threw it at him, reaching for the weapon holstered at his side. Dmitri batted the box aside, ducking faster than the human could move. He kicked out, sweeping out his opponent's leg, following it with a punch to the face before the man could hit the hardwood.

The guard groaned, his head lolling on the floor, but he made no move to get up again. None of them did.

Dmitri surveyed the human wreckage scattered around him.

Ragged breathing filled the air. He hadn't killed anyone. But if there was some justice in the world, they would never be the same again. Wilcox, in particular, would suffer. He might have borrowed someone's life force, but he hadn't magicked himself into the body of the Rock. He was going to feel that punch for months to come.

There was no guilt. The only innocent in these rooms had been the nurse, and he was dead. As far as Dmitri was concerned, Wilcox deserved worse. *You could end it right now,* he thought, but then pictured Nina's reaction if she ever found out.

He swore under his breath, sending up a prayer to the Mother that someday, somehow, Wilcox would get what he deserved. His only regret was he wouldn't be the one to ensure the old man paid.

The nurse's body was lying on the floor now. He'd been covered with a white sheet. Dmitri forced his eyes away from the corpse, taking stock of his surroundings.

The steel box proved to be the custom case for the collar. Dmitri stripped a pillowcase off a pillow to use as an extra layer between him and the cursed necklace. He didn't want to touch it, not even with his gloves.

He picked up the hellish adornment. Bitter cold seeped through the layers. "Fuck," he muttered, dropping the thing as if he'd been scalded.

After seeing the stone glow so brightly, he'd thought the metal would be warm. However, this odd chill didn't surprise him either. The collar may have breathed new life into Wilcox, but it had done so by stealing another's life force. It was an instrument of death.

Death is always cold.

Trying not to think about it, he shoved the collar into the padded steel box, securing the handle to his belt with a length of polypropylene rope. He made a quick egress from the balcony before any of the victims could stop him.

He hopped over the balcony of his rented suite, rapidly collecting the glass and bottle of vodka, wiping down anything he might have touched. After stashing the steel case with the collar in a larger suitcase, he headed down to the basement parking lot, just another resident leaving for the long weekend after picking up his luggage.

In a few months, Dmitri would have the few furnishings and fake photographs packed up and carted away by a group of movers—long enough for the fervor of the theft to die down. Cass would take care of the details, as usual. In the meantime, he would need her to look into something else.

"What do you mean you're not turning over the item to the client?" Cass's voice rang with indignation.

"Exactly what I said. I won't be giving it to him."

Dmitri maneuvered the car through traffic, narrowly avoiding getting a love tap from a delivery truck. He shook his head, a failed attempt to jostle the image of the dead nurse out of his head. Horns blared as he refocused on driving, switching lanes with greater care.

"What was that?" Cass snapped. The woman was in a wheelchair, but her hearing worked just fine.

"It's nothing. I hit a spot of traffic," he muttered. "Listen, I just saw this thing in action. I don't know what Edward Lawrence plans to do with it, but whatever it is, it's not good."

With halting words, he explained what he'd seen—the collar's true purpose.

There was silence on the other end of the line. "That's not really up to you, is it? You get paid a lot of money not to ask questions." Despite her no-nonsense tone, but he could detect a small thread of uncertainty

"This is different," he growled.

"How exactly?" A normal person would have been cowed by his tone, but this was Cass. She always spoke her mind.

"Because we're dealing with a magical artifact—black magic to be precise."

"And you think it's the first time?"

Shit. She had a point. Swearing, Dmitri unfastened his best. He was at his destination, one he'd chosen unconsciously. The Caislean Hotel valet came around to the front of the car.

"Your keys, sir?" he asked politely.

Dmitri transferred the call from the car to his Bluetooth headset before opening the door. Cass waited with uncharacteristic patience on the other end of the line. He was in the room he'd rented before she continued.

"Dmitri, we've taken plenty of jobs where we had to acquire a black-box object—unidentified packages we outright stole or acted as courier. We've always handed them off, no questions asked. It's why your services come with such a high price tag. People need to know they can depend on you. In this line of work, reputation is everything."

She wasn't wrong. It was mere chance that they had learned the true nature of the collar. He'd been trafficking in stolen goods for a long time, mostly gems and the like. People killed for those every day.

Perhaps there'd been something of this nature before and he simply hadn't known.

It doesn't change anything. The fact was he did know, and he couldn't let Lawrence have it.

Dmitri opened the case to examine the collar. The blood rubies winked under the bright track lighting that illuminated the room.

"The Elementals don't take kindly to thieves. Alec knows I was on the trail of this thing. He's expecting to get it back."

Cass sniffed. "Well, if they hadn't lost it in the first place, you wouldn't be in this position. Can you delay returning it?"

Dmitri frowned. He wanted the collar gone yesterday. "I can feel the dark magic coming off this thing like toxic smoke. The less time I have to spend with it, the better."

"Why not give it to Lawrence for a short while? You can always steal it back after a few days."

"It's an idea," he murmured, pacing at the foot of the bed to view the collar from different angles. "But..."

Cass sighed heavily. "But what?"

He shook his head. "I just don't like the idea of handing this thing over knowing what it takes to make it work."

"Now there's something to consider," Cass mused. "We know what

Wilcox wanted—a fountain of youth. He must have been at death's door, or else he wouldn't have killed Genevieve Burgess."

"Agreed," he said, staring contemplatively at the glittering stones.

He'd almost forgotten—it wasn't just the nurse's blood on Wilcox's hands.

"I assume she knew what it did because she was a witch. I'm not sure why she wanted it. I didn't smell the taint of illness on her body. She died from blunt-force trauma."

"Maybe she wanted to study it, or she was saving it for a rainy day —the why isn't important in her case. Not with her background. What matters is how Wilcox and Lawrence learned about it. They're both human, aren't they?"

"Yes."

"Could Lawrence be sick?"

"If he is, he doesn't know it yet." His nose would have picked up those telltale scents of impending illness long before any diagnostic test. He hadn't picked up a whiff of anything amiss, not even diabetes which was almost a given in this country's love of fast food and the vast amounts of hidden sugar in manufactured meals.

"Then it's the son."

Dmitri blinked. "He's not sick either."

Or at least, he didn't think so. He hadn't gotten close enough to be absolutely certain of course. He'd been playing it safe. Too much contact with the groom and he might give in to temptation to knock the git senseless. He was Nina's ex after all.

"But he's a doctor," Cass pointed out with a frustrated snap of her jaw that was audible even over the line.

"So?"

"So, isn't he up for a prominent position?"

"Nina mentioned they were competing for a post," he confirmed, mulling it over. "Nina is the frontrunner, but her friends were concerned Lawrence Senior might make a play to buy the post for Junior with a big donation."

"Well, that's it then?"

"What is? Lawrence Junior does have a shot, but only cause of the cash his father is willing to throw around. I plan on making a competing donation to even things out."

Cass sniffed. "Maybe you should leave things alone. Let the money talk, then Lawrence won't need the collar to make his son look good."

The lightbulb belatedly went off in his head. "That's why he wants it, isn't it?" He swore aloud. "Lawrence knows his doctor son can't win the job on his own. Nina is the superior surgeon. In fact, she's so good she's getting famous. Even if the donation gets the younger Lawrence the job, everyone will know he didn't earn it. But if he starts pulling off a few miracles, then it won't be strange when the hospital brass gives it to him."

"It gets worse," Cass said in her voice of doom. "You said the collar transfers a person's life force. With it, Lawrence could save his own patients, but he'd have to sacrifice others in order to do it."

He almost groaned, finally understanding what his pessimistic partner was trying to tell him

"Of course," he muttered. "Lawrence Junior could get a leg up, but it might not be enough—not at this stage of the game. Nina's reputation is too solid. It could survive a competitor having a sudden hot streak. He'd have to discredit her at the same time."

"Yes," she agreed. "The choice of who died wouldn't be random. He'd kill her patients to save his own."

CHAPTER TWENTY-TWO

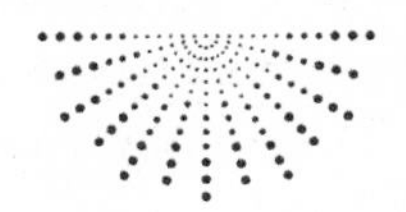

Dmitri rubbed his face, pacing the spacious bedroom of the Caislean hotel. "Well, at least we both agree. The Lawrence family can't have the collar."

"I didn't say that," Cass muttered.

"You can't be serious. Not now that we've figured out what they want it for." Dmitri wrinkled his nose, giving the collar the side eye. The stones winked malevolently in the light.

Cass cleared her throat. "That's a given. But why not make the reason he wants it irrelevant? Tell your mate the truth. Tell her to withdraw from consideration for the job. If she's such a good doctor, she can get another one, someplace where you can live and run free. Your real mate would understand—Boston is untenable for one of our kind. Well, for one of our kind who can still shift."

"Shifting is like breathing," he pointed out. "You just haven't tried since the accident. But it's not something you can just forget."

"And what if I can shift?" she whispered.

Dmitri winced. He could feel her pain across the line.

"My rear legs would drag behind me, completely useless," she continued. "This isn't a temporary injury shifting can heal. I've consulted the best doctors among our kind. I'm paralyzed from the waist down."

His eyes were drawn almost unwillingly to the collar. "Are you thinking what I'm thinking?"

"*No.*" Her answer was sharp and immediate. "I would never trade someone else's life for my legs. How dare you even suggest it?"

"I wasn't really," he lied.

What if he found someone who deserved to die, like a murderer? He stumbled across them from time to time.

"Sure you weren't." Cass knew him too well. "Forget it. Focus on the real problem."

I need a drink. Sometimes talking to his partner gave him a headache. "Well, according to you, the solution is to give up."

"I didn't say that. I just think we need to figure a way out of this mess, one that minimizes the body count and keeps your reputation intact."

"I don't give a damn about my reputation," he said.

"Well, I do," she snapped. "Not all of us have enough tucked away for retirement. The medical bills after the accident ate away at a lot of my nest egg."

Fuck. He hadn't thought of that. "I promise I won't retire until you're all set up, whether that means retiring yourself or continuing on with other clients."

"My other clients don't earn as much as you."

"Some have the potential I'm sure." He didn't know much about the other men and women Cass worked with, but they had to have a fair amount of talent. Otherwise she wouldn't have chosen to associate with them.

"If I pull back on these high-priced jobs in order to spend time with my mate, one of them can step up to fill the void. They just need the right person out there, booking those jobs."

"Maybe..." Cass sniffed. "But let's not forget the matter at hand. Crossing Lawrence may have consequences. You were stupid enough to show your face to him. And your mate is mixed up in all this."

"Like I could forget that. But you've forgotten that Alec and the

Elementals are waiting for this thing. Crossing them is a thousand times more dangerous. However, I think I've come up with a plan," he said, leaning over to study the central stone more carefully.

"Is it a good one?"

"Under the circumstances... But you're not going to like it." He stood, facing the mirror. "I need you to go to my vault."

"Which one?"

"The big one, the one I call my retirement fund. It's the only one with a ruby this size. Send it to me ASAP."

"You're going to swap the stones?"

He nodded even though she couldn't see him. "It takes a lot of dark magic to create an artifact like this, usually a human sacrifice. The stones are a part of that. They would have absorbed the death and been turned into conduits. From what I could tell, the stones focus the energy during the life-force transfer. If I take one out, it should render the thing harmless."

At least, he hoped that was the case. But he didn't have a choice. He had to try. "I'll give the original stone to Alec and the altered collar to Lawrence."

I hope the ruby I have is a close match. The stones on the collar were a distinctive shade, the color of blood, but Lawrence only had a photograph as a reference.

He pursed his lips. If his memory served, the stone in his vault was a little brighter and lighter in color, but only a touch. He didn't dare swap it with a fake synthetic stone. He strongly suspected the client would be able to tell the difference.

Cass sighed. "Before I drag my ass all the way to your bank upstate, you should tell your mate the truth and see if she accepts you first."

"I will tell her as soon as I get a chance. I'm just waiting for the right time."

Nina was a strong and intelligent woman. He was confident she would accept his true nature...but making sure she learned about it under the ideal circumstances was the best course of action. Setting the right mood was important, almost as important as when and where a man proposed.

First things first. "Cassandra…I need that stone."

"Fine. I'll go get it, then have it sent out by special courier."

When she huffed, the wheelchair made the tiniest of squeaks, one he'd noticed in their last few calls. Cass was on the move. He made a mental note to oil the wheels the next time he saw her.

"I sincerely hope this human is worth it," she added waspishly.

"She is."

Something was wrong with Dmitri. Nina was sure of it, although why she was so certain, she couldn't really say.

Her swaggering Russian lover was still his effortlessly charming, incredibly oversexed self. Dmitri was provocative, entertaining, and fun. She would come home after a long day in surgery with the desire to do nothing more than take a bath and sleep. He could turn that around in minutes flat, either making her laugh over a dinner he prepared or joining her in the shower, making her scream in ecstasy at least twice in the process of getting clean.

Her neighbors officially hated her, but she ignored their dirty looks. Nina had never experienced so much joy and pleasure in a partner.

But there was something was off. She couldn't pinpoint it, but it was obvious it had to do with whatever job he was doing in town. Her Russian loved to talk, but whenever she asked about his work, he grew tight-lipped. All he said was he was waiting on a delivery before he could wrap things up. Then he would change the subject or distract her by making love to her.

Other than this mysterious delivery he was waiting for, Dmitri appeared at ease. He'd thoroughly ingratiated himself to her entire family. He was a great favorite at their gatherings. Her aunt Toni baked him an extra sweet potato pie to take home. Nina couldn't think of a time she'd ever done that for Matt.

Even her parents adored Dmitri. In fact, they liked him more than they liked her at the moment.

Nina had done her best to mend the rift with her sister; she really had. They spoke whenever the two happened to visit their parents at the same time. Despite her busy schedule, she'd made time to see them, strictly hit-and-run visits. But Nina hadn't been able to accept their many dinner invitations because she knew her new brother-in-law would be there.

Her mom and dad wanted to pretend all was well now. Mom seemed to think that now that she had Dmitri in her life, Nina had no reason to be bitter. The humiliation was over and done with. As her mother said—she had a man now, too. Couldn't she just get over it?

Nina strongly suspected Dmitri shared her mother's opinion, but he was smart enough to keep quiet about it.

Should a new relationship erase all the wounds inflicted by an old one? Wasn't that too much of a burden on the new partner?

It was true her scars were healing, but what was going to happen when the fellowship was announced? Hospital gossip had the contest narrowed down to her and Matt. Most were surprised that the winner hadn't been decided yet, but the administration seemed to be dragging its feet.

She and her ex were barely on speaking terms, but regardless who was awarded the Downey prize and the job that went with it, the outcome was going to strain their already-tense relationship. Matt had never liked being upstaged. He'd like it even less if it was by his former girlfriend. *There you go counting your chickens.* It was hardly a done deal, not with Edward Lawrence writing six-figure checks to the hospital.

Think about it later, Nina ordered herself sternly as she scrubbed up outside of the operation suite. She had two surgeries scheduled back to back today. Neither was particularly complicated, but things could change on a dime on the operating table.

She walked into the surgical suite, nudging the head nurse with her hip. "Give me a beat, Jason."

A happy pop tune began to play. Nina got to work.

Hours later, her feet aching, Nina decided to shower at the hospital. She normally preferred to bathe and eat at home, but dinner had come and gone hours ago. Her last surgery had taken longer than planned due to a few added complications—including a blood clot in a hard-to-reach vessel.

With most any other doctor, the elderly patient probably wouldn't have survived. At the very least, their prognosis would have been substantially dimmer. But Nina was tenacious in the OR. She never closed up a patient until she was sure she'd given them their best chance.

Staying late wasn't an issue for Dmitri in any case. He'd texted he was going to be home late so there wouldn't be a shot at hot shower sex anyway.

That was probably for the best. She really needed to talk to him. If all he was waiting on was a delivery, then it was just a matter of days before it was finished.

He won't leave. Well, that wasn't quite true. Dmitri wasn't about to end their relationship, but he might actually leave, resuming his work as a marshal.

C'mon, even you aren't this stupid. She knew air marshals didn't run around town doing mysterious errands. They spent their careers in the air, flying from city to city. If that was what Dmitri did for a living—even part time—then he'd barely be able to spend any time with her. Instead, he'd practically moved in. He hadn't even mentioned the air marshal job after they arrived in Boston. It was as if he'd stopped pretending.

So, what was her new boyfriend's true employment? She closed her eyes under the stream of water, trying to recall all the minute details he'd let slip about his work. Those weren't many. More significant was what he *hadn't* said.

Dmitri was a criminal. There was no point in denying the obvious anymore. The question was, what was she going to do about it? Sooner or later, she was going to have to confront him. Either he would lie, or he would tell the truth. Once that happened, it would all be over.

Yes, Dmitri cared for her, but she wasn't fool enough to believe he'd give up a life of crime for her.

Nina turned off the shower, grabbing the towel and drying herself roughly before leaving the stall. Her thoughts a tangled muddle, she wrapped the damp cotton around herself and stepped out only to come face to face with a man waiting a few feet away.

Unfortunately, it wasn't her current lover intent on surprising her. It was the former one.

CHAPTER TWENTY-THREE

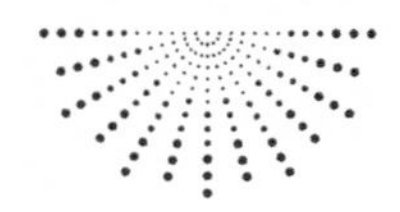

Nina hitched the towel up higher in a vain attempt to cover the cleavage threatening to spill over the suddenly small length of cotton.

"What the hell, Matt?" She glowered.

He was leaning against the sink, his arms crossed and a distinctly dark expression on his face.

"What?" he asked, his lips twisting derisively. He straightened. "It's not like I haven't seen it all before. I wouldn't have to ambush you like this if you weren't avoiding me."

What right did he have to be annoyed? She was the one naked and dripping wet under her towel. The bathroom in the doctor's lounge was unisex, but that didn't mean common courtesy didn't apply. Crowding someone in the small shower area was bad form.

"I'm not avoiding you," she snapped. "As far as I'm concerned, the last time we spoke in depth—the time you told me you were breaking up with me, so you could marry my sister—was the last conversation we needed to have."

She didn't mention what he'd said at the wedding. His stupidity was his own cross to bear.

He sighed dramatically. "We are still colleagues, or did you forget?"

"Obviously I haven't. The fact we have to work together is the only reason I haven't run you over with my car."

"Really, Nina…" He huffed. "I thought we were past this."

Adrenaline coursed through her, and she clenched her fist. Nina had been in a single fight back in grade school. The elementary school bully had wiped the floor with her. After realizing there would always be someone bigger and stronger, Nina resolved to work out her problems by talking things through. But right now, she'd give her left tit to be able to punch him. But she couldn't do that without exposing herself.

I need a bigger towel. Or a robe.

"Speaking of being past this," she muttered, brushing by him with a hard shove. Her clothes were on a bench near the window. "You may have seen all this before, but you risk a lot by assuming you get a free pass now."

"Will your new Russian boyfriend beat me up?" he said, a hint of a sneer in his voice.

"Yes," a deep voice rumbled.

Startled, Nina's head snapped up, clutching her clothes to her chest. Dmitri had appeared as if by magic. He filled the doorframe, towering over her and Matt.

Crap. How long had he been standing there?

Apparently, it was long enough. He took one step and reached out, grabbing Matt by the neck and lifting him like a recalcitrant puppy. A low animalistic growl emanated from him, vibrating her teeth, as he drew her hapless ex-boyfriend closer to his face.

The noise was low and full of menace—a predator's warning. It was so real she whipped her head around to make sure a bear hadn't suddenly joined them in the little room.

"*Shit.* Dmitri, put him down."

"Yes, put me down." Matt's voice was strained, but Nina was relieved he could still speak. It meant Dmitri wasn't crushing his windpipe.

Reluctantly, Dmitri set Matt down. Her ex jerked away, rubbing his neck. "I just came to tell her the decision for the Downey fellowship has been delayed. Dr. Strickland, the head of the committee, is going out of town again, so they're postponing till he gets back."

"Well, that's convenient for you," Dmitri said, his disdain clear. "It gives your father more time to maneuver, to get his plan in place."

Matt scowled at him. "I don't know what the hell you're talking about. I'm going to leave now." He turned back to Nina. "By the way, Kate wants you to call her."

Right. Nina's sister would never have Matt pass on that message. Kate was still too insecure with Matt to encourage any kind of contact between them if she wasn't around.

Matt turned to the door, attempting to edge past Dmitri, but the stubborn Russian just stood there, an immovable mountain with eyes that promised death.

He leaned down. "Remember your viewing pass is revoked. If you even look at Nina sideways again, I will know, and you will regret it."

Even Nina shivered at the icy tone.

"Enough already." Her concern and edginess sharpened her tone. She lifted her pile of clothes in an unmistakable get-out gesture. "I'm cold, and I want to change."

Dmitri nodded shortly, moving to the side just enough to let Matt squeeze past him. He turned back to her as the other man's footsteps faded. His expression warmed lasciviously.

Nina blinked, shaking her head. Dmitri's eyes were almost luminous in the low light, but whatever alchemy was running through him was channeling his aggression in another direction.

"Allow me to help you," he murmured.

She held up a hand, laughing in spite of herself. "*Niet.*"

Nina put down the pile of clothes and picked up a shirt, shaking it out before throwing it on. She hurriedly tugged on her panties and pants after, wondering why she was so happy when she should have been annoyed. It just wasn't rational.

"As you can plainly see, this place isn't private."

He didn't seem to care. Dmitri wrapped his arms around her, nuzzling the skin next to her ear until she squirmed. "I locked the door."

"*No.*" Dmitri continued to nuzzle her neck, lowering her IQ with a few practiced moves. Desire thickened her tongue and she blinked at him stupidly. "Um...what was I saying?"

"That you were going to take off your pants again."

"No, I'm not."

Her stupid hormones disagreed. A few bone-melting kisses later and she was wiggling out of her pants like a cat in heat. Dmitri unzipped, hoisting her up before she could think better of it.

Nina gasped as Dmitri pinned her to the wall, her legs wrapped around him as his cock nudged her entrance.

Time seemed to slow down, and her vision misted over. The flood of chemicals in her brain were making it difficult to speak. All she could do was hold on. "What...is...wrong...with...me?"

"There's nothing wrong with you. You're perfect." Dmitri kissed her throat with parted lips. He licked and nibbled as he rocked, his length pushing past the constricted ring of her entrance.

Nina melted around him, clutching his shoulders. "I wanted to have a serious talk with you."

How did he do this to her? She'd wasn't the type to get derailed, but all Dmitri had to do was touch her and reason flew out the window.

Dmitri slid in slowly, clearly taking care not to hurt her. Accommodating someone of his size was always a little difficult, which was why she was grateful he made sure she was wet and hot for him before he took her.

"What could be more serious than this?" he asked hoarsely. He cupped her bottom, squeezing as he pulled her in tighter to deepen his penetration.

He made a very good point.

Sparks flew behind her eyes as her sheath gripped him tight, rippling across his cock in a heady prelude of what was to come. Nina panted, her body helplessly straining to meet each devastating stroke.

If anyone walked in, Nina could kiss her fellowship goodbye. Maybe even her job. But those considerations seemed small and petty when she was in Dmitri's arms, being fucked within an inch of her life.

She laughed and then moaned, her lips parting. This wasn't going to kill her. It only felt like she was dying.

"You're going to kill me," Dmitri gasped, doing his sex mind-reading thing. He pushed in a little deeper, rubbing her G-spot in a prolonged move that made her toes curl. Her ass banged against the wall as she cried out, spasming around him as her climax rolled through her.

Dmitri kept going, fucking her through her orgasm until his neck corded and he gasped, pumping deep as his cock jerked inside her. Warmth spread through her core as his seed coated her womb.

"Hold me tighter." Dmitri flexed his hips again, making her arch instinctively.

Hypersensitive, Nina could feel every distinct tile pressing against her back. They were growing colder, too, the steam from her shower condensing into beads and drops than ran between her and the wall. Dmitri's arms were like iron around her. They didn't tremble or shake despite the exertion of sex. She, on the other hand, was still shivering in the wake of that mind-altering orgasm.

She pressed against his chest gently to make him let her go, inadvertently flexing her hips in the process. Her channel caressed his cock. Even soft, he filled her well. Hunger roared, and she gasped again, clinging to him. Dmitri groaned and flexed, murmuring in Russian. Despite just climaxing, she could feel him hardening inside her.

"*Wait. Stop.* We can't. We have to get out of here." Nina pushed at him more insistently, cursing in her thoughts. Why did she always lose her mind when he touched her? Her passion burned out of control with Dmitri, like a white-hot flame instead of a yellow and gold one.

Those are the most destructive kind.

"No one can come in now," he pointed out, moving his lips to her earlobe. "The door is locked."

She prodded harder. "And no one ever locks it—not unless they're doing what we're doing."

True, the doctors on staff were generally too busy for that sort of thing, but it was a high-stress job and people needed to release every once in a while, particularly if they didn't get it at home. Hook-ups were not uncommon among the staff, but they normally found more private places to conduct their business. Only the truly brazen used the room adjoining the lockers.

"Did you and your ex ever lock this door?" Dmitri's tone was suspiciously even, but it didn't fool her for a second.

"No. Never."

It was the truth. She had been too staid to have sex at work before the crazy Russian. The culprit had usually been Dr. Wagner and one of his subordinates. He'd burned through the interns like tissue paper, but he'd moved on before it could become an HR issue.

"Hmm." Dmitri didn't appear convinced, but his mouth relaxed. With some reluctance, he finally withdrew, setting her on her feet.

Nina cleaned up as he fastened his pants. She dressed in record time. Heat flamed across her cheeks and down her neck as she tentatively opened the door.

There was no one else in the locker room. Breathing a sigh of relief, she tugged an amused Dmitri along. His grip tightened on her hand as they walked past the busy nurses' station.

"Have a good night, Dr. Briggs," Jennifer called from the desk. A few of the other nurses were staring knowingly in their direction.

"Good night," Nina said, trying to rush Dmitri away from the curious eyes.

He waved to them, a little smile on his face. "Everyone is so friendly."

"They sure are," she said from behind gritted teeth. The charge nurse wasn't usually so enthusiastic, but then Nina didn't have a hot muscular Russian in tow every day.

"What's your rush?" he asked, allowing himself to be tugged along. "I want to meet your coworkers."

"You met a fair amount of them at the wedding," she said, making for the exit nearest the employee lot. "And we don't need to stop so they can take a closer look at us. No one else needs to know what we were doing in the shower room."

He laughed, but medical staff was trained to notice the minute changes in a patient's body to determine their prognosis or recovery. Spotting signs of recent sexual activity was easy by comparison. There were no secrets in a hospital.

She hurried out, heading in the direction of her car, but Dmitri pulled her in another direction. "Let's go across the street," he said. "There's a quiet little pub a few blocks down. I need to talk to you."

Nina drew up short. "All right. Like I said before, I need to speak to you, too."

"Sounds ominous," he said, using his grip to guide her in the other direction.

"I've been thinking…" she began.

"I advise against that whenever possible," he joked, glancing at her sideways as they joined the light evening crowd on the sidewalk.

"I'm serious."

"As am I—about you. So, if this is about our relationship, start there," he said softly.

Wow. Nina swallowed, nodding. "Your directness is refreshing."

And slightly terrifying.

They walked a little further. When she didn't say anything, he exhaled. "Well, I guess I'll begin. I wrapped things up with my client in town today."

Nina tripped on a crack in the sidewalk, nearly falling flat on her face. But Dmitri caught her easily, hoisting her up with the hand he still held.

"I see," she said, clearing her throat.

"I meant what I said earlier. It doesn't change anything between us. I'll be where you are—here or in another town should you need to leave Boston."

She stopped. "Why would I leave?"

He pursed his lips. "Are you really going to stay if your ex gets the job you're after?"

Damn. She'd almost forgotten. "I haven't thought about it in great detail...I guess I assumed I'd find something else in Boston. I've lived here my whole life. It's where all my family and friends are. Why do you ask?"

He swung their arms in a small arc, establishing a regular oscillation. "I have some land in Oregon, just outside Portland. It would be an easy commute to downtown, shorter than the one you have now. I have a cabin there, but I was planning on building a bigger house later."

"Are you suggesting I move to Portland with you?"

He shrugged. "It's an idea, not an ultimatum. After today, I have every confidence you're going to be given the job here."

She studied his face. He seemed extremely confident. "How do you know that?"

"Let's just say I'm certain." He paused, his expression sobering. "Which brings me to what I wanted to tell you."

There was more than Portland?

Dmitri took a deep breath. His posture had altered. There was a distinct tightening around his eyes and his shoulders were a little higher than normal, as if he were bracing himself for something.

She stood up straighter, pulling him out of the crowd and a little down the mouth of an alley on their right. Glancing around them furtively, she made sure no one was close enough to overhear them.

"If this is about your profession as a criminal, I put it together on my own," she said quickly, the words coming out clipped and a little harsh.

Her heartbeat quickened. Despite her resolve, she was starting to panic. "I'm afraid I do have an ultimatum to make. If we stay together, you have to stop making your living that way. I can't be with someone who might be arrested at any moment."

She was expecting anger or even a denial, but Dmitri just smiled. "I won't pretend I haven't skirted the law at times, but the people I deal with aren't angels. None of them would dream of calling the authorities should a deal go south."

Oh God. It was worse than she thought. "Dmitri..." she began.

"Wait. There's more. There's something else you need to know about me—something pretty important. Maybe when I finish explaining, you'll understand. You need to have the whole picture before you decide on what our future is going to look like."

Nina frowned at him. He seemed pretty damn confident there was going to be a joint future.

"But—"

She didn't finish her sentence. Dmitri snapped his head up, his face contorting.

In the near distance, glass shattered. People started screaming. Red bloomed on the red cotton of Dmitri's shirt. The popping of the gun didn't register to her ears until after he started to fall.

CHAPTER TWENTY-FOUR

The world spun out from beneath Nina's feet. Head whirling, she registered a roar, like the growl of a wild animal and rapidly shifting bricks.

Her head thudded against the brick wall of the alley. Pain exploded across the back of her head. Her vision blurred as she reached out. "*Wait.*"

Her hands touched something soft and warm. It was fur. Sucking in a breath, Nina blinked, trying to focus. And then she nearly wet her pants.

She was halfway down the alley, pinned between a dumpster on her right and the brick wall at her back. In front of her was a massive wolf.

Nina stifled a scream, clamping her lips tightly shut. Pressing hard against the wall, she held her breath, willing the animal to move along.

It wasn't paying attention to her. The great grey and white beast stared at the street where tires squealed. The screams died down as the noise of an engine grew fainter.

For an endless moment, neither moved. Then the wolf swung its muzzle toward her.

She gasped, feeling faint. Shock blossomed throughout her, making her fingertips buzz. *I know those eyes.*

"N-no." Nina shook her head in disbelief, her heart dropping in her chest.

Was it her imagination or was the wolf frowning at her?

It chuffed like a big dog, its hot breath on her skin, but then it staggered, settling on its haunches before its front legs gave out. Alarmed, she scrambled to her feet.

There was a huge dark splash of red on the far side of its muzzle.

Nina didn't know that much about canine anatomy, but her agile mind did a quick translation—on a human, that would be high on the chest, right next to the shoulder.

"No fucking way," she breathed. It couldn't be. That was impossible.

The wolf studied her with its big amber eyes, nodding weakly as if to say *yes way*. It whined, but the sound was fainter now.

"Dmitri?" Her voice shook as she reached out to put pressure on the wound. She almost snatched her fingers away at the feel of his fur.

"There's too much of it," she said nonsensically.

How could she assess the damage with all this thick fur in the way? She couldn't even tell how much blood he was losing. Whatever was being spilled was matting his fur.

She swiveled her head, gauging the distance to the mouth of the alley. How the hell had he managed to get her down this far?

Law enforcement was arriving at the scene, judging from the wailing sirens. She blocked them out, turning back to the wolf—she couldn't think of it as Dmitri just yet. Nina dug through his fur, parting it more aggressively to get a better view of the bullet hole.

"Fuck," she muttered, tears obscuring her vision.

She wasn't a vet, but it looked bad. Very bad. The wolf wasn't even moving now. It lay at her feet, panting as if it had just exerted itself.

Of course he exerted himself, you idiot. Despite being shot, Dmitri had somehow carried her out of the line of fire. He'd saved her life.

"You have to turn back into a man," she said, pressing harder on the wound. Anxiety sharpened her voice to a razor edge. She was almost hysterical, not quite believing anything that had happened. Was she dreaming? Had she hit her head harder than she thought?

The wolf's head lolled.

"This is not a negotiation. I need to take you back to my OR. I can't treat you like this."

The animal whined, shaking its head again.

"Damn you, it's not a request!" she cried. "We need to get that bullet out of you. I can't do it when you're like this, so you better turn back. *Do it now.*"

This time, the wolf didn't shake its head, but the little huffing sound it made sounded like a negative.

"Dmitri, so help me God, if you don't turn back into something I can safely operate on, I'm breaking up with you."

She pointed at the mouth of the alley. There was a uniformed police officer visible in the distance. He was starting to direct traffic, so they could cordon off the area.

"I'm fucking serious." She got to her feet. "If you don't turn back into a man, I will *walk*. And I won't look back."

Could wolves sigh or was that just what she wanted to hear?

Nina held her breath. A cold ball of ice had formed in her stomach. She felt as if she were freezing from the inside out, but then the wolf rolled and went blurry. Her eyes watered as the fur disappeared and the torso lengthened, but it was as if her eyes refused to focus. She rubbed them hard. When she opened them again, Dmitri was there.

His bare chest was covered in blood. Where the hell had his clothes gone?

A white t-shirt ominously stained with red was on the far side of the dumpster, but Dmitri's jeans were only a few feet away.

"Holy Mother," Nina muttered under her breath, grabbing the pants. She gulped. "Now, get up. We're going to the hospital."

"No, take me to your place," he growled, glancing down at himself as if bleeding to death was a minor irritation.

"Are you crazy? You need surgery."

"No human hospitals—not if we can avoid it." He was panting now. "I heal faster as a wolf. Just take the bullet out."

"I can't!" She needed her tools. She didn't have so much as a toothpick on her. Kneeling, she tried to lift him, but he was too heavy.

"No h—hospital." Dmitri's eyes fluttered, but then widened as if he was forcing them open.

"Shut up," she yelled, letting go of him.

Turning, she ran to the officer. He was in the street now, but he swiveled when he heard her calling for help.

By the time they got to Dmitri again, he was unconscious.

Matt was hovering as Nina scrubbed her hands furiously in the sink.

"Nina, you can't be serious," he hissed. "You can't possibly operate on your boyfriend. It's against hospital policy to operate on loved ones. I'm the on-call doctor tonight."

She didn't spare him a glance. Releasing the foot pedal that turned on the sink, she backed up, arms up to stay as sterile as possible before the nurse helped her gown and glove up.

She turned to the door, but Matt blocked her path. "Nina, stop. You're not being rational. Let me do this."

Nina finally met his eyes. He flinched, his head drawing back as he read—quite correctly—the promise of violence in her gaze.

"Get the fuck out of my way," she said, enunciating each word very carefully.

"I know you're upset, but that's no reason to risk your job. I can do this."

She narrowed her eyes. In the periphery, she could see bodies in scrubs moving. They had gathered an audience. "You're not fucking touching him."

"Nina, be reasonable."

Her face felt like stone. "I am being reasonable. If you want to see unreasonable, keep standing there. I dare you."

Glaring at her, he held out his arms, blocking the door.

"On my worst day, I am ten times the surgeon you are, so I repeat —*get the fuck out of my way.*"

Finished, she pushed past him impatiently. "Jason! Glove me up. *Now.*"

The OR nurse scrambled to obey. He tied the surgical mask around her in a rapid, practiced move, then he threw open the door for her.

The surgical team was waiting, wide-eyed. Two exchanged knowing glances as she stalked in instead of Matt.

Ignoring the charged atmosphere, she stepped up to her patient and held out her hand. "Scalpel."

The nurse hesitated for a fraction of a second. He blinked, but then rushed to hand her the instrument.

Nina stared down at Dmitri. Her team had done a decent job of cleaning him up. She could see every wound clearly now. He'd been struck twice. The one high on his chest was in an extremely dangerous place. In any other man, she'd give him a one in a hundred chance.

But this wasn't a man, was it? *Stop that. You're not just any doctor.*

Bending her head, she pressed the scalpel to his chest. When she spoke, her voice was flat and hard. "Let's get to work."

Dmitri should have died—his wounds were that severe. Everyone in the operating suite knew it, but no one dared to say a word. Her fingers flew as she worked. Only the hum of the machinery broke the silence.

Her OR was a bright place. Nina liked to play music while she operated, and she encouraged the rest of the team to talk and make observations. True they held a person's life in their hands every time they worked, but she'd learned long ago that maintaining a heavy and oppressive attitude was not conducive to an efficient team. She wanted these people to enjoy working with her. It was a critical factor in their success.

But now the only words they spoke were acknowledgments to her commands. She didn't even lift her head when she gave them. All her energy was focused on Dmitri, open on the table in front of her.

She'd been shocked when she went to recover the first bullet. The path was no longer clean. It was as if his flesh had begun to close and knit over the wound. She took it out easily before beginning to work on the second.

I heal faster as a wolf. The words reverberated in her head as she was forced to cut the thin threads of healing tissue to access the bullet —once and then again. The wolf might heal fastest, but the process was still swift as a man.

A sudden intake of breath on her left distracted her, but she didn't lift her head.

"Focus, Jason," she muttered, aware that on some level, the nurse had realized something was not right.

There it is. Clamping her forceps around the bullet, she swore. It hadn't pierced his heart or a major artery, but the fucking piece of metal had shattered into more than a half a dozen pieces that Dmitri's body seemed determined to absorb.

Methodically, she removed each one. It was a race against the unnatural, and a test of endurance she hadn't expected.

The surgery taxed her skill, pushing her to her limits, but she managed to clear his body of the foreign metal, every last damn piece.

Repairing the damage they had done was another story. Nina struggled, suturing and cauterizing, but she had to work against Dmitri's body to do it.

Stop fighting it. Sucking in a breath, she took a step back.

"Is everything all right, Dr. Briggs?" Jason asked.

"Yes." She moved back to the operation table. "Everything's fine."

She'd just been doing everything wrong. It was one thing to cut away the crazy magical healing tissue to remove the bullets—those had to come out. But now she'd removed them, she needed to work with his body to finish.

That was the moment everything changed. Within minutes, the staff had rallied, sensing the shift.

"Turn on the radio. I need some Beyoncé," Nina ordered, using her elbow to turn off the monitor that allowed everyone to see a magnification of what she was doing.

No one commented about the monitor as the music began to play, but someone started humming along as Nina bent over her patient.

This time, she worked in concert with Dmitri's supernatural healing ability instead of against it—realigning vessels and ruptured veins, letting them reknit themselves whenever possible. She sutured sparingly, helping only when it was clear the damage was too great for him to overcome on his own.

An hour later, she put the last stitch in place, closing him up. His prognosis was still serious, but he was going to make it.

A wave of exhaustion crashed over her as she put her instruments down.

"We'll take him to recovery suite C," Cathy, the junior nurse, said. "It's the nicest."

Too drained to respond, Nina nodded, tossing her gloves and surgical mask aside as she exited.

Dr. Ryan, the co-chair of surgery, was waiting for her outside. He didn't look happy.

CHAPTER TWENTY-FIVE

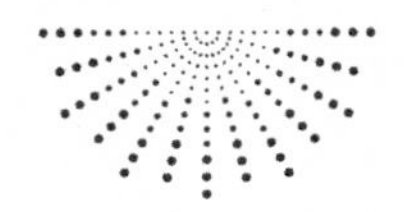

Nina leaned forward in her seat. Now that the surgery was over, she'd allowed the numbness to creep over her—residual shock over the shooting no doubt. Nevertheless, something like outraged disbelief was starting to crack the icy shell.

In the main surgical conference room, she sat across from a hastily assembled panel of her superiors. She should have expected this, but these things usually took time. There was only one reason they would assemble the board to reprimand her for performing surgery on a loved one literally minutes after she'd finished.

I've just given them cause. She knew it the moment she took her seat.

They had been searching for an excuse not to give her the job, but hadn't been able to come up with a legitimate one. Not until today.

"I'd do it again," she said aloud.

The comment wasn't directed to them, but Dr. Ryan exchanged a speaking glance with Dr. Carlson before answering as if it was.

The only words she caught were *'a serious infraction'*. Nina tuned him out, staring into space.

Of course she'd do it again. Dmitri was worth whatever this cost her career. A formal reprimand was nothing compared to getting him back in one piece. No other doctor would have stood a chance. They wouldn't have understood what needed to be done because they hadn't seen the wolf.

Hell. Her boyfriend was a werewolf. That was the right term, wasn't it?

It was almost too insane to believe, but Nina was a scientist and she trusted what her eyes told her.

The world suddenly opened up, a myriad of endless possibilities running through her mind. If werewolves existed, then what else was out there? Vampires? *Ghosts*?

She should have been afraid, but her curiosity was engaged now. She needed answers—and one of the first questions she was going to ask her secretive lover was why the hell he'd just been shot. Because the idea that it was a random drive-by was out of the question.

She glanced at her watch. Dmitri wasn't due to come out from under the anesthesia for hours yet, but there was so little she knew about his physiology. His metabolism had to be off the charts. *At least you know why those readings from his earlier medical tests were so weird.*

"Are you even listening to us?"

Nina blinked, surprised to see Matt glaring at her from behind the line of office chairs where the board was sitting.

"What are you doing in here?" she asked, taken aback.

"Dr. Lawrence reported the incident," one of the board members said.

"Of course he did." She sighed, crossing her arms. "Telling tales."

Dr. Carlson cleared her throat. "If Dr. Lawrence hadn't, someone else would have. That was a rather serious breach of protocol, not to mention the language you used..." The woman sniffed, tucking a strand of grey hair behind her ears.

Nina's lip quirked, but she wasn't tempted to smile. "I did what was necessary."

"Dr. Lawrence could have taken the surgery. You should have stepped aside and let him do it."

She shook her head. "No. I couldn't have."

"Why not?"

"Because it was beyond his skill."

Matt scoffed, and she narrowed her eyes at him.

"We both know it's the truth," she said softly. "No donation by your father is going to change that, no matter how much money he throws at this hospital."

"Really, Dr. Briggs, there's no need for that sort of thing," Dr. Strickland said, shifting uncomfortably in his chair.

"You wouldn't be chastising me for that comment if I had a penis." she pointed out.

It was no less than the truth. Surgeons were notorious for having big egos, but most of the braggarts were male. Not all, but most. Matt had been relatively modest by comparison.

Nina had decided long ago to let her work speak for itself. She'd obviously miscalculated because now these people felt like they could walk all over her.

She let her gaze sweep over the assembled group. "It seems some of you are still in denial over the fact I am the best surgeon in this hospital. I may, in fact, be the best in the state, although Dr. Lahor at General is right up there as well. However, since she's also a woman, I doubt anyone else here will acknowledge that fact."

She leaned forward. "But Dr. Lahor wasn't here. I was. My fiancé had been shot multiple times in front of my face. In fact, he saved my life today. There was no fucking way I wasn't going to repay the favor. I sure as hell wasn't going to let anyone else operate on him."

"You were there when he was shot? Jesus, Nina." Matt rubbed his face.

"That was all the more reason to let Dr. Lawrence do the surgery," Dr. Ryan exclaimed. "You operated on your own fiancé!"

"So, let me get this straight? I was supposed to let my ex-fiancé operate on my current one?" Nina's brow drew down.

"Yes," Dr. Simmons pronounced, but her eyes were sympathetic. "Witnessing something so traumatic and then having to perform surgery on that amazing specimen of a man—" She broke off when the person next to her gave her a hard nudge.

"What?" she muttered. "We've all seen him."

Dr. Ryan snorted derisively. "The point is anything could have gone wrong, and your mental state could have been cited as the reason. That's why we don't operate on family. We can let that slide for minor surgeries, but with something so major, we're left exposed to a lawsuit from Mr. Ivanov's family."

"I'm his only family," she said flatly. "So that's a moot point."

Well, there was the mysterious Cass. *I need to find a way to get in touch with her.* She would want to know what had happened.

Dr. Strickland coughed. "Yes, well, regardless. Normally we would have to suspend you for something like this, but under the circumstances—the stress of the shooting and your subsequent state of mind—we're content to let you go with a reprimand. However, I am afraid it will go in your file. Of course, it may affect any future decision the committee makes regarding the Downey fellowship."

And there it is. Matt had the grace to turn away.

Dr. Phelps scowled at the others. "Excuse me, this isn't the fellowship committee. Nothing is decided yet," he said before launching into a full-blown argument, detailing her many victories in a vain attempt to acknowledge how lucky they were to have her.

Nina tipped her head back, trying to listen to her mentor. It was kind of him to fight for her, but after today, she knew it wasn't necessary anymore. She was beyond it.

"No," she interrupted.

"What?"

"I said no." She frowned at the assembled doctors. "I think—or rather, I know—that I don't want to work here anymore."

"Nina, don't do anything rash. Losing the fellowship is a minor career setback at best," Matt interjected.

Nina shrugged. "That's not it. Don't get me wrong. I get it—politics are politics. We all have to play the game to some extent. It's the nature of every profession. What I'm no longer willing to do is work in a place that buries talent in favor of money and the old boy's network."

She narrowed her eyes at Dr. Ryan. "Lisa Pope should be head of Obstetrics, and everyone knows it." Nina turned to Dr. Kelso. "And you know Maria Daughtry should be running the morgue. She's a far superior death diagnostician than the current guy. As for the two of you, I personally think it's long past time you retired. Your misogyny is holding the hospital back."

Ignoring the gasps of outrage, she stood up, checking her watch again. "Consider this my notice. I'd give you two weeks, but I honestly don't want to work here any longer than I have to. I'll be leaving the hospital the minute my future husband checks out—and that will be quite soon, I think. I expect we'll be leaving town shortly after."

Matt tried to stop her. "Nina, you can't be serious. Your family is all here. Where do you think you're going to go?"

She paused at the door, feeling a smile stretch her cheeks. "I'm thinking Portland."

Dmitri stirred at her touch. Nina had half been expecting him to wake early, but she was still surprised when he opened his eyes and briefly smiled at her. He reached for her hand, holding her fingers weakly as he shifted groggily.

It was unbelievable. She was right about his rapid metabolism. It certainly explained the amount of food he could put away and the rapid healing she'd witnessed in the OR.

But he wasn't ready to get out of bed yet. Mythological creature or not, he needed the healing properties of sleep

"For now, I want you to rest—doctor's orders. You're going to be fine," she whispered, aware they were visible to everyone at the nurses' station just across the hall. Recovery suite C was coveted for that reason. Patients who stayed there did better because they were more closely supervised than other patients, but in this case, it might be a bad thing.

It was too much to hope the nurses wouldn't take an undue interest in the recovering Russian. Her gorgeous and mysterious new man was a patient under their care. They wouldn't be able to resist hovering and checking on him every two minutes. She could feel their many eyes on them now.

Dmitri murmured something indistinct, his eyes fluttering closed. Slowly, he released her fingers as his body grew slack in sleep.

Cathy, the night nurse, came in. "Is it true that you quit, Dr. Briggs?" She sounded aghast.

Nina was gratified by the horror in her voice. Cathy had always been nice, but distant. Nina wouldn't have believed she'd be this upset.

"It's true," she confirmed with a small smile.

"*Oh*." Cathy was quiet for a moment. "We're sorry to see you go."

"Thanks." Nina stood, her eyes on the steady rise and fall of his chest while Cathy checked the IV drip. "Can you tell me where his personal effects are? I need his phone."

"I'll get it, Doctor."

After Cathy fetched the phone, Nina went to the third floor, to the balcony that doubled as a smokers' lounge.

The phone rang several times before a curt voice answered with a snappish, "Talk to me."

"Cass?" she asked.

"Who is this?" the woman asked suspiciously.

"It's Nina Briggs."

There was a dead silence.

"Is he dead?"

"No, but it was close. He was shot. I got all the bullets out. He's in recovery now. I expect he'll be up way before I'm ready for him to be."

There was a sigh that sounded like relief. "So, he's going to be okay?"

"Yes." Nina struggled to find the words. "Are...are you like him?"

There was an indrawn breath. "So, you know?"

"I just found out—when he was shot." Nina checked behind her to make sure no one else had come out on the balcony. "So...are you?"

More silence. "Not anymore."

"Oh." Nina didn't know what to say to that. "I know he was shot because of that job he was doing in town. Is he still in danger?" she asked.

"Yes."

Short and to the point. Clearly, the woman had spent a lot of time with Dmitri.

"What do I do now?" Nina asked in a whisper. "How do I protect him?"

"Not sure you need to, knowing him." Nina heard the click-clack of the keyboard. "I would send someone to watch his back—Nash is available, but if big D is going to be up and around as soon as you say, there's not much point. He'll take care of the problem himself," Cass added, sounding irritated. "That won't be good for business."

This was too confusing for Nina's exhausted brain. "I see… So he's not in immediate danger?"

"He might be. I wouldn't let your ex anywhere near him in case he's in on it—and I don't see how he couldn't be. He'd have to know if he was going to use the necklace on your patients. But Edward Lawrence will probably wait and see if this attempt takes before trying again."

"Wait, *what?*"

CHAPTER TWENTY-SIX

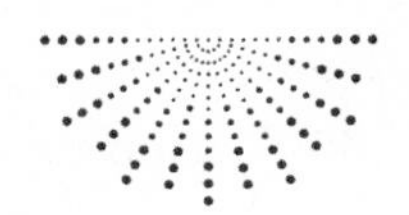

Dmitri knew the hand feeling his pecs wasn't Nina. He grabbed it and opened his eyes, meeting the startled gaze of an unfamiliar nurse.

"*Heeey*," the man said, an expression of a child caught with his hand in the cookie jar on his face.

Not the sex Dmitri had been expecting, but he wasn't about to make an issue out of it. Finding his mate was a priority.

"Where is Nina?" he asked, his voice extra rusty from disuse.

The male nurse reared away, adjusting the pillows to cover his copping a quick feel. "Dr. Briggs? I'm not sure she's still here after everything that happened."

Shit. The man had a point—a much larger one than he realized.

His memories of the shooting were pretty hazy, but he was certain of one thing. Nina had seen his wolf.

He racked his brain, trying to remember every detail of her reaction, but there wasn't much. He'd been hurting too badly to take it all in.

Fuck me. Here he'd been waiting for the right time, the perfect opportunity, and instead she'd seen him at his most dangerous, a snarling beast writhing under a hail of bullets. He'd been cornered, fangs out, an animal reduced to his most primitive protective instincts.

It didn't really matter it was her life he'd been trying to save. Wounded animals weren't exactly rational. But he knew he hadn't hurt Nina. It simply wasn't possible. She was his mate. Even at death's door, he'd chew his own arm off to keep her safe. But she didn't know that.

He shuddered, praying to a God he didn't really believe in. *Don't let her be afraid of me the way Mother was afraid of Father.*

What if Nina ran? Sure, she'd made sure he received medical help. She was a physician. That *do-no-harm* and help people oath doctors took was a part of her. But that didn't mean she wasn't freaking out somewhere, losing her mind after the fact.

The human psyche was a fragile thing.

No, not her. Nina was strong. Her mind was flexible. She hadn't just dumped him here and left.

It was quiet so long Dmitri forgot he had company. The nurse was staring at him wide-eyed, and it was more than sexual interest. He seemed amazed.

Dmitri lifted an eyebrow. The man coughed, closing his mouth. "Sorry, it's just such a pity Dr. Briggs is going to be moving on. She's such an amazing surgeon." Breaking off, he gestured to encompass Dmitri. "I mean...look at you up and around already."

Dmitri's lips parted, and he peeked under his hospital gown to see the rows of neatly precise stitches, two sets of them. "Nina did my surgery?" he asked.

"Yes." The man's face was bright with admiration and awe. "The surgical team on call is whispering about it—they say they've never seen anything like it. She was so quick, so sure. You should have died."

"Huh," Dmitri hummed. He didn't doubt the nurse's assessment. His healing ability was good, but it may not have been two-bullet-wounds good—not where these stitches were.

What if the bullets had been silver?

Luckily, they had been standard bullets. And Nina had been the one to remove them. That spoke volumes for her state of mind. At least, he hoped it did.

He narrowed his eyes at the nurse. "What did you mean by she's moving on?"

The man leaned closer conspiratorially. "Oh, it's all over the hospital. Dr. Briggs quit. They tried to reprimand her for operating on a loved one. It's against hospital policy, you see. They were trying to railroad her."

"*Fuck.*" Dmitri had a bad feeling about what was coming next.

The man nodded sagely. "Exactly."

"What happened?"

"Well, they were just using it as an excuse to give Dr. Lawrence the big Downey fellowship, but Dr. Briggs called them on their bullshit. She quit instead. Said she was moving to Portland."

The dread pooling in his gut dissipated. Dmitri could breathe freely again. "She did? Nina specifically mentioned Portland?" Moving gingerly, he threw his leg over the side of the bed.

"Oh, no." The nurse hurried forward. "Bad idea. You're fresh out of surgery. You can't get out of bed yet."

"I need Nina."

Something in his tone convinced his gossiping new friend he meant business. "All right. I'm not sure if Dr. Briggs is here, but I can page her and find out."

"Bring my pants while you're at it," Dmitri called after the guy as he left the room.

His clothes came long before Nina did. By the time she arrived, he was dressed, sitting up in bed, with his rapidly healing bullet wounds covered by a clean pair of scrubs someone had managed to find in his size. His shirt had been full of bullet holes and covered in blood.

"Where have you been?" he growled at his mate as she finally came into the room. He checked behind her to see if they were alone. Across the hall, the nurses behind the desk were pretending not to watch them.

He lowered his voice. "From now on, you don't leave my sight," he hissed, forgetting to be grateful for his life.

Nina huffed, checking his chart just like a doctor on television. "You're not really in a position to give orders."

He motioned her closer. Instead of coming into his arms, she checked his pulse. Dmitri grabbed her hand, holding it tight.

Their fingers were both cold, but they warmed quickly in each other's hold. "We need to get me out of here," he whispered conspiratorially.

She leaned in as well. "Because you're a werewolf? Yes, I *am* aware of that." Nina twitched the neckline of his shirt, moving to peek down it instead of making him remove it in front of their audience.

"I love you," he said.

"I know," she said blandly before whistling. "You've done almost three days of healing in as many hours. So, yeah, we will be checking out before anyone else has a chance to realize what's happening."

All right, that was a little…clinical.

Under the circumstances, that was to be expected. Her analytical mind would step back and consider the situation from all angles. *It isn't necessarily a bad thing,* he told himself.

"There's more," he said, pushing aside his misgivings about her weird attitude. "We need to make sure anything with my blood is burned. Everything with any trace of me—fluids, tissue, the whole shebang."

Nina took a deep breath. "Believe it or not, I know all this. I just got a little crash course in the rules of your world. The hospital autoclaves its medical waste. I tossed your blood-typing kit in a little early. There will be no trace of you after it's treated."

He heaved a sigh of relief, but immediately regretted it. Despite his advanced healing, the bullet holes ached and stung when stretched. Ignoring the burn, he cocked his head. "From who?"

"From Cass."

Nina reached into her pocket, then handed him his phone. Her lips firmed as he took the device.

Dmitri didn't ask how she'd unlocked it. He'd used severed fingers to get past lock screens before. Thankfully, Nina had only borrowed his fingers while he was unconscious.

There was a glint in her eye he didn't like.

"Cass was very helpful," Nina continued. "I found her very informative."

Ah crap, she knows everything.

It was a contest of wills, a battle unlike anything he'd ever faced. If he didn't prevail, he would lose everything.

Nina narrowed her eyes, drumming her fingers on the Caislean's small breakfast nook table.

Their hurried exit from the hospital had been interesting, to say the least.

He'd checked out AMA—against medical advice—but since he'd been taking their best surgeon with him, there hadn't been serious arguments to try to stop them. Not from the doctors, anyway. The nurses had been a little more vocal, but they had cheered as he rode past them, waving from that inadequate little wheelchair. Nina's friend Jesse had pushed him out as if he'd been a celebrity.

"I'm waiting for the explanation you promised," she said, her voice carrying an edge that rivaled a surgical instrument for its sharpness.

He leaned back, adjusting the cushion she'd provided for his comfort. "I'm trying to figure out exactly where to start."

"Start with the person who hired you. How long have you been working for Matt?"

He drew his head back, insulted. "I'm *not* working for your ex. I was working for his father, Lawrence Senior. However, I didn't know that at the time we met. The transaction was meant to be anonymous —on my end, anyway. I always check out my clients thoroughly. I found out at the wedding he was connected to you. It was a rather rude awakening, actually. I make it a point not to mix business with pleasure."

Dmitri shifted again. "But even if I had known, I would have taken you anyway. You are my mate, my heart, my life. For you, I will always make an exception."

She didn't say anything, just kept watching him from across the table. The air felt heavy as he waited for her judgment. Couldn't she feel the truth of his words? If only she could smell it like he did, then things would be so much simpler.

Guilt beat at him as tears glinted in her amazing brown eyes. "Then our meeting wasn't faked?"

"What? Faked how?"

She rocked in her seat. "You were on that plane because of your business with Edward Lawrence, but you didn't orchestrate running into me? He didn't tell you to…I don't know…distract me?"

"Hell, no!" Dmitri was furious. He wanted to pull her into his arms, to show her that she was wrong. However, the holes in his chest forced him into uncharacteristic restraint.

"Meeting you was pure chance—and a hell of an inconvenience," he said.

"I see," she said, her mouth tightening.

Fuck. He was screwing this up. That was the problem when he tried to use words to make his arguments. Dmitri took a deep breath and planted his feet on the ground, forcing himself to stand.

Nina's head snapped up. "What the hell do you think you're doing?"

She rushed over, trying to urge him back into his seat. He refused to cooperate, pressing her into his side instead, the only kind of hug he was capable of at the moment.

"I didn't mean it that way, love," he murmured. "I should explain. I've always been pretty blasé about finding my mate. *Weres* only get one true life mate, you know. We're actually more faithful to our partner than real wolves."

Nina snorted lightly. He pushed her away a little, so he could see her face. He needed her to read the sincerity in his eyes.

"If I'd known you were the one waiting for me, I would have searched for you," he said, realizing it was the truth. He was just like those ridiculous love-at-first-sight shifters after all.

"But I wouldn't have chosen to meet you on a plane," he continued. "That's the worst thing that could have happened."

The cute little line between her brows deepened. "Why?"

A corner of his mouth lifted. "Because you smell too good. It was all I could do not to tear your clothes off the minute you sat next to me—before then really. I could smell you the second you walked into the airplane door."

Her expression of incredulity made him want to laugh.

"I can't smell that good."

"You do to me. That's how shifters know our mates, by their scent. Yours is unmistakable and unforgettable. I could find you in a crowded room with my eyes closed—provided there was nothing truly disgusting in there—like copious amounts of pepper spray or anything like that."

"*O-kay*. Do I smell that way to other *Were*s? There are other male werewolves, aren't there?"

"There are," he said, the muscles in his neck tightening involuntarily. He made an effort not to sound like a jealous ass. "Why do you ask?"

Nina rolled her eyes. "Not to replace you, douchebag. I just need to know if I should expect a similar reaction if we run into more of your kind."

Well, that was a legitimate concern. He calmed down. "You'll smell appealing to most single male *Weres* until we finish bonding, which is why I'm glad we haven't run into any yet. My kind avoids cities for the most part. We need open spaces to run."

Nina ran her fingers over the table. "So...what do we have to do to finish bonding?"

He smiled, pleased to detect an uptick in her pheromone levels. "More of the same. A lot of lovemaking and then..."

"Then what?" she asked.

He touched the base of his neck. "I bite you here."

Nina scowled. "I thought you said you were a werewolf, not a vampire."

"I'm not going to drink your blood," he said, sniffing disdainfully. "I'm just going to get a quick taste. Once my saliva is in you, your biochemistry will change. Our scientists have studied this, but it's still a bit mysterious. I won't pretend to understand the details, but your scent will alter—it won't be as potent for our males. More importantly, there will be something of me in there. They'll know you're taken. The power of your scent will wane a bit for me as well. It'll become easier to live with."

Her mouth dropped open. "You mean you can't live with it now?"

She sniffed her armpit surreptitiously. He tried not to laugh, but only because it hurt.

"Nina, love, do you think I usually walk around with a hard-on—twenty-four-seven? I've been shot, and I *still* want to jump your bones."

"Oh."

He loved the blush on her cheeks. Dmitri touched the spot at the base of his neck again. "I wanted you to have a choice about bonding, the one my mother didn't get."

Nina's face clouded. "What happened?"

He scanned back through his memories, eyes unfocusing as he dragged buried recollections to the surface.

"My father was a dangerous man—wealthy and immensely powerful. In his part of the world, he was almost a king. And kings are used to taking what they want. Mother was his true mate and she was strong, so she adapted in time, but I understand that those early years were extremely hard on her. I didn't want that for you, so I kept waiting for the right opportunity to reveal myself. I was going to tell you everything after dinner. My plan was to bring you back here and show you, but I guess I waited too long."

"Yes, you did." Nina ran her teeth over her upper lip as she considered everything he'd said.

He waited. The tick of the clock on the wall seemed very loud suddenly.

Dmitri couldn't wait any longer. He had to know. "So, will you do it? Will you bond with me and be my mate forever?"

CHAPTER TWENTY-SEVEN

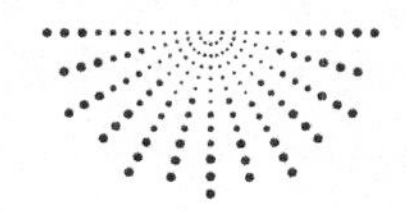

Nina's lips parted. She sucked in a deep breath, her mind working and reworking all the facts Dmitri had shared.

He was waiting for an answer.

Every second she hesitated hurt him. He didn't say so, but it was almost as if she could feel his burgeoning pain. It was like a living, tangible thing.

And this is before this bonding bite. What would she feel from him afterward?

Despite having been engaged before, Nina had always been a self-contained person. She'd loved Matt in her own way, but it didn't compare to what she felt for Dmitri.

You won't lose him to another like you did Matt. This bonding was the ultimate insurance policy against infidelity. But there were other ways to hurt people, other ways to lose them.

Dmitri had just been shot. Whatever web he was tangled in, it was dangerous, lethal.

The only way to protect her heart was to walk away from the bonding and Dmitri now. *Stay or go, you'll be devastated either way.*

She needed more information. "Tell me about this deal with Edward Lawrence."

Dmitri's disappointment was palpable, but he leaned back with an air of resignation. He knew she wouldn't be able to make a life-changing decision without all the facts.

"He must have found out I double-crossed him."

A niggle of unreality stole over her. It was one thing to find out her boyfriend was a werewolf—it was quite another to believe that the staid and snobbish Edward was involved in anything criminal.

Another thought struck her. Her head drew back. "Wait. Am I supposed to believe *he* is the one who shot you? Because Edward is a lot of things, but he's not exactly the hot-blooded get-revenge type."

Her ex's father was almost Victorian in his sensibilities. Descended from German and English nobility, the man had been an arrogant prick from the day she'd met him. That had been one good side to her breakup; she didn't have to pretend to like him anymore.

"I don't really think there's another strong suspect," he said. "Don't get me wrong—I do have enemies, but I've been careful. Most don't know where to find me or what I really look like. I'm afraid I tipped my hand with Lawrence. I shouldn't have confronted him, but under the circumstances, I thought it was the right thing to do. I realize now it was a mistake, and I'm sorry. Honestly, I didn't think he had it in him. I didn't mean to put you in danger."

Unbelievable. "You were the one he shot."

"Lawrence isn't the type to do the deed himself. I'm sure it was a paid shooter, most likely local talent."

"Well, I won't argue with your expert assessment," she said, pointed sarcasm creeping in despite her resolve to stay objective. "But why? What is it you were doing for him?"

Dmitri took a deep breath, but then winced.

"Be careful with those stitches," she muttered, waiting.

He nodded. "They are moving to the itch-like-mad phase. What did you tell your coworkers about my being wheeled into the ER naked?"

"I told them nothing. They probably assumed the EMTs cut your clothes off." She folded her arms. "Now quit stalling. What did Lawrence hire you to do?"

"I was supposed to acquire something for him. That's the sort of thing I do."

"You're a *thief*?" she gasped. It was almost a relief. Her imagination had painted a much darker picture.

"Sometimes. Sometimes I'm just muscle, but I'm the intelligent kind. Force should be applied judiciously and only when all other options are exhausted. Or if they would take too long. I pride myself on efficiency. My clients pay a high price for it."

The arrogant charm was wearing a bit thin. "So you failed to get this item you were meant to steal? What was it?"

Dmitri smacked his lips. "I didn't fail, but the item wasn't where it was supposed to be. Things got complicated. I had to wade through a few bodies to get to it. That's when I decided to find out what it was."

He fished out his phone, swiping a few times before turning it so she could see the screen.

Puzzled, she took the phone to study the picture of a bejeweled bronze piece. "It's a crown, right?"

"No, it goes around your neck like a collar."

"Are those stones rubies? How much is it worth?"

"A few million for the stones alone, but that's not where its true value lies. It's what it does that makes it worth killing over."

He reached for the phone, shaking his head at the picture. "After I learned what I was searching for, I did some research. My contact told me the item had been stolen from some powerful people...and they wanted it back. Before I could retrieve it, I saw the ghastly thing in action. I saw it kill."

There was something about the way he said the words that made her catch her breath. A shiver ran down her spine. "What do you mean?" she whispered, lowering her voice instinctively.

"It's a product of black magic. It can save your life but only by taking someone else's first. These damn cursed objects always exact a price. In this case, it's a life for a life."

Nina was horrified and fascinated all at the same time. "How does it do that?"

He shrugged. "I'm not a practitioner, so I can't really say. I buy my spells. Aside from shifting and rapid healing, I don't have magic, not that kind."

"*Really*?" she asked.

"Well, aside from being magic in bed."

Nina snorted at his irrepressible grin. "You saw this collar being used?"

"Yeah, unfortunately. I saw it bring a bedridden old man back from the brink, but it killed his nurse to do it. I retrieved it right after he used it, but I knew I couldn't give it to Lawrence. Edward may be human, but he obviously knows what it does, or he wouldn't be trying so hard to get it. I'm not an easy man to hire, and my services cost a mint."

"So, what did you do to fool him exactly?"

"My contact was adamant the item be returned, but I decided to play it safe." He broke off with a self-recriminatory sigh. "I should have tossed the damn thing in the river—told Lawrence it had been lost. Instead, I tried to trick him by removing the center stone."

"Did you think that would deactivate it?"

"Black magic is almost reliable that way. Someone had sacrificed a lot of goats to get that thing to work—or worse. Take out the center ruby and it might still do something nefarious, but I was willing to bet it wouldn't kill anymore. I even replaced it with a ruby of the same size. It was a close match in color, but not close enough. I was hoping Lawrence would think it had photographed darker, but he must have realized I tried to pull a fast one."

"But Edward Lawrence is in perfect health. Why would he want something like this? And how did he find out about it?"

"As for the last, I can't really say. There aren't that many humans who know these artifacts are more than myths and rumor. Sadly, a surprising number of old money farts are looped in. Not many, but enough to cause problems every once in a while. Money talks, even to my kind. I also have some idea about what he wanted to do with it."

He grabbed a bottle of Stolichnaya from the makeshift bar he'd set up on the cabinet and slid it over to her.

"You may want to have a swig before I tell you."

"No thanks."

He reached over for the bottle, uncapped it, and took a healthy swallow. "It's just a guess, of course, but we think Lawrence Senior was going to give it to Junior so he could use it at the hospital."

"What? No—Matt would never do something like that, not at that cost. He's a jerk sometimes, but he's not a killer."

"You know him best, but you shouldn't underestimate a man's ambition—especially if he can make his superstar ex-fiancée look bad in the process."

"No, he's not involved." Nina was sure of it. Matt was a cheater, yes, but he wasn't a murderer.

"He *isn't*," she protested when he threw her a sardonic glance. "Killing a patient on the table—that is something some doctors have to deal with. Doctors kill people every day. But not on purpose and not with some black-magic hoodoo. Matt is too conventional to touch that stuff. Trust me, he's not capable."

"Lawrence Senior could have someone else do it—a nurse or an orderly. Hell, even a candy striper gets a few minutes alone with certain patients. Hospitals aren't known for their high security."

"That's true," she muttered grudgingly. "But stop calling him Lawrence Senior. Matt isn't named after him, so he's not a junior. That's really bugging me."

"Sorry." Dmitri's smile was wry. "I know precision is important to you."

"What happens now?"

"Lawrence doesn't know what I really am. If he did, those bullets would have been silver."

Damn. "That's not an old wives' tale?"

"'Fraid not, love. Silver is poisonous to us. We can recover from a small amount—say one bullet in a non-critical place—but you have to dig it out quickly because it will kill the tissue around it if you leave it too long."

He took another swig of the whiskey bottle. "I'll heal faster than Lawrence will expect. I'll deal with him as soon as I'm able."

"Are you going to kill him?" she asked.

His glance was one of pity, as if she was being naive. "I will remind you that he tried to kill me."

"I just want to know." Nina had stopped shivering, but it felt as if there was a big rock pressing on her chest. They were talking about killing a man she knew. No, she didn't like him, and her own lover's life would be in danger as long as he lived, but where did they go from here?

"I don't know yet. We have a number of options. Cass can help. That woman's mind is devious. There are ways around killing."

"I'm glad to hear that." She stood, making her way to him. "Take off that shirt."

He complied with a little tightening of his chin. She examined him quickly, biting her lip to keep from commenting on how quickly he healed.

"I'll be calling that Doctor Kiera now that I know what you are. I assume she'll be able to tell me how to best take care of you from now on."

He was quick to jump on that. Dmitri sat up a little straighter. "Does that mean what I think it means?"

Nina turned to face him. "I gave notice at work."

"Yeah, I heard. Please answer the question. Are you coming with me?"

It felt as if she was about to step off the ledge of a tall building. "I don't intend on knocking around the world indefinitely the way you do. I'd want to work again at another hospital if possible. You mentioned Portland."

"That's right. It's my retirement plan."

"How do you feel about retiring young?"

"As long as you're with me, I feel good. I feel really good."

Nina went up to him, putting her hands on the sides of his waist, where there were no bullet wounds.

"Then, as soon as you're healed, yes—I will bond with you."

CHAPTER TWENTY-EIGHT

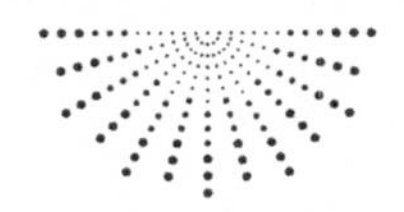

"Are you fucking paying attention?" Cass hissed.

Dmitri plugged his USB into the desktop computer. It was nearly three in the morning, and he was back in Lawrence's office. He was alone this time. Edward and his high-society wife were asleep somewhere upstairs. If he woke, Dmitri would hear him the second he stepped on the wooden floor.

Almost two weeks had passed since the shooting. He and Nina had been living it up at the Caislean ever since.

Dmitri had kept close tabs on Lawrence. So far, the man hadn't made a move against them despite knowing he survived the shooting. Perhaps he wasn't planning further retaliation. That or he was bidding his time. Dmitri was betting on the latter. *Better safe than sorry.*

"Not really," he muttered. The computer was the top of the line, with a fancy biometric security system it had taken him less than a minute to bypass with a lifted print.

"I don't like this. The man tried to kill you. You should get rid of him now, *permanently.*"

"Yeah, you've made that clear." He'd heard this particular argument from her for days now. "I told you… I don't want to start off life as a bonded man with blood on my hands. If there's any way to deal with Lawrence using the human authorities, I want to try that first."

"You forget I spoke to your precious Nina. For fuck's sake, she's no fainting flower. Just tell her the truth—that Lawrence needed to go. She'll understand. Hell, you laid it all out. She chose to bond with you, no tricks or traps. You didn't even have to blackmail her."

He snorted. "She knows my worth. Blackmail wasn't necessary."

"Don't knock blackmail. It's how my dad got my mom back in the day." She sniffed loudly. "Plus, there's no guarantee your plan is going to work."

"It'll work," he said, downloading the incriminating files onto the computer.

The data in the files was genuine. He and Cass had enlisted a hacker friend to do some digging. They'd found evidence of some serious SEC violations and a little light embezzlement. Edward had concealed the crimes with some skill, which was where Dmitri came in.

Once they were finished transferring, Dmitri was going to conceal them—badly, of course. They'd be easy to decrypt.

Now for the breadcrumb trail, he thought, opening the web browser. The authorities always checked the search history. This one was going to be highly informative.

"Trust me, the securities and exchange commission are going to lap this shit up," he told her.

"And what if Lawrence has enough clout and cash to make this all go away?" Cass asked, always the pessimist.

"Not this time. My guy there owes me a favor."

He didn't bother to tell her that if this plan failed, he'd think of another, and then another. He'd do whatever he had to protect his future with Nina. Unfortunately, that included keeping Lawrence alive. He wouldn't have the man's death casting a shadow over their beginning.

"This might not be necessary. The man got what he wanted—his son got that cushy job at the hospital and the cash prize that comes with the fellowship. The little shit doesn't even need it."

Dmitri glanced around the office. It was decorated with expensive antiques. "No, he doesn't. But those with the most tend to be the greediest."

"How is your mate dealing with unemployment?"

Dmitri raised his brows. Cass almost sounded interested. "Nina's fine. Well, fine for her. She spent days organizing her things for the move, but now that everything is packed and shipped off to Oregon, she keeps rearranging my guns."

At first, she'd been put off by his large suitcase of weaponry, but then she surprised him. She started watching online videos on how to clean and shoot guns. Dmitri had little choice but to teach her how to use the damn things. She'd done very well at the gun range, but when he asked her if she had fun, she'd shaken her head.

"I see too many gunshot wounds to be able to enjoy this," she'd said. "Right now, I'm doing this to learn how to protect you. I hope I never have to use one. In fact, I wish aliens would invade and melt down every single one."

Aliens. If only she knew…

"A woman like that can't stay idle long," Cass said, cutting into his reverie. "If I were you, I'd cut the honeymoon trip around the world short, so she can start at the new hospital."

He murmured something unintelligible, aware his honeymoon would last only as long as it took for the hospital in Portland to finish remodeling their cardiac wing.

As predicted, several hospitals had been thrilled to offer Nina a position. The one at Portland Irving had a cardiac surgeon on the brink of retirement. Their aged surgical suites had been almost as old as he was.

Nina's impending arrival meant more expensive surgeries would be done there, so they were investing in new surgical suites furnished with the latest equipment. They'd even asked Nina for her input on the process. She'd spent hours on the phone and her computer, exchanging emails and going over blueprints and photos for most of the last week.

"I'm done," he said, beginning to pack up. He went out the way he came in, through the kitchen. Gliding out through the garden, he kept to the shadows. Dmitri jogged the half mile to his car in a few minutes.

"Like a ghost," he bragged as he got behind the wheel.

Cass made a wet raspberry sound. "Don't forget you got shot, asshat. So, you're a tattered ghost at best."

He grinned. "What would I do without these great pep talks?"

"You know you need me," his assistant delivered dryly. "Who else is going to keep you humble?"

He shrugged, driving the long way back to the Caislean. "Nina does a credible job."

This time, it was a fart noise. "That's not what mates do. A mate pumps you up, makes you feel invincible and, by extension, stupid."

"You haven't met Nina. Her sheer greatness is humbling."

Cass sniffed. "Well, at least you didn't end up with one of those ass-kissing dish rag types."

He laughed. "I knew you liked her."

"Here's to Nina and the wolf-man," Jodi yelled at the top of her lungs.

"Shh. Not so loud. The whole bar can hear you." Nina admonished with a laugh, wondering why Jodi had chosen that nickname for Dmitri. It was almost as if she knew something…

They were back at Red's, the hospital hangout. Dmitri had wanted to have their bon-voyage party at the Caislean or at a fancy restaurant, but since they had done that for their wedding reception, she had lobbied for the bar instead. She wanted to make it easy for her old coworkers to drop by and say goodbye.

Nina would've been content to be married at City Hall, but Dmitri had organized a small and decadent ceremony at their hotel instead. Only close friends and family had been invited.

It had been a surprise. Their guests had been told it was just a casual get-together, only to be ambushed with a wedding. Her parents had been there, but Kate had been a no-show, most likely because Matt had been scheduled to work. He'd been in back-to-back surgeries at the time. Nina suspected Jodi had made sure of that. Her friend had been the only one who didn't appear shocked when they made the big announcement.

Nina returned Jodi's next toast with a ribald anecdote. Liquor and laughter flowed freely for the next hour. Dmitri hugged the bar, watching approvingly as she took leave of all her friends and a few frenemies.

Nina was having a little too much fun. She'd just decided to switch to water when Jesse poked her sharply in the ribs.

"*Ow.*" Wincing, she rubbed her side and glared at him. He jerked his head to the door.

Kate.

She stared at her sister in surprise. It must have been longer than she thought because Dmitri leaned in. "Do you want me to come with you?"

"No, of course not."

Kate hesitated at the door. Jodi was shooting Nina's sister a dark and dirty look from across the room.

"Simmer down," she murmured, patting her friend as she walked past.

Her sister skirted the edge of the crowded bar, around the many wooden tables that filled the space between her and the front door. Kate sat in the only empty booth in the place.

"I'm sorry I missed your wedding," she murmured after Nina sat next to her.

Nina leaned closer. "That's okay. I'm sure you would have been there if we'd warned you in advance that we were getting married."

Kate nodded, her eyes flicking from her to Dmitri and back again. "Congratulations. He seems like a fine man, no matter what Matt says."

Nina laughed. "He is."

Kate took a deep breath. "You didn't have to do it that way—a small ceremony. We could have done a big party like my reception. Mom and Dad can afford it. I could have done the flowers."

Now Nina felt like crying. "I'm sure they would have been lovely, but I wouldn't have enjoyed that. I hate having that many eyes on me. It's one of the reasons Matt and I could never agree on a venue back when we were planning our reception. He always wanted big and glamorous. It's better he married you. This—" She broke off, gesturing to the bar. "It's more mine and Dmitri's speed—a small group of real friends."

Tears glittered unexpectedly in her sister's beautiful eyes. "I'm sorry we're not friends anymore."

Nina sighed. "That's not true."

It was a lie, but it was the kind of lie that was needed to live.

"Everything is different now because of what I did." Kate sniffed. "Mom and Dad act like everything is all right, but the way they look at each other when they think I'm not paying attention… They think I'm selfish."

"Kate…you are selfish."

Her sister blinked. Nina grinned, reaching out to take her hand.

"But we helped make you that way. After what you had to go through as a child—what you still have to go through—you get to be selfish sometimes. Just not all the time."

Kate sniffled. "You're a much nicer person than I am."

Nina thought about that. "I'm not sure I am. Things have worked out for me. My future bears no resemblance to what I thought it was going to be, but I'm so much happier now."

Nina was honest enough to admit the truth. If she hadn't met Dmitri, she'd still be bitter. Her crazy Russian werewolf hadn't just given her another chance at love. He'd given her the means to repair her relationship with her sister.

"I shouldn't have been that way about Matt," Kate whispered. "I think we both realized it was a mistake right after the wedding. I don't know if we're going to make it. I may have ruined our family for nothing."

"We're not ruined." Nina sighed. "Well, we're not ruined anymore.

We're still rebuilding. I don't know how long it will take, but I will always love you."

Kate wiped her cheek with her fist. It was a familiar gesture, one she'd done as a child.

"What about Matt?"

"Him, I don't have to love anymore," Nina said flatly.

Kate laughed, and Nina squeezed her hand. "I think you're better suited to the life Matt wants than I was. He always complained that I never needed him."

That and he'd always tried to push her into a supporting role—more like a prop than a partner. Kate made a much better trophy wife. It was kind of the role she'd been born to play. If she accepted it. Nina couldn't do that for her.

"I'm going to miss you," Kate said tearfully.

"I'm moving, not dying." Nina leaned back in the booth. "Do you want something from the bar? A soda maybe?"

Kate's mouth twisted. "I know it's hard for you to think of me as an adult, but I've been legal drinking age for years now."

That was true. But in Nina's defense, Kate didn't always act like an adult. Something told her that might be about to change. At least she hoped so.

"Then let's go get you a drink." She gestured for Kate to follow her to the bar, so they could join the others.

Kate got to her feet. "Oh, before I forget, I brought grandmother's needlepoint pillowcases for you. I left the bag in the trunk. I don't know why Mom thought I would want them now that I'm married. They don't really go with anything in our new place. But you always liked them. Do you want to take them with you?"

Nina thought about the intricately stitched scenes. Her grandmother had taught her how to sew and knit. She owed her precise surgical sutures to that training. "I'd love them."

Nina waved to Dmitri, pointing to the door to let him know she was stepping out with Kate. She followed her sister to the side of the building. The narrow alley allowed for a single row of cars to park at a slant. They had to wait for a car to make the turn before reaching the sporty little coupe her parents had bought Kate.

Her sister was chattering cheerfully now. Nina let the conversation wash over her, making a mental note to remind Kate's cardiologist to keep her apprised of any changes in her sister's condition.

The roar of the car engine came out of nowhere. It was so loud she snapped to attention, expecting to see a speed demon barreling down the cross street. But it was turning at the corner. It raced toward them, showing no signs of stopping.

Time slowed down as a half-ton of black steel tore down the alley. Kate was safe next to the driver's door. She'd gone there to pop the trunk from the front seat controls.

Nina had just enough time to register those details before the world blurred. Warmth enveloped her as colors bled and blended. The sky raced above just before her body landed, the impact jarring her senseless.

CHAPTER TWENTY-NINE

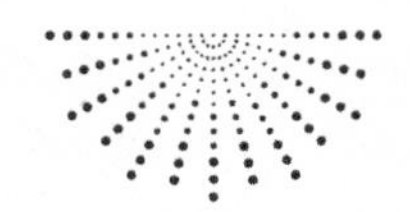

The shriek of grinding metal on metal and breaking glass nearly deafened Dmitri as he cradled Nina in his arms. To his relief, she groaned and swore under her breath.

He was on his back, holding her to his chest. He was bleeding from the glass embedded in his back. Out of the corner of his eye, he saw the SUV veer into the wall of the adjoining building, cracking the brick and mortar. Then it backed up and continued down the alley as fast as the damaged engine could go.

Kate was screaming her head off. He winced at the ear-splitting noise, but he didn't let go of Nina to cover his ears.

He was oddly numb. It was either the shock of nearly seeing Nina mowed down or the fact he'd vaulted over a car to get to her, pulling her out of the oncoming vehicle's path. They'd landed on the rear windshield of what he guessed was Kate's car, cracking and flattening it like rock candy someone had stepped on.

"Can you stop that, please?" he asked Kate. His mate's sister was one of those talented humans who could hit the frequency that made ears ring without even trying.

Dmitri had been calm when Nina stepped out with her sister, pleased the interaction was going well for her. It made him feel better that she could forgive the younger woman. It told him she had truly moved on.

He didn't know why he tensed when the door closed behind him, but the second Nina disappeared from his sight, he was on his feet, following. Dmitri was still alive because he always listened to his intuition. And now Nina was, too.

Except she wouldn't have been in any danger without me and my brilliant plan.

Tears were streaming down Kate's cheeks as she grabbed at Nina. "Are you okay? That crazy asshole nearly killed you."

Nina groaned again as he set her on her feet next to the car. "Ow. I feel like I got hit by a brick wall."

"You pretty much were," Kate wailed, waving at his chest as their party rushed out of the bar.

They were surrounded by the others. Dmitri was forcibly reminded they were all doctors and nurses as stethoscopes and penlights appeared.

"I'm fine," Nina assured Jesse as Dmitri pushed an unknown doctor's light away.

"You might have a concussion," Dmitri protested as he crowded Nina, pushing closer to her sister.

Kate's eyes widened as he came to a stop next to them. "How did he do that?" she hissed, her eyes on him even though the words were clearly meant for her sister.

He ran his hands over Nina, double checking she hadn't broken anything. He fished out his keys before pressing them into her palm.

"Take your sister and go to your parents' house," he said in her ear before pulling back.

Her frown was immediate. "Where are you going?" she asked sharply.

He walked backward, wanting to keep her in sight as long as he could. "I'll meet you there soon. Wait for me."

"Dmitri, don't you dare leave!"

He flinched, but didn't turn back. By the time he got to the street, he was running.

"Where do you think he went?"

Nina hummed noncommittally, staring out the window of her parent's house. They had a mid-sized townhouse in Cambridge, but both were away for the weekend for a friend's wedding in North Carolina. Dmitri must have forgotten that detail when he sent her here.

"Nina, is he normal?"

She turned to frown at her sister. "Is who normal?" she asked, her mind on Edward Lawrence and the mess he'd made.

Why hadn't he let it go after having Dmitri shot? Had he decided that killing her was adequate revenge or was he going after Dmitri, too? Would he keep coming after them?

Regardless, Lawrence had just signed his own death warrant. She barely felt bad about it anymore. *Almost dying has a way of changing your perspective.*

"I mean Dmitri, of course," Kate said. "Is he on steroids?"

"He's a werewolf," Nina muttered, her eyes still on the street. How long was this going to take? Were they going to have to go on the run after this?

Screw that. There was no way she was doing that.

Kate sighed and stood. "Fine, don't tell me. I'm going to call Matt and make some tea."

Nina whirled around. "Don't call him."

"What? Why not?"

She walked closer, putting her hand on her sister's shoulder. "Don't call him. Text him, but don't mention me or where you are, okay?"

Kate scowled. "What's going on?"

I didn't want to do this. "I have to tell you something, and you're not going to like it."

"What is it?"

Nina braced herself. *Please let her believe me.* "Today wasn't an accident. Someone tried to run me down. Maybe you, too. I'm not sure."

Kate paled. "On purpose?"

"Yeah."

"Who?"

"I have reason to believe it was Edward Lawrence."

Kate's face twisted as if she had smelled something sour. "*What*? Why?"

"It has something to do with Matt getting that fellowship. He hired Dmitri to get him something that was supposed to give Matt an edge—this was before I met him. When Dmitri met me, he decided not to give it to him. Now Edward is angry."

"What is the thing?"

"It's a device," Nina said, deciding to leave out the magical aspect. "It's something that can save people when they're at death's door."

Kate was perplexed. "It's a machine? Not a drug?"

"No. It's definitely a *thing*."

"Oh." Her sister glanced away, her brow creased. Kate put her hand on the counter, mulling it over.

"They've been going through a lot of the latter lately,"she offered eventually with a little shrug.

Nina was incredulous. "Do you mean Matt and Edward? What drugs have they been using?"

"None. It wasn't for them. The drugs were for Constance."

"Matt's *stepmother*?"

"She's ill. I think it's serious."

Nina stared at her sister uncomprehendingly. Constance was fourteen years younger than her husband. She was also old money, from a prominent New England family. Nina had never warmed to her. She was too much like Edward.

Kate coughed. "I'm sorry. I should have said something but I was trying to be supportive. I thought Matt and Edward would appreciate me more if I was discreet.

"But she seemed fine at your wedding." Nina hadn't spoken to Constance much that night. It had been too awkward.

Kate nodded. "I don't think they've known very long. I noticed she was starting to tire easily when we were planning the reception. She was all over everything in the beginning, but then kept backing off and letting me handle more and more of it as time went on. That was a huge red flag given what a control freak she is. But I don't have to tell you what she's like."

A control freak was putting it mildly. *Damn it.* If only she'd been speaking to Kate when they were planning the reception. She would have learned this detail long ago.

This changes everything.

"I didn't think Matt knew about the device," Nina said carefully, "but if this is true—if Constance is gravely ill—then I'm not sure of anything anymore."

Kate appeared troubled for a moment, but then her expression cleared. "I don't think he does. He's been warning me for months that he wasn't going to get the fellowship and that we should start looking for houses out of state. He kept saying the same thing right up until you quit, and they gave him the job. He's been really quiet ever since. He doesn't say so aloud, but I know he feels bad about the way things went down. He's been drinking more."

"Good." Nina sagged under the weight of her relief until she caught the glint in Kate's eye. "I don't mean it's good he's drinking. But at least you don't have to get a divorce."

Kate smiled, but it was grim. "That is good, I guess." She sighed. "I'm not that fond of Constance, but I don't want her to die. Maybe they should use this device."

"What if I told you that using it would cost another life in exchange?"

"Like a sacrifice?"

"Yes."

Her sister stared at her skeptically.

"It's true," Nina whispered, infusing all her conviction into the few words.

Her sister's face blanched. "Holy crap."

Kate touched her chest, fingers over one of the many scars she had from the many medical procedures she'd undergone as a child and in her teens. "Then no. They can take their chances on Western medicine the way we had to. Or they can try acupuncture or Eastern medicine. But not something like that. Not at that price."

Something tight and anxious unfurled in Nina.

Even now, Kate lived with the constant threat of her condition worsening. She could have pleaded for Nina to try to use the collar to cure her.

Most people would kill for that. Nina was grateful Kate was not one of them. Yes, she could be selfish, but she was still decent.

At least for now. If Kate took a downturn, would her attitude change?

And despite his doubts at the wedding, Matt was still with her. Under other circumstances, it could have easily been Kate that Edward was trying to cure. What would she have done then?

"What is Dmitri going to do now?" Kate asked. "If the machine is broken, then there's nothing Edward can do about it, right?"

"No, I guess not."

Dmitri had sabotaged the necklace to save lives, undoing a great evil in the process. She didn't want to think about what it had taken to make it in the first place.

What would it take to restore such a thing?

More death, no doubt. Suffering. And someone capable of channeling those negative acts, trapping them in stone and metal.

It would take a wicked witch.

Wood splintered under Dmitri's hand as he drove his fist down on the shining surface of Edward Lawrence's desk.

The computer on it was gone. So were Lawrence and his wife. The house was empty, closed up as if they were about to move. Half-packed boxes stood in every room, sheets covered some of the pricier large pieces of furniture.

Whether his ploy had been discovered, Dmitri didn't know. It was possible Lawrence had somehow detected the hidden files and thrown the whole lot away.

It wouldn't solve the problem entirely. One didn't frame a person for securities fraud without evidence. Facts had to be verified out in the real world. But without the files he planted on Lawrence's computer prosecution would be that much more difficult. Not impossible, but damn harder.

In the meantime, Lawrence had run, or at least retreated.

It could be a feint. Never forget what Sun Tzu taught you. War is an art.

Impulsively he yanked opened the top desk drawer. A sheet of paper fluttered over the tray on pens and paperclips. He snatched it.

Give back the ruby or be prepared to lose her.

Dmitri swore aloud. Lawrence wasn't done going after Nina. She was still in danger.

CHAPTER THIRTY

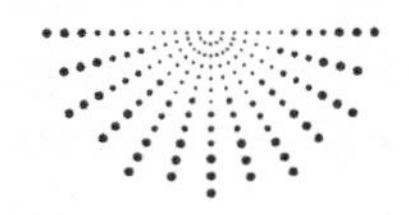

Nina's noodles were cold.

"Aren't you hungry?" Kate asked. "You've barely touched it."

They hadn't fixed anything to eat until nearly midnight. Kate had texted Matt, told him that she was going spend the night with Nina, to help her pack.

Nina pushed the plate away. "I was starving, but I guess I'm done now."

Her own voice grated on her nerves. Outside, the slight wind seemed like a howling torrent. *I hope wolf hearing isn't contagious.* Her human senses might be duller than Dmitri's, but if this what a little wind sounded like when you were mated to a werewolf, she'd have to invest in earplugs.

Nina got to her feet, starting to go to the window before backing away quickly. Staying out of sight was the first thing Dmitri would tell her to do. Rubbing her arms, she went to the kitchen to put the kettle on.

"What's wrong?" Kate asked, rising to follow her.

She'd done a much better job of clearing her plate. Despite not living with her for several years, Nina still checked.

Nina had no idea why she was suddenly so hypersensitive. She was like a guitar string that was wound too tight. Any second now and she would snap.

She reached for the box of teabags on the shelf. Kate shook her head, taking the box of Earl Gray away.

"I don't think so. You're already on the edge, and it's starting to make me nervous. Try the chamomile."

Nina smiled. Kate was taking care of her for a change. It was a nice feeling, albeit an unfamiliar one.

She was making tea for them both when she heard it.

Glass was breaking somewhere in the house. It wasn't the kitchen or the dining room—it was farther. *The living room.*

She whirled, grabbing Kate by the arm. "Get in the basement," she hissed, shoving her sister in direction of the door.

"Wh—" Kate began. She hadn't heard the subtle crack at all.

Shit, my hearing is better.

"Go." She pushed Kate harder, opening the door to the basement. Her sister paused on the top step, her crystalline eyes huge. There was another crash—this time from the salon on the other side of the living room.

Whoever it was, they weren't trying to maintain their stealth. "You have to hide, too," Kate said, holding onto her sleeve. Nina shoved the restraining hand away.

"I love you, but for God's sake be quiet," she said, shutting the door. With luck, they wouldn't look down there.

She had just enough time to grab a knife from the butcher block before the intruder burst into the room.

He was tall and muscled with broad shoulders. All his clothes were black, the better to blend in with the night. His heavily muscled form filled the space, making the large kitchen seem small.

Without the extra thickness at the waist, she might have confused him for Dmitri. They were the same height and almost the same weight. And both could intimidate with a single glare.

Terror stiffened her muscles. It was almost painful, but she pressed back against the kitchen counter.

Please don't let this be another werewolf.

Nina might be able to escape a human assailant, but she knew in her bones that if this man was a shifter, she'd never make it out of this alive.

"Are you the one who tried to run me down earlier?" she asked. Her voice was high and thin, but it didn't waver.

She could only see the man's eyes. He wore a half mask over his mouth, but she could see his eyes crinkle up when he smiled.

"That was merely a warning. If I'd wanted to hit you, I'd have succeeded." He took a step toward her. The only thing between them was the square butcher-block island in the center of the room.

She held the knife higher. To her relief, it was steady.

"I'd put that down if I were you." She could hear the laughter in the stranger's voice. "You might hurt yourself."

If he comes another step closer, he won't be laughing for long.

"I'm actually exceptionally good with knives. Years of training." She edged closer to the door, but she knew running would be a mistake.

He's not like Dmitri. She didn't know how she knew that. He was still a predator, however, of the human variety. She wouldn't get far.

The man seemed amused by her bravado. "I'm shaking in my boots. But there is no need for dramatics. I need you alive. This is going to be a simple exchange. You for the item in your fiancé's possession."

"Edward wants to trade the ruby for me?" Would putting it back in the collar work…or had the evil been undone by the act of removal?

The man's lashes fluttered, and she realized he hadn't known what Edward wanted. He was hired muscle, not a confidante.

"Your employer didn't tell you what this was all about?" she asked. "The stone he wants is this big," she said, holding her finger apart. "It's worth a fortune—several fortunes."

Yes, it might suck his soul out of his body, but right then, that didn't seem like such a bad idea.

"Is that so?" the man mused.

"It is. Perhaps we can negotiate…"

She tried to make her words enticing, but it was hopeless. Nina wasn't good at cajoling or persuading. She'd never wrapped a man around her finger in her entire life.

No, her skills were of a different sort. She gripped the knife a little tighter.

The silence stretched as the man considered her offer. But he shook his head. "Sorry. It's my understanding that your lover has a nasty habit of double-crossing people. Best if we stick to my original plan. I know it won't take the man himself all that long to get back here."

He darted toward her. Nina sucked in a shaky breath, bracing herself. She couldn't let him disarm her. If he did, all was lost.

The pounding steps on the basement stairs were very loud.

"*No*," Nina cried. She was already moving, trying to get between the door and the man, but it was too late.

The door swung open. It hit the counter hard, but Kate held it open with one hand. In the other was an exceptionally large gun.

Nina registered the bright orange barrel a second before sparks shot out, burning out her retinas momentarily. The man dived out of the way to avoid the ball of fire racing toward him.

He failed. It hit him in the chest as he landed on the floor with a loud crash.

Dropping the knife, Nina raced to pick up the copper frying pan on the stove. She ran around the kitchen island, then swung it with all her strength at the man beating a small fire off his chest. He collapsed with a groan.

"Is he dead? Please say yes!"

She turned toward her sister. "What the hell was that?"

"It's the flare gun for the emergency kit you bought for Dad's boat."

Nina threw up her hands. "That's supposed to be on the actual boat."

"Well, thank God it wasn't!" Kate gestured with the orange plastic gun. "Aren't you going to check his vitals?"

Nina's lips parted. "No. I've watched too many movies to get anywhere near him again. Let's get the hell out of here."

She grabbed Kate's arm, pulling hard. They exited the kitchen back door, bursting into the backyard at a run.

"We can call the cops from the neigh—"

Nina crashed into a wall of flesh and muscle. Her lips parted to scream. This was her parent's neighborhood. People knew her and Kate here. They would help them.

She registered the familiar heat a moment later.

"Nina!" Dmitri cried, enveloping her in a crushing embrace.

"I still can't believe your sister saved you," Dmitri said, double checking the ropes that held their would-be kidnapper. Good knots were one of his specialties, but it paid to be cautious.

Nina laid out her instruments on the metal tray. "Kate is a Briggs, after all. She's more like me than not."

Dmitri's mouth quirked. "Well, she has potential," he conceded, adding an extra knot to the ropes binding their guest's wrists.

"Although, I was kind of surprised she agreed to keep everything from her husband. After the way he acted that morning, I thought she'd crumble and spill everything."

Kate, on a silent signal from her sister, had not mentioned the unconscious man in the kitchen when Matthew Lawrence had rushed to the house. No one at the hospital had told him about the hit-and-run attempt until after he'd gotten out of surgery. When he heard, he went straight for Kate.

To his surprise, Matthew Lawrence expressed a fair amount of concern for his wife—enough to satisfy Nina. Despite everything that had happened, his mate was still an overprotective big sister.

Despite being genuinely glad the two sisters were getting along better, he didn't see frequent family get-togethers in their future, a detail he was selfishly grateful for. It meant he would have Nina largely to himself. She would always have friends and her family, but their everyday life would belong to him and whatever cubs they had.

His sunny mental image of a pack of rambunctious boys and girls was interrupted by a loud groan from their guest.

"Are you sure this is going to work?" Nina dropped her voice into a whisper. She gestured at herself in the navy-blue scrubs. "Do you really think I'm going to be all that frightening?"

Dmitri grinned, examining the man suspended by the ankles from the bare steel beam. His arms were bound at the wrist, a tight gag in his mouth.

They were in an abandoned warehouse somewhere in Sommerville. Cass had found it for them, so they could conduct their interrogation in private.

He was still a little confused as to how he'd let his mate talk him into allowing her to join him for this part.

They'd had a rather spirited argument in her father's BMW. They'd used it instead of his SUV because of the car's spacious trunk. Somewhere between West End and Framingham, his mate had decided to come with him. By the time they got to the abandoned building, she'd had him wrapped around her little finger—and he'd been half-convinced the whole thing had been his idea.

It was no doubt a harbinger of things to come. Dmitri had a feeling he'd be losing a lot of arguments that way, but given how deftly she manipulated him this time, he probably wouldn't even notice. That was a skill that would improve over time. Nina was a fast learner.

He was looking forward to it.

"Trust me," he told Nina, examining the shiny medical instruments laid out on the metal tray in front of her. "There are few things more frightening than a woman with a knife in her hand. Throw in the fact you're a doctor—people are afraid of seeing their physicians for a reason."

Nina sniffed. "An ignorant and outdated attitude. But for our sakes, let's hope our friend here hates going to the doctor."

Dmitri nodded. "We're ready. Time to wake him."

Nina grabbed a syringe. He hadn't thought to ask what was in it, but there seemed to be an endless supply of useful things in her medical bag.

She backed away after administering the shot, hurrying around the bench and putting on a surgical mask.

The hired muscle woke up with a start, the sudden jerking movement sending him swinging from the rafter.

Dmitri smiled as the man started yelling behind the gag. The words were muffled, but he could make out each individual swear word.

He whistled. "Do you kiss your mother with that mouth?"

Reaching out, he checked the man's momentum. "Allow me to introduce myself. I'm the one who was originally employed by Edward Lawrence."

He turned to gesture to Nina. "You've met my lovely lady."

Nina put down the scalpel to wave. Their guest grunted something foul, but Dmitri could see his eyes flare when she picked it up again.

"I have some question for you. I'd like to know where Lawrence is, and I hope for your sake you know."

There was distinct *go-fuck-yourself* from around the gag.

"I was afraid you were going to say that. It's too bad because that is a Sterling Evolution rope, and I don't want to get blood on it. I use it when I climb, and it's kind of expensive."

He leaned against a concrete pillar. "It so happens this gorgeous woman is a skilled surgeon. Very skilled, which is a stroke of luck for you. Why do you ask? Well, it's because she's going to be removing some of your organs. Don't worry. We'll start small and nonessential…"

CHAPTER THIRTY-ONE

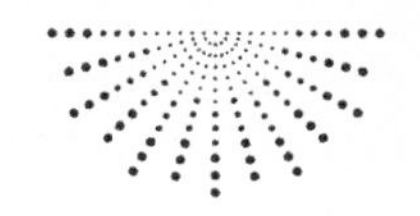

Nina collapsed on the Caislean's king-sized bed.

"I can't believe that worked! I was sure he would call our bluff—seriously, I thought I was going to pass out when I walked toward him with the scalpel. But he folded like *that*," she said, snapping her fingers.

"It was a lucky stroke on multiple levels," he murmured, enjoying the way she was languorously stretching out on the crisp white sheets.

The kidnapper, who went by the ironic moniker 'The Crusher,' had wisely decided he wasn't being paid enough for his loyalty. He hadn't been able to provide Lawrence's location, but he'd given them something far more valuable—the burner phone he'd used to contact Lawrence. Apparently, in his haste to reacquire the ruby, Edward dropped some of his precautionary measures. There'd been no middleman using encrypted back-channels between the two this time. Edward had likely been counting on the substantial paycheck he'd been offering to guarantee his anonymity. He was supposed to call for an update in a few days.

When he did, Cass would find him.

There had been another item of particular interest to Dmitri in the phone, one he didn't tell his mate about. Cass found a recording of

Lawrence giving The Crusher information that would help him kidnap Nina. The only reason Dmitri wasn't preparing to rip the older man's throat out was his strict instruction that Dr. Briggs was not be harmed. He only wanted her detained and secured while Dmitri brought him the missing ruby.

The whole exchange was a smoking gun, but Dmitri was saving it for a rainy day—specifically if the SEC charges didn't stick.

Their new friend The Crusher was currently on a trip south of the border to a little prison in Nayarit, courtesy of another one of Cassandra's clients. The warden of the Mexican prison owed him a favor. When The Crusher got out, there would be a small cash sum to tide him over. With careful planning, it would be just enough to get him back to the US.

If The Crusher had hurt Nina, it would have been a vastly different story. But he hadn't, so Dmitri was willing to be lenient.

Lenient—but not stupid. Cass was keeping close tabs on their friend. If the guy entertained thoughts of retribution, he'd get a not-so-subtle reminder that it was a bad idea.

"Do you really think you're going to be able to find Edward with the phone?" Nina asked, kicking off her shoes.

"Cass is incredibly good at what she does. Plus, Edward left town in a hurry. People running scared don't cover their tracks that well. It's more than enough for Cass. I've seen her find criminals who have been in hiding for years with far less. Plus, she's as stubborn as a tick. Once she has his scent, she won't stop till she finds him."

It was part of her nature. Cass might not have the use of her legs, but she was as cunning a hunter as any other alpha.

But Dmitri had tired of talking about his assistant. Nina was running her hands over the Egyptian cotton sheets, glorying in their softness. He could smell their freshly laundered scent from where he stood but he still smiled when Nina buried her nose in them and inhaled deeply. She was such a tactile little thing—always reaching out to stroke and explore different surfaces. *A thousand little touches and constant exploration*. She used her nose, too, which delighted him to no end.

Humans didn't behave that way anymore. Most focused on sight and some on taste, but more and more they were letting touch and smell atrophy...another side effect of too much civilization.

Watching his mate roll around on the bed was too much for his paper-thin self-control. He grabbed her ankles, dragging her toward him. She yelped and grinned, twisting away playfully. Dmitri let her go, tugging off his clothes quickly before climbing on the bed.

He stalked her over the short distance between them, loving the way her eyes widened as she took in his hair roughened chest and the sculpted ridges of his ten-pack.

When her gaze drifted to his hard length, she licked her lips. He damn near came then and there.

Down boy, he ordered himself sternly. She started to reach for him, but he pinned her wrists against the bed.

"I want to taste you," she whispered.

Fuck.

"And you will—later. But if you touch me now, I'm going to disgrace myself...and I want this to last."

Nina flushed. He bent to lick her rose-tinted cheek before moving to her neck, inhaling deeply as her pheromones spiked. The scent of her arousal was like a drug. He was already an addict.

He reached for the fastening of her pants. Dmitri slipped his fingers into the waistband of her panties, dragging them slowly down the length of her legs. She wiggled out of her T-shirt herself. The bra was all him. He tossed it over his shoulder.

The mounds of creamy cocoa skin were too much for him. He ran his palms down her shoulders, cupping her glorious breasts. Always responsive, Nina's lips parted as her breathing picked up. She squirmed under his touch.

He let his fingers drift to her waist. Her stomach wasn't flat. It had the most endearing curve to it. Her hips were also wider than what was fashionable, but they were perfectly proportional to the exaggerated arc of her delectable derriere.

Dmitri parted her legs, stroking the humid heat he found. He pumped his cock lazily, running his blunt head along her wet lips, teasing her clit repeatedly. Every time he did, she shuddered.

"I love you, Nina," he breathed, sliding into her velvet with a slow surge.

Her mouth gaped, her eyes rolling back and closing as his thick cock slid home.

"I love you, too," she gasped, whimpering as he withdrew only to thrust back in, faster and faster.

Dmitri threw back his head, letting his own sense of touch take over. A creature of instinct, he fucked her slowly, driving deeper and deeper until he was touching her womb. With each stroke, he caressed her G-spot, enjoying the way she moaned and writhed until she was begging for release.

But he didn't let her come—not yet. He built her hunger and pleasure like a master, a virtuoso playing the instrument he'd been born to play. She was his mate after all. No other man would ever be as in-tune with her body and its needs than him.

He could feel the fluttering of her inner muscles, the sign her orgasm was almost on them. He withdrew and flipped her, pulling her onto her hands and knees. He pushed her hair off her neck, putting his fingers on the pulse there.

"Nina, it's time. Are you ready to be claimed?"

"*Yes*," she said, shuddering as he caressed the rounded globes of her ass.

"This may hurt a little," he warned.

"I don't care," she said, staring at him with glazed eyes. She pushed back against his dick, willing him to penetrate her again. She was so swollen now it was harder to work himself inside. He thrust in a little roughly, shifting to hold her neck as he bit down.

Nina cried out as his teeth broke the skin, marking her very blood with his pheromones. Her channel tightened and spasmed violently, climaxing instantly in that moment of his ultimate possession.

Heat and testosterone raged for an instant, blinding him. He surged forward involuntarily, pressing her hard into the mattress.

Mindlessly, he pumped, pounding against her rounded cheeks until the bed frame groaned.

His heart was pounding so fast it might give out on him, but he couldn't stop. His hunger was sharper than his claws. It had dug deep, and it wasn't about to let go until she came again. Dmitri took hold of Nina's hips, flipping them again so he was on his back and she was draped across his chest, gazing up at the ceiling.

Nina cried out again as he cupped her breast, pinching her nipple gently. With his other hand, he reached down to stroke her clit, parting her lips wider so she could see his thick cock driving into her, branding her as his...forever.

Her body rocked in time with his thrusts. "No. Not again. I can't so soon," she panted, knowing exactly what he wanted.

"Yes, you *can*."

Dmitri held her tighter with one arm under her breasts before lunging up and grinding inside her. His palm circled her clit and she splintered, shuddering as he exploded. His cock jerked, erupting. His seed splashed against her womb as her nails dug into his lower thighs, marking him the same way he'd marked her.

It was a long time before he came down. Nina was still sprawled across his chest, her breathing deepening, growing less ragged.

"I think I'm dead," she said, trying to lift her hand before letting it flop back.

Dmitri rolled again, carefully laying Nina on her side without leaving her body. He wrapped his arms around her, exultant. She was his now. He could feel it in every cell of his body.

The perfume of their lovemaking was all around them, but it was different now. The change was subtle, but his nose recognized it. The signature of their bond was there now—both advertisement and warning to others of his kind.

Nina laughed, rubbing her toes down his leg. "You smell different."

"I do?"

"Like leather and cinnamon. Is that normal?"

His heart beat a little faster. Dmitri had heard of certain pairings where the human female had taken on some of their mate's traits and abilities. They had faster reflexes and enhanced senses. In at least a few cases, they were more *connected.*

"*Dmitri.*" Nina jostled him. "Is this normal or am I having a stroke?"

"I think it's normal." He laughed, racking his brain for what little he knew about the mate bond.

She poked him in the side. "You *think* it's normal?"

He rolled over her, trapping her in the cage of his arms. "I have a little confession. I don't know as much about this as I should."

"What about your parents? Didn't they explain their bond to you?"

This time, his laugh was sardonic. "My parents didn't have the healthiest of relationships. When he met my mother, my father forced the bond on her without explaining. It took them years to get to a good place with it, but theirs was always a volatile relationship."

"Oh." She stroked his cheek. "I'm sorry, I had no idea."

He shrugged it off. Dissecting his parents' complicated bond was the last thing he wanted to do. "I should have paid closer attention to the *weres* I know who have been through it. I'm afraid I got into the habit of tuning out the smug bastards. Now I am one of them."

Her mouth quirked up at the corner. "Dmitri, I hate to break it to you, but I would bet any amount of money that you were a smug bastard *before* our bond."

He laughed. *I was right.* The universe had given him the perfect mate.

CHAPTER THIRTY-TWO

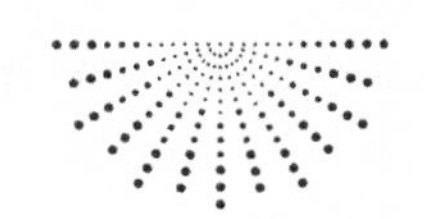

Nina put the final box in her former vehicle's trunk. "Is that the last one?" Jesse asked.

She nodded, her body relaxing. It felt as if a great weight had been taken off her shoulders.

That's got to be a good sign. A lot had changed in a few days. Edward Lawrence was wanted for questioning by the SEC. At this point, it was still a preliminary inquiry, but Dmitri assured her his trap was working. Fortunately for Kate, Matt had gone in another career direction as his father so there was little chance of this spilling over onto him.

They were scheduled to fly out to Portland tomorrow morning. It was a first-class flight, the better to accommodate Dmitri's height. Although being crammed in next to him in coach would be fine with her.

"Yes. Finally," she said, expelling a loud breath. "Who knew I had so much stuff around here?"

She'd worked here for years, but hospitals weren't places that encouraged people to make themselves at home. Clearing out her office had taken much longer than she'd planned, which was why Jesse had offered to drive her to the hotel. Nina had sold her economical hybrid to him at a substantial discount. Their new house in Oregon wouldn't be deep in the woods, but there was enough rain in that part of the world to make four-wheel drive with higher ground clearance a good idea.

"Thanks for giving me a ride," Nina told Jesse, climbing inside. It was a little strange to sit on the passenger seat instead of behind the wheel, but it made sense for Jesse to drive so he could get used to the vehicle.

"It's no problem," he said, pulling out of the lot. "I'm glad I get to spend a little time with you before you fly away tomorrow. I am going to miss you, girl."

"I'm going to miss you, too. And tell your mom I'm sorry I didn't stop to see her before we left. Things just got too crazy."

"You can say that again," Jesse muttered. "She's sorry she didn't get to see you either. She's been feeling a little run down lately, else she would have come to the going-away shindig. You know it killed her to miss all the action."

Nina patted his arm. "It was a little too much action. I hope she feels better soon. I love your mom."

He nodded. "I know. Everyone does... Hey, do you want to drop by and see her real quick? It's on the way."

The city sped by the window. Nina was going to miss Boston, but she was looking forward to Portland. "Sure, but I can't stay too long. Dmitri said he had something special planned for our last night."

Jesse turned the wheel. "Just a quickie then. No problem." He turned up the radio, humming along to the latest pop tune instead of belting it out the way he normally did.

Nina leaned back, tired from packing. Her mind turned off for a long while. She didn't notice the thinning buildings until they were far out of the city center.

"This isn't where your mom lives, is it?" The view out the windows was more industrial than suburban.

Jesse swallowed. "Did I forget to tell you she moved? The rent is almost nothing out here, and she needs every penny these days."

"I'm sorry to hear that," she said, but she was starting to get unnerved. There was something in his tone. It was low and flat, not at all like the lighthearted singsong that usually characterized him. He kept his eyes on the road, never glancing at her once.

She waited for him to crack a joke or turn around, but he ignored her. A tear welled up and slid down his cheek.

"We aren't going to your mom's place, are we?"

"No."

This was bad. Jesse was one of her best friends. They told each other everything. He was one of the most talkative people she knew. The fact he was monosyllabic alarmed her like nothing else.

"What's wrong?" she whispered.

He took a deep breath. "You're going to be fine," he promised. "I just need to keep you here for a little while. It'll be over soon."

Tears started running down his cheeks. He didn't say anything else.

Nina fought to stay calm. Jesse meant what he said. Wherever they were going, he believed she wasn't going to be hurt. *Please let it be true.*

A short while later, they pulled into a parking lot. There was a nondescript concrete building at one end. It looked like an abandoned warehouse, save for the large men in dark jackets sweeping the outside in a regular rotation.

"Is Edward in the building?" she asked. Jesse didn't answer.

He must be. Why else would there be so many hired guns out here?

"Can I borrow your phone?" Jesse asked, wiping his cheek with his cuff.

"Why?"

He shrugged. Nina handed it over, her eye on the nearest guard. This one was less sleek than the one who'd broken into her parent's house. He was shorter and nowhere near as muscular. There was a distinct paunch spilling over his dirty jeans. The others were of similar caliber.

"Dmitri should be here soon," Jesse said, handing back her phone. "As soon as he gives Edward the ruby, you can both go home."

Nina thought about running, but there were too many guards.

She'd never find help in this isolated neighborhood. More than likely, she would get a bullet in the head for her trouble.

Jesse urged her out of the car, past the low-rent guards, and into the building.

Edward was waiting at the other end of the large square room. He was seated on a folding chair, talking on the phone, flanked by two armed guards wearing identical smug expressions. One of them leered at her.

Edward waved at Jesse dismissively, indicating the buckets and overturned crates near the entrance. Jesse led her to them, taking a seat.

Nina was incensed. "That fucker isn't even going to talk to me?"

She should have been pleased not to have to deal directly with the man, but somehow this was more of an insult.

"Hey, asshole," she yelled. "Dmitri is going to remove your head from your body—he's going to use it as a soccer ball!"

She finished by flipping him off, sitting down with a loud humph.

She couldn't make out every detail, but Nina was fairly certain Edward's lip curled. Other than that, he didn't react.

"*Nina*. Don't make him angry," Jesse hissed.

After a minute, her blood stopped boiling and she was able to think clearly. How had Jesse gotten mixed up in all of this? Her mind cast back, racing over all the details of the last few weeks. *Of course.*

"Your mom is sick, isn't she?"

Jesse hiccupped, stifling a sob. "It's cancer."

It was all the explanation she needed. "How did you find out about the collar?"

His mouth twisted in disbelief. "Dmitri told you?"

"Of course he did."

"Oh." Jesse's narrow shoulders slumped.

"Did Edward promise you could use the collar to save your mom?"

He sniffed and nodded. "It was just a crazy story at first, but he got desperate after his wife got sick."

"But you heard of it before?" she asked, puzzled. *Wait*. "Were you the one Edward recruited to use the collar at the hospital? Was Dmitri right about that?"

"I'm so sorry. If it makes any difference, I thought he was insane at first. A necklace that saves lives? It was obviously made up, but he believed it. He offered me a lot of money." He buried his face in his hands. "Those cancer meds are so expensive…"

"I know." The price of those life-saving drugs in the US was astronomical.

"I didn't think of it as betraying you because I didn't think it would work. And then he sent me to work at Wilcox's penthouse."

Nina started. "What? When? He didn't even have the collar in the beginning. His people stole it after murdering the winner of the auction."

"I didn't know about that. But Edward knew Wilcox was sick. He figured he won the auction because he was the most desperate. But Wilcox hadn't won. He had to steal it. I was still doing shifts there for extra cash when his men brought it to the penthouse."

Nina shuddered. "Damn it, Jesse! It could have been you that got soul-sucked and not that other nurse."

"I know." He sighed. "But at the time, I still thought it was a fake… right up until it got stolen from them. After it was gone, the guards couldn't stop talking about it. One of them let me see the security footage."

Nina's eyes closed. "You were the one who told Edward about the swapped stone. You realized the ruby had been switched because you'd seen the collar."

He shook his head. "Honestly, I hadn't gotten close to it, but I did see Wilcox. He's so active and looks thirty years younger. After he couldn't make it work, Edward guessed it had been sabotaged. He realized the setting around the ruby in the middle had been messed with."

Shit. Dmitri told her he'd done the work himself instead of going to a jeweler. The less people who saw the vile thing the better, he'd said.

Jesse grabbed her arm desperately. "I promise you that I won't let

Edward use innocent people. We're going to sacrifice criminals—people the world is better off without." He leaned in closer. "I think he's going to use one of these guards. They're all thugs and killers."

Nina was still reeling. "Does Matt know about any of this?"

"No. Doc McWhiney still thinks he's the shit, despite everything. Edward doesn't want him to know he planned on giving him a leg up. I don't think he's going to have me use it at the hospital anymore anyway. He's just focusing on his wife—I would never have guessed he liked her that much! I figured he'd bail on her. Get a younger model like all those other old-money types."

Nina huffed. "Love makes you do crazy things."

He wiped his tears again. "Everything is going to be fine as soon as Dmitri gets here. You'll go off to Portland together and live happily ever after."

Poor deluded Jesse. "Edward is never going to let me leave this room alive. I know too much."

"No! He thinks you don't know about any of this. He thinks Dmitri is the only one who knows the collar works, and that he won't tell you anything. I mean, it's magic and you're a scientist at heart. He thinks if Dmitri told you about the collar, it would only drive you away."

Nina couldn't decide if she wanted to laugh or cry. Believing in a life-force-swapping necklace had been easier than accepting her man was a werewolf.

She still had a million questions. "How long has your mom been ill?"

Nina thought they were best friends, but she'd clearly misjudged how close they were if he hadn't said anything.

"I—"

"*Hey.*"

Nina glanced up. Edward had just noticed they were talking. "Enough conversation." He gestured for one of the guards to cross the room and stand next to them. Despite the hulking brute's presence, she flipped him off again, just to annoy him.

Jesse made a teary choking sound. "Please stop that."

"Fine." It probably wasn't very smart. If she got hurt, Dmitri would absolutely start killing people. Nina peeked at the muscle guarding them out of the corner of her eye. He hadn't reacted. If anything, he seemed amused.

She relaxed, but decided to keep her lips shut until Dmitri arrived. Knowing him, it wouldn't be long.

CHAPTER THIRTY-THREE

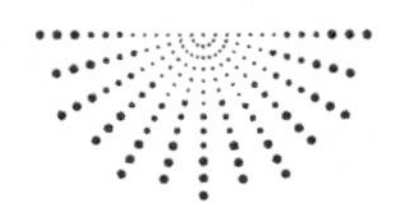

The hired muscle was going to be a problem.

Dmitri was on four paws at the lot next door, watching the warehouse where he'd been ordered to bring the ruby.

He'd received the ransom text from Nina's phone less than an hour ago. He'd been holed up at the Caislean on the phone with one of his sources, trying to track Lawrence in whatever tax-shelter shithole he'd fled to.

The bastard hadn't even left town. Dmitri had fallen for the oldest trick in the book, and Nina was in that warehouse paying the price.

Stop panicking. Edward is too smart to hurt her. If he did, then there wasn't a hole he could hide where Dmitri wouldn't find him. On some level, Lawrence had to know that. He hoped...

Not that it was going to get that far. The fact the man hadn't decamped was proof he wasn't willing to give up his power and position over this. When this was over, he was expecting to resume his place of power among Boston's elite. If anyone noticed his absence, he'd brush it off as an unexpected business trip. Maybe he'd heard about the SEC investigation, and this was his reaction.

Whatever had spurred this foolhardy move—it was a mistake. Lawrence was out in the open. He wouldn't get away this time.

The men Lawrence had hired were local, just a step above amateur. There were four guards out in the lot, two were patrolling in front of the building entrance and two more were hidden out of sight in a beat-up van parked near the door. No doubt they were meant to surprise him the moment he arrived.

Seriously? Even if he couldn't smell them, he would have known they were there from the way the other men would glance over at the van periodically.

He'd come empty-handed, leaving all his guns and knives behind in the car. The last thing he wanted was to precipitate a firefight.

Dmitri raised his head, tracking the second man patrolling the exterior. He was going to be the first one Dmitri took out—he was too twitchy and keyed up, almost as if he could feel the silent menace stalking him. That man would be the first to pull the trigger.

When his chosen victim turned the corner, Dmitri padded after him, a ghost stalking him like a shadow.

He kept low to the ground, but it was almost unnecessary. The discarded trash in the next lot, piles of old carpet rolled up and discarded furniture, provided more than adequate cover. He skirted around a broken washing machine, coming up on his mark's right to avoid casting a shadow. Then he struck.

His attack was swift and soundless. He crossed the distance to the guard in two bounds, leaping and hitting him with all his bulk. The man toppled over under the unexpected weight, hitting his head on the cracked pavement twice before he could scream. Dmitri raised his muzzle once he was safely unconscious.

The body in the back lot served as an adequate lure for the second. Dmitri was on the second guard's back before he could sound the alarm—he was depending on the men in the van to do that part for him.

Once the coast was clear outside, he shifted back to human just behind the trash line. The van was old with high tinted windows. He used the ancient and heavy washing machine, hefting it and throwing it at the door. Buck naked, he streaked to the other side, punching the lock on the driver side door hard enough to bend the metal in an attempt to jam the lock. With luck, they'd have to push the washing machine away on the other side to get out.

The van window exploded, and he felt a burn on his shoulder. *Fuck*. The men inside had reacted faster than he thought. He threw himself down, then rolled to reach the cover of the side of the building before rounding it at a dead run.

He didn't enter through the back door. Instead, he scaled the wall freehand to the second-floor window, hurling through it and shifting into a wolf simultaneously.

Dmitri assessed everything with a sniff—Edward was nearest him, with the guard in between him and Nina. Sitting next to her was Nurse Jesse.

The second Nina saw him, she grabbed her friend and pulled him after her. They huddled in the corner as Dmitri chased down the armed guard. Despite a softness around the middle, this was the most dangerous of the hired muscle.

He could always tell a killer at a glance.

Dmitri ignored the startled Edward, leaping after the gun for hire. The man had turned at the sound of broken glass, his eyes widening in horror as his mind registered the two hundred-plus pound nightmare flying straight for his throat.

He clamped down, making sure the man's head would take the brunt of the impact like with the others before shifting again. As soon as he had an arm in which to do it, Dmitri disarmed the man, slamming the other's arm onto the ground and prying the gun out of his grip. When the man grunted and struggled to get up, Dmitri cold-cocked him with the gun. His opponent slumped unconscious as the other two came in.

There was a reason this pair had been stuffed in the van. The second gun, an overweight and sweaty number, tripped over the first, narrowly missing shooting his cohort in the head as he fired wildly in Dmitri's general direction.

His return fire was rapid and calculated. He went for the extremities, the hands that held their weapons and their knees. If he shot them in the chest or gut, Nina might feel obligated to operate.

Dmitri managed to catch one man in the fist, blowing off his trigger finger. The other one, still unbalanced from nearly being knocked over by his buddy, dove for cover. Dmitri was faster, using his bulk to knock him into the wall. His head and shoulder cracked the plaster with the impact and he went down. A kick to the head made sure he didn't get back up again.

He picked up the gun next to the guy whose finger he'd shot off. A punch and the fat man's caterwauling abruptly ceased mid-wail.

"Stop!" Lawrence screamed.

Dmitri spun around to face his nemesis. Edward was pale and sweating—a change from the irritated but collected mien he'd worn when Dmitri first busted in. He was holding a gun, but he was obviously not familiar with how to use it given the awkward and shaky grip.

"I don't know what the hell you are, but I want what you stole from me."

Dmitri fingered the pouch around his neck. "Don't you mean what I stole *for* you?"

Lawrence's eyes went to the black leather. Dmitri snapped the thong that had secured the drawstring to his neck. "Can I ask you something? Why do you want this so bad? You can't use it without creating a significant body count. What is the point of that when your son already has Nina's job?"

"Just give it to me!" Spittle flew out of the corner of his mouth as he shrieked bloody murder.

He could feel Nina moving just behind him. "Dmitri, his wife is sick."

"Stay back," Dmitri growled, waving her away without turning around. In his business, it wasn't smart to take eyes off the man with the gun.

He held the pouch a little higher as the details clicked. Apparently, Lawrence had something to lose here. He almost felt sorry for him. But the deal was over and done with. He'd shipped the ruby to Alec yesterday by special courier.

Dmitri opened the bag, then threw a spelled stone at Lawrence with all his strength.

Human smoke bombs were large canisters. The ones in the movies had pins that had to be pulled before they were tossed. This one, courtesy of Salvador, like all his best toys, was primed by rapid movement and detonated on impact. When the rock hit, Lawrence was enveloped by a noxious smoke. It would only last a dozen seconds at most, but it was more than Dmitri needed.

Lawrence choked and stumbled, clutching the gun. He fired wildly, but his eyes were tearing too badly to even see where he was aiming. Dmitri disarmed him in nothing flat before punching him in the head.

He pulled it, of course. He didn't want to kill the man in front of Nina.

Lawrence crumpled to the floor. Safe at last, Dmitri turned back to his love, prepared to take her into his arms. One look at her face told her something was wrong. She was nervous.

"What is it?" He turned his head, checking for another threat, but the only people left standing were Nina and Jesse, who sat in the corner.

Her eyes flicked to Jesse, who was sitting on the crate frozen. "He's a…he's a…he's *naked*. He did all that *naked*."

"Never mind, Jess." Nina edged in front of her gangly friend—instead of rushing to him.

"What's going on?"

"Uh…" Her tension was palpable. Nina's mouth opened once before closing.

Dmitri took in the way she was standing in front of the other man, as if she was protecting her friend from him.

Awareness dawned. *"Don't tell me he's in on it."*

He had assumed Jesse had been kidnapped alongside her, but the little fucker wouldn't meet his eyes.

His growl filled the room, rage heating him until he could almost melt the floor underneath them all at a glance.

He started toward them, but Nina spread her arms out. "No!"

The cords in his neck stood out. *"Nina, move."*

She sighed and shook her head, the expression in her eyes heartbreaking. "Lawrence promised to use the collar on his mother. She's dying."

"That's no excuse." Lawrence would have clamped the collar around Nina's neck in a heartbeat to save his wife.

"I know, but I love her, too. She's like a second mom." Nina waved to Lawrence. "Even Edward genuinely loves his wife. She's a little bitchy and a complete snob—they're perfect for each other. They were desperate. I almost can't blame them."

Of course Nina would be sympathetic. She was a healer by trade and too soft. "I can."

She shook her head. "I don't want you to hurt him."

Nina wiped away tears before turning back to Jesse. "I'm going to call my friend Sam. He's the best oncologist I know."

Jesse didn't look up. "It won't help. We've been to four different doctors. They all say the same thing."

Dmitri rubbed his face with an abrupt hard motion. He surveyed the human wreckage lying around him, sighing dramatically. "Do you have a piece of paper?"

"What?" Nina asked, the little crease between her eyes deepening.

"I can't believe I'm fucking doing this," he muttered, rubbing his forehead. "I need a piece of paper or a phone. No, *his* phone—"

He broke off, snatching Jesse up by the collar. The device was in his pocket. Dmitri opened the contacts, then typed a phone number. He thrust the phone back at Jesse, none too gently.

"What is this?" he asked.

"It's the number of a witch doctor I know—who happens to be a real witch. It's a little ironic. He's from the same family that started this mess, but he keeps his nose clean. Most people don't trust him because of who his people are, but he's the fucking best. If your mom has a shot, it's with him"

He threw Lawrence another disgusted glare. "You can take his wife with you if you want. *Just her*. Don't you dare tell Edward when he wakes up. His involvement ends here."

I'm getting soft in my old age. Cass would read him the riot act when she found out about this. But it was worth it for that little spark igniting in Nina's eyes. She was incandescent, staring at him as if he'd hung the moon. "Thank you," she said.

He nodded shortly, accepting her gratitude as his due. "Let's go."

Nina's eyes ran over him. "Uh, you know I like the view, but do you have pants?"

He wrapped an arm around her. "No one is going to arrest me for indecent exposure in this neighborhood."

They started for the door when Jesse sprang up. "Nina, are you going to go with him? He's a—a…"

Nina hesitated. "What do we do about him knowing what you are?" she whispered.

He sighed. "I normally have something for these kinds of occasions. A little drug that helps people forget several hours, sometimes entire days at a time based on the dosage. But we can't use it now or he'll forget the number he has to call."

He raised his head, slinging an arm around his mate. "Talk to your friend Jodi," he told the male nurse. "She can explain a few things. And for God's sake, keep your mouth shut about everything else."

"*Jodi*? What does Jodi know?" she asked, bewildered. But Dmitri was already ushering her away. "What about Lawrence? He also saw you change."

"That smoke was infused with some of that drug—an added precaution."

"Then let's get the hell out of here." She almost raced him to the door. He managed to catch her before she ran outside. He stopped her, pushing her behind him in case the men outside had regained consciousness.

They hadn't.

The SUV was still where he'd parked it. He tossed the keys at Nina. "I'd drive but shifting so many times in a row saps my energy."

Her eyes widened. "You're letting me drive?"

"Seems only fair we take turns after each life-threatening emergency."

She snorted before climbing behind the wheel. He sat in the passenger's side, closing the door behind him. Nina wasted no time, starting the engine. Once they were a few miles away, he relaxed.

Without meaning to, he drifted off, letting his mate drive them off into the sunset.

EPILOGUE

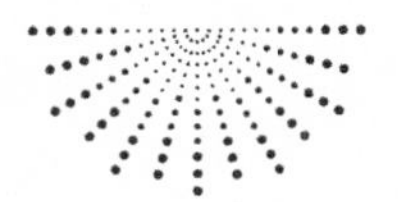

Nina walked into the kitchen, expecting to find Dmitri at the stove the way she usually did after she got home from work. It smelled delicious, but there was no sign of Dmitri or their dinner. She found his note pinned to the refrigerator.

Come find me in the backyard.

She and Dmitri had moved into their home last month the minute construction was finished. The sprawling two-story house resembled a big ski lodge with its treated pine exterior and big picture windows. It had six bedrooms, two offices, and the biggest kitchen she'd ever seen in a private home—not that she ever used it. Dmitri was an excellent chef, something she told him at every opportunity so he'd keep cooking, a chore she hated.

The best part about the house was the fresh-cut wood smell. She didn't know how long it would retain that pine scent, but for now, she was enjoying having the smell like Christmas every day.

On impulse, she grabbed a bottle of wine and two glasses, hoping she wasn't in for a hike. Their backyard was several acres of heavily wooded forest.

Fortunately, Nina found her new husband a few hundred yards away in a tiny glade just out of sight of the house.

The little clearing had been transformed.

"I had no idea you were a carpenter," she said, admiring the wide platform that had magically appeared overnight after handing up the wine and glasses to him. It was like a small deck with enough room to walk around the California king mattress he'd laid in the center. The structure was surrounded by fairy lights and huge candles.

"When did you have time to do all this?" she asked, turning around in wonder.

"It didn't take long," he said, lighting a final candle.

"Are these citronella?" she asked, sniffing.

"I wouldn't want my new bride to get bit."

"What about you?" She grinned. "Let me guess…they wouldn't dare bite you cause you're too much of badass werewolf?"

"Only if they want to burst into flames. I have very potent blood, but you knew that."

"I do." She laughed, her eyes devouring every precious detail. "This is amazing."

The long hours spent in surgery instantly melted away. She inhaled deeply, loving his scent combined with the clean crisp air of the woods. "What's the occasion?"

Dmitri grinned, standing at the edge of the platform and pulling her up. He poured her a glass of wine, then handed it to her, lifting his own in a toast.

"It is six months to the day when we first met. Here's to getting bumped from first class—the best damn thing that ever happened to me."

Far too short to put her arms around his neck, she settled for putting a hand over his heart. "I can't decide why that's unbelievable—because it feels like yesterday or because I feel like I've known you all my life."

Dmitri blinked, turning away to wipe his eyes. He was still distinctly misty when he reached out to take her glass.

Clothes melted away with the breeze.

Nina's heart swelled until she could barely breathe. She took

Dmitri into her body and her heart, their bodies melding under a carpet of stars.

She undulated, lifting her hips to meet his thrusts the way that made him growl and swear. Her breath caught, her body rocking in time with her husband's, the cool night air a delicious contrast to her over-heated skin.

Nina reached up, clutching at his broad shoulders, loving the way the steel of his muscles felt under her fingers. Gripping his cock with her inner muscles, she reveled at the feel of him inside her, the taste of cinnamon on her tongue. The spice was a part of her blood now.

Dmitri kept the pace slow, sliding out of her and twisting a little to maximize the friction. Nina moaned, the light of the stars above winking as she closed her eyes briefly. They were so bright here; the muting effects of the city was so far from this space in the woods behind their home.

It wasn't the frenetic, almost-desperate lovemaking from when they first met—although they frequently indulged in fast and furious sex. But this wasn't one of those nights. Tonight, Dmitri's pace was deliberate, leisurely, like sampling at a feast that lasted for hours.

His big hands moved across her body, teasing and touching possessively before turning them over so she was on top. She threw her head back, gripping him tighter, marveling at the decadence of the wind caressing her bare breasts. Then Dmitri's mouth closed over her nipple, and she was transported.

It was as if she'd melted. The scent of the forest spiked with notes of cinnamon and musk became tangible, a sensuous invader that seemed to dissolve into her.

On some level, she was still aware of her body. She could feel the hardness of Dmitri's hips between her legs, the steel of him moving inside her as she rode him. One orgasm blended with another and another until the wave broke and she sank into oblivion.

When awareness returned, she was cuddled in Dmitri's arms, their swiftly cooling bodies covered by a down comforter.

"So how was your day?" he asked.

Nina laughed, running her foot up his leg. "I don't remember."

His smile could have melted the remaining candles. "Did you like your surprise?" he asked, gesturing to the platform.

"Very much. I especially like how sturdy it is. Something tells me we're going to be spending a lot of time out here."

He shrugged, running his fingers down her thigh. "Every couple needs their own traditions."

She leaned over and took the wineglasses from the side of the platform, refilling each. Then she handed both to him. "Drink up."

"Both of them?"

"Yes."

He raised a brow. "Why?" he asked, his stance widening.

Nina took a deep breath. "Because I remembered how my day went. I…uh…I heard from Jess."

"I see."

She pulled the cover tighter around her, feeling the chill coming off him.

"His mom had a checkup today. Her oncologist is amazed. He'd given her a few months, but now she's in complete remission. I don't know how your friend did it, but she's doing amazing. They're even planning a trip now, a little vacation to celebrate."

"That's good," he said unenthusiastically. "They're not coming here, right?"

This was an old argument with them. Nina had forgiven Jesse. Over the course of her career, she'd seen so many families struggling when their loved ones were sick and dying. She understood their grief and desperation only too well.

"No, not this year," she said with affected carelessness. "Maybe next year."

His mouth turned down. "How about the year after?"

"Deal," she tossed back with a grin.

With a sigh, he shook his head. "I knew you were going to be trouble the second I saw you."

She preened, taking it for the compliment it was.

"Any word on Mrs. Lawrence?" he asked. "How's she coping with Edward in jail?"

"Jesse hasn't heard from her since they saw your witch doctor friend together, but Kate thinks she's having a grand time sunning herself in the south of France."

She tsked. "It's like she didn't learn her lesson the first time!"

They had belatedly learned from Kate that Constance had been in the preliminary stages of skin cancer. But the people who'd been given so much in life didn't always appreciate the second chances they were given.

"Babe, you can lead a wolf to water, but you can't make him wear sunscreen."

Nina sniffed. "Well, after all we went through, she damn well better be wearing SPF a thousand this time around."

"And your sister?" he asked.

"She's fine, too," she said. She crawled toward him, straddling him. "Have I ever told you what a wonderfully understanding man you are?"

He stirred, hardening beneath her in a way that should have been biologically impossible. "I shouldn't have to keep reminding you that I am not a man."

She tilted her hips, sliding her heat across him until he sucked in a breath. "Believe me, I haven't forgotten."

There were distinct advantages to being mated to a werewolf—and she was going to spend the rest of her life enjoying all of them.

The End

Read more about Dmitri's world and see his first appearance in the award-winning novel Fire: The Elementals Book One!"

“A hot-tempered heroine and the charmingly undead prove a winning combination." - Kirkus Reviews
"Reminiscent of a hard-boiled detective novel, Fire is gritty, sharp, with an edgy quality and a snarky humor." - Liz Konkel for Readers' Favorite ★★★★★

Start the Adventure Free on Kindle Unlimited Today!”

ABOUT THE AUTHOR

Lucy Leroux is another name for USA Today Bestselling Author L.B. Gilbert.

Seven years ago Lucy moved to France for a one-year research contract. Six months later she was living with a handsome Frenchman and is now married with an adorable half-french toddler. Her family lives in California.

When her last contract ended Lucy turned to writing. Frustrated by the lack of quality romance erotica she created her own.

Lucy loves all genres of romance and intends to write as many of them as possible. To date she has published award-winning paranormal, urban fantasy, and gothic regency novels. Additionally, she writes a bestselling contemporary series. The 'Singular Obsession' books are a combination of steamy romance and suspense that feature intertwining characters in their own stand-alone stories. Follow her on twitter or facebook, or check out her website for more news!

www.authorlucyleroux.com

Made in United States
Orlando, FL
20 March 2023